Dearest Jayne,

The Life of Failure Mcfadden

by

Timothy Ross McDonald

Thank you so much for supporting Brunello. Since
meeting you I've had infinite wonderful story time. I
miss Jet immensely, but I'm happy to still
see you ever today. This book is my
first, and I love it.

Sincerely,
Tim McDonald

P.S. You're Amazing

Timothy Ross McDonald
www.failuremcfadden.com

ISBN-13 978-0988356900

First Timothy Ross McDonald trade paperback edition
November 2012

Cover design by Chris M Roberson
Interior text layout by Tim McDonald

Printed in the United States of America

for my family, with love
through myriad
trials and tribulations

Preface

This novel began actually as a short story about overcoming the fear of failure in baseball, which I am well acquainted with. I wanted Orville to recognize his fear, how it came about, and to do something to overcome it. When I had attempted two drafts, I realized that it was no longer a short story; there was too much I wanted to explore. Thus, the novel was born.

I knew I wanted Orville to travel abroad at some point as a way to find himself. I had been to New Zealand and England, and a few other cozy countries, but nothing that suggested the change I was looking for—so, I decided to move to South Korea to teach English. That was where I would write my novel and gain the experience I needed to write a real account of Orville's travels. Orville ended up in Vietnam wherein I spent a month traveling from Hanoi to Saigon.

I wrote this book as a means to understand and heal from a life of fear, an amalgamation of experiences that have created one Timothy Ross McDonald, a man seeking the answer to the eternal question, *Who am I?*

Part I
Chapter 1

"What happened that night?"
"It's difficult to say. I know what happened, but I don't know *what* happened to me."
"Let's try to piece it together."

***

Clink. Clink. Clank—the cup met the saucer. I opened my eyes from the sweet slumber of innocence and relished in the soft sound of swishing tea meeting porcelain. It was still dark out and the heat of the glowing fire warmed the small house.

My grandmother smiled, her cheeks glowed like big, red Christmas bulbs. "Awake at last—children sleep so peacefully."

"What time is it?"

"It's tea time." She poured two cups, one black as night and one with added milk, the only way I'd drink it. "Like the English," she said.

"I'm English."

"A long time ago, your family was."

"But I talk English," I said.

"You speak English, but you're an American."

Clunk, clunk, clunk—the rain pitter pattered off the gutters—a perpetual waterfall streaming down the walls nourishing nature. It was October and chilly and we holed ourselves in playing Go Fish. My father was out of town and my mother had worked late at the hospital the previous night so my sister and I stayed with our grandmother. A creak and a door opened and my sister emerged with Theodore the stuffed bear.

"Come have your tea Abby," my grandmother said.

"I want hot chocolate." She yawned.

"At grammy May's, we have tea—with milk if you'd like."

Abby wrapped herself up in a wool blanket and lay down next to me on the couch. We three sat in sleepy silence sipping the steaming tea. Our shadows flickered on the art of Man reaching out to God as the rain poured down and dripped off the sides of the white umbrella of a house that shielded us.

"Can you read us a story grandma?" I asked.

"Oh, I suppose I could." She lifted her strong, stout legs from the green armchair and went to the bookcase against the wall. "A bookcase is a portal. If you read, you'll be transported," she mused. "But, you must always come back for there are things to do in this world." She perused through the books until she came to a thick orange book with a wicked witch holding the neck of a turkey on the cover. "Today, we shall go to a faraway place, to the land of *Little Red Riding Hood*." She sat down and snuggled back into a quilt she had knitted and began, "Once upon a time..."

My sister and I skipped down the sidewalk in galoshes and raincoats, twirling our umbrellas. A shivering murder of crows overhead saw three black flower petals drifting along a river stream. They cawed and skipped along the wires—and I knew they were waiting to swoop down and take off our heads. The school bus came and pulled up next to the sidewalk just in time I was sure.

"Why doesn't Orville have to go?"

"Preschool is closed today. Remember when you were in preschool?—you had days off too."

My sister stuck out her tongue and then clambered up the steps with her book bag and umbrella, found a seat next to another girl and instantly lost herself in the chitter chatter of a seven year old. We waved her off and then walked hand-in-hand under grandmother's grand parasol back along the sidewalk. The day was mine.

I hunched down and crept along the line of bushes

that guarded my grandmother's front yard. I was defenseless. I slowly raised my head and peered in at the cottage. Its two large, square eyes moved side-to-side, menacingly, searching. Its rectangular nose twitched as a faint breeze carried the scents of fallen rain, salt and worms, and the green curling beard wrapped around its white face slithered to and fro, to and fro. The cottage was nestled amongst sentries—a grove of quaking aspens, poplars, and pine trees. My grandmother had told me when people died, their souls went to heaven, but their bodies turned to trees.

I gripped a stick I had found and it flashed fiery as a brilliant sword and I made a dash. I jumped over a tree stump and heard the cottage growl, hungrily. I hid behind a large pine tree and counted to ten. My grandmother had told me that that pine tree had been my grandfather. He watched us and protected us, but I knew the cottage's power was immense. I dashed by the stacked fire wood, passed the budding rose bush and into the backyard. I was safe.

It wasn't long before the sun rose like a magical golden egg through the trees and the grass glistened with the morning dew, and a soft sea breeze smelled of adventure. The birds began their daily gossip as they hopped along on the branches of their homes, and the squirrels began gathering the nuts that had fallen the night before. I was a knight of the highest order. And that day I went on my most daring quest.

I stopped. My sword drooped down beside my leg. I felt some strange power. The world blurred as I twirled around and around trying to focus on all that was there. The trees whispered through their leaves and crept closer, the very land beneath my feet quaked, forging a path deep into the woods, and the creatures scampered and flew about me as if I was the water at the waterhole. And I soaked up that exceptionally serene, rare, and peaceful moment when the world was still and everything was right.

This was a magical place. And I was its lifeblood. I gave it the very thing it needed to survive—belief. For magic was in nature. "That's God speaking to you through trees and flowers," my grandmother said when I had asked her about the strangeness. But I knew that God and magic were two different things. God was everywhere but real magic could only be found in nature. It was magic's home amongst the trees and rocks, the rivers and mountains. It was a haven for the mind's curiosity, the mind's questions, a place to gather and surmise. It was the connection of colors and the art that transpired. The magic of nature was through the connections, the utopian world—the way the green bristles were perfect with the brown bark, the way the red rose was perfect in the mid-afternoon sun.

I raised my gleaming sword and took the dirt path deep into the forest, a part of the forest that held tremendous power and tremendous danger for that was where the trolls, giants, and enormous spiders lived. But the greatest treasure was there too—the fountain of knowledge and life. Whosoever drank from this fountain would be given one more day and one more secret.

I had traveled deep into the wood. The path narrowed and the raspberry bushes grew tremendously large on both sides, their sweet aromas enticing me, their prickly thorns cutting me, but I slashed my way through with my sword until I came to a part of the forest where the overhanging arch of trees was so thick that even the sun could not penetrate through it.

I was close.

I walked a bit farther and came to an eerily quiet hollow. I looked down and saw a brown cylinder Coffee-Mate can. I picked it up and put it over my left arm and it transformed with a flash of brilliant light into a protective gauntlet.

Across the hollow were two massive raspberry bushes and hiding between them was a small opening. I crept through. I came out into a smaller grove. "I finally found it," I whispered. There, in the grove surrounded by vines was the fountain of eternal life and knowledge, where the birds sat and drank their fill, hundreds of years old, telling tales of past generations, where the squirrels came to share their nuts and talk of the trees...and, where a huge, ugly, mean troll sat staring at me with piercing yellow eyes. It had black, leathery skin with flowing auburn hair and carried a massive club with four-inch spikes darting out from the sides. It slowly got to its feet. "You've finally come," it said.

I vanquished the troll even though its strength was mighty and I drank of the fountain. Then I retreated back to the cottage because it was time for lunch—grilled cheese sandwiches and tomato soup with saltine crackers and apple juice. My grandmother grilled the sandwiches while I sat at the kitchen table and tried to shuffle the cards to play Go Fish.

"Dear, will you go and get some tomato soup from the cellar?"

"But there're monsters down there," I said.

"There're no monsters down there. There haven't been for ages—I beat them away a long time ago."

"But sometimes I hear noises," I said.

"Someday, you'll have to go down there by yourself."

"But not today?" I smiled.

"It's those freckles and dimples that get me," she said.

She led me to the back of the house. I heard the trickle of rain water pass through the gutters as we made our way through the kitchen, passed the refrigerator where she kept liver and chicken hearts, bratwursts, and worst of all, blood sausage. We passed the bathroom and came to the cellar door where monsters hid. The lighting was poor, and the floorboards creaked under our feet.

She reached down and took the door handle and opened it; a haze of dust fluttered up into our eyes and noses. We both looked down into the cellar and saw stacks of garbanzo beans, pork and beans, canned corn, beets, and carrots, pumpkin pie mix, and soup cans. There were no monsters, but I knew they mostly came out at night. I went down and grabbed two cans of tomato soup and quickly ran back up.

"See, no monsters, just food to fill our bellies."

"No monsters *this* time."

I awoke to the gentle rocking of grandmother's hand on my shoulder.

"We need to head to the shop."

"Can we get Skittles and pumpkins?" I asked.

"Of course," she said.

Her hands were moist and her face red from gardening. She always said, "If you find God in nature, do a little gardening."

"What does God look like?"

She shrugged her shoulders. "God takes many forms—sometimes a tree, sometimes an insect, sometimes the rain, the sun, but he's always within our hearts."

"Really? How does he fit?"

"That's a good question—I don't know. He just does."

"Even sometimes an insect?"

"Yes, which is why you must never kill anything unless you absolutely have to. You never know if it's God knocking on your door."

My grandmother parked her brown Oldsmobile into the gravel driveway while I ate my Skittles. Mr. Akre from across the street was raking orange and brown leaves into small piles. He waved to us, then set aside his rake and came over carrying a large box.

"Howdy May. Howdy Orville. Have some apples for you." He was a frail, elderly man who wore blue suspenders and a white shirt. He set the box of apples on a tree stump in grandmother's front yard and handed a package of Oreos to me.

"See you got some sweets there already. Don't eat those Oreos all at once and make sure to share with your sister."

"You shouldn't have Thomas. You're always bringing us things, and what do we ever give you?"

"I believe you gave me some wonderful beef barley soup just the other day," he said and winked at me. I smiled with a mouth full of yellow, green, and red teeth.

"Oh that?" she said. "That was easier than waking up in the morning."

"Humph, I find waking up in the morning harder and harder," he said.

"Well, we certainly appreciate it. And it just so happens I'll be making some butternut squash with a touch of brown sugar tonight just the way you like it. Why don't you just stop on by?"

"May, you know I can't resist your butternut squash, but tonight I'm going to have to go hungry. I have to pick my daughter up at the airport. She's coming in from Anchorage. Wouldn't you know it of all nights?— butternut squash."

"Well, I'm sure I'll save you a bit," grandmother said.

"I'll just keep bringing those apples by," he said.

Just after three o'clock, as the lazy orange October afternoon sun spread its mustard through the trees, my grandmother and I walked out to the sidewalk to wait for the bus that dropped my sister off from school. It was my favorite time of day: the leaves shone gold and the sun fought to stay. The bus rolled down the street and my sister and two other girls got off giggling.

"How was school today Abby?" My grandmother asked as she took both our hands in hers.

"Remember that boy I told you about...he gave me a paper heart today."

"Well, that was sure nice of him," my grandmother said.

"It's gross. He eats his boogers and smells like dog."

"Abby, that's not nice. I'm sure he's a nice boy."

"Abby has a boyfriend, Abby has a boyfriend," I chanted.

My grandmother took out the knife carving set—knives with small blades so Abby and I could carve our own pumpkin faces. My favorite part was taking out the guts. I reached into the first pumpkin and squeezed the seeds and slimy orange guts through my fingers. I reached for Abby—

"Stop," she screamed. "You're gross."

"Gross. Abby has a boyfriend. Abby has a boyfriend."

"I don't," she screamed.

We finished carving the pumpkins and my grandmother put a candle in each and lit them. We placed them on the stoop outside the front door. Around five o'clock, she started making the squash. Abby helped while I looked at pictures from Dr. Seuss books. We ate the sweet squash by the stoked up fire. The nights were getting cold, but we had plenty of wood—Mr. Akre and I had chopped firewood the other day and there was a large stash alongside the house. When finished, we set our plates aside and lingered lazily about the couch in warm bliss.

***

"At least that's how I remembered it," I said. "Warm fires, magical forests, fountains of eternal youth and knowledge, that sort of thing."

"What changed?" Dr. Fields asked.

"That's not how the world is—I was shown the real world."

***

Creak. I opened my eyes, fluttering my lids to adjust to the dim light. The house was warm and the embers in the fireplace glowed hot. Grandmother had her quilt wrapped around her and a book open, but her eyes were closed and her head bobbed from sleep. I looked at Abby whose eyes fixated on the hallway, the impenetrable shadow leading to the cellar where monsters hid. Creak.

"What is it?" I whispered.

"It's coming from the cellar," Abby whispered back. "Grandma said sometimes raccoons nudge the backdoor open."

Creak, creak, creak—they were footsteps, slow and heavy. And then something appeared out of that shadow. It was the most hideous troll I had ever seen. It had patches of dark facial hair around its chin, upper lip, and cheeks, its eyes were bloodshot and it wore torn blue jeans and a red and yellow checkered shirt. It carried something in its hand.

My grandmother opened her eyes and looked at us looking at it. It moved slowly in front of the kitchen light casting a dark shadow over the back of my grandmother's chair. She quickly turned around and gasped—"Wha..."

It sprang like a wild cat and put its hand over her mouth. "Sshhee," it whispered.

"What do you want?" she cried through its grimy fingers. She managed to slide her body out of the chair and made a move towards us, but it swung its body around and into her and with its right arm threw her back into the green chair with a harsh thud.

"Don't move, don't say a fucking word." And then I realized that this was real; this was a man. He stood over my grandmother, breathing hard. I couldn't turn away from my grandmother's frightened face; her eyes, wide and terrified stared straight back up at the man who rotated a large steak knife in his hand over and over. "Don't move now."

The man turned slowly around and looked upon Abby. He looked at her little white dress, her black tights. He stared so fiercely I thought his eyes were going to pop out from his head. She was holding my hand and it felt like a wet squid. My body was paralyzed and it oozed deeper and deeper into the couch trying to escape through the cracks—my arms were straight next to my legs, which dangled off the end. I looked pathetic.

The man bent over my sister and took a deep breath, smelling her hair like an animal. He fingered her ponytails in his dirty, grubby fingers. I smelled the stench of the sweat that had soaked into his shirt. His odor permeated the room, choking my senses. Abby started to cry and he put his grimy hand over her mouth. I saw the dirt caked under his finger nails and the black stringy hairs covering his knuckles. "Sshhee," he whispered.

"Don't you touch her," my grandmother whimpered.

The man straightened back up and sighed as if my grandmother were an annoying pest that hovered about, preventing him from completely enjoying himself. "Shut...the...hell...up. Shut up. I told you to sit there and shut up." The man turned back to Abby and reached his hand under her dress, tugged hard and pulled out her tights and underwear. "You're sick," he said. She had wet herself. "You're so sick."

"Oh honey," grandmother said.

The man stood up fully erect and started to unzip his pants. He kept the knife in his hand. I couldn't look. I turned away and stared at the burning embers, wondering if I could reach them and burn the man. But I couldn't think clearly; I couldn't do anything. I wanted to move, to help, to run, but my body went numb.

"Oh please don't do this—please. Not her—what do you want?"

"Shut—the—hell—up," the man screamed. And then he swung around and struck my grandmother in the face with his bare hand. He struck her so hard she crashed back into the chair, her eyes closed and her head toppled down. I thought she was dead.

The man ripped down his pants and leaned over Abby. I don't know what happened next—I was paralyzed with a fear I had never felt before. My head started to hurt and my body started to shake. And then I heard a horrifying scream. I didn't know what was happening. I

16

couldn't look. I didn't know what to do.

Her screams pierced the house, reverberated the walls. I had never heard anything like it, like a wild animal shrieking in the night. I looked and saw that her legs and dress were covered in blood. Then I heard my grandmother scream something, a horrifying, animalistic scream, and then she jumped off the chair and ran into the kitchen. I had never seen her move so quickly. She came back with a frying pan, which still had the remnants of the eggs we had had, and I sat there as my sister screamed repeatedly and my grandmother hit the man over the head as hard as she could. The man staggered into my sister and then reared up and rushed towards my grandmother.

"Run!" she screamed at me. "Run Orville!"

Abby's hand slipped out of mine. I grabbed it again, but I couldn't pull her. I looked at her and there was blood rushing from her neck and her head had lolled to the side. She was covered completely in blood; everywhere was blood. I didn't know what it all meant, but I knew she was dead. I knew then that my sister was dead.

The man wrestled the frying pan away from my grandmother and raised it above his head. He swung savagely down over and over again, and it was like beating bloody meat.

"Orville, run," she stammered.

It was strange, as if my legs weren't my own, my body wasn't my own. It sprang suddenly up from the couch and ran to the front door—I wrestled with the lock. I heard the screams of my grandmother and the savage grunts of the man as I ran out into the night, out into a world I didn't know, a world of fear and death. I didn't know where to go so I ran to the one place I thought I could hide. I ran through the raspberry bushes as they cut up my arms, legs and face. I ran passed the trees and into the small grove where the water fountain of eternal life and knowledge was.

Voices were heard a short time later and flashlights scoured the outside of the house, but I was too scared to move out from under the bushes. The police found me as their yellow lights lit up my eyes, big and bright like a nocturnal animal.

Welcome to my world, said Fear.

Everyone you'll ever love will die, said Death.

Chapter 2

We met in austere, white-walled rooms furnished with brown leather couches, televisions mounted in the corners of the walls, and small plastic white desks with matching plastic chairs. Dr. Fields sat across from me comfortably with her legs crossed in gray pants and a white blouse. She rested a note pad on her lap.

"How do you think you got here?" she asked.

"You mean literally or figuratively?" I asked.

"I think you know."

"I don't know. Everything sounds cliché," I said. "My thoughts are jumbled. I don't even know where to begin."

"Did you choose to come here?"

"No, not literally. I think it was inevitable—the hands of fate twisting maniacally—as usual."

"Why do you say that?"

"I think everything in my life has led up to this point. Rather that point at the bridge I mean. This, I don't know what this is. Limbo I guess."

"You believe that you, being here, happened because of fate."

"Yes, I was fated to fail."

"That's interesting. And now you are twenty five years old and have failed. So what will you do next?"

"What do you mean?"

"Well, you've already accomplished failing at life and yet you're still alive and have many years ahead of you so if this was all fate, there must be a reason for it all still right? So, what will you do?"

"I don't know," I said. "I haven't thought it through that far."

"Let's figure it out. Let's figure out this chaotic mess of a life and connect the dots. Tell me what happened after your grandmother and sister were killed."

***

Memories through time become sporadic images, clips from the movie of life. The murders were chapter one of mine. I saw blurs—colors, events clouded by a dark fear—events that became imaginative interpretations so powerful that they lodged themselves into a deep memory bank, but through time, even they became opaque stories blurring the lines of veracity and falsity. I saw what I wanted to see.

I was born from a deep well within the earth filled with imaginatively fantastical manna. Inside this seemingly free floating space were undecipherable images of unexplainable things: the void. They traveled through me and I absorbed them into my body, my mind, my very being. They welled up inside me, and when the world opened its gaping maw, I was born as an untapped mine with mythic apotheosis, rich in story and creativity. The natural world whispered the language of the supernatural, and I felt most at home, comforted, happiest within the forests, around rivers, rocks, and sand dunes. It was a world of goblins, trolls, giants, a world of castles, fortresses, and secret doors.

After the murder, I spent much time alone in this world.

It was a sweltering Independence night in 1987. I pitted two green tanks against each other and lit them at the same time; one inevitably blew the other to smithereens, catching fire and burning to a heap of black ash. It was a good start to a night of roman candles, wheels and stars, and sparklers. Weeks before, I had organized the fireworks into an order. It was important to save the best for last.

But soon I had exhausted my meager supply of fireworks and was about to call it a night, but down the street a ways, the sky was lit afire by a barrage of glowing reds, whites, and blues. I saw a group of people

20

scrambling about the house that had been for sale just a short week ago. Someone must have moved in. I asked my parents if I could go watch.

I crept down the street furtively like a ninja, clad in black and using the shadows as cover. I wanted to be the unobserved observer. I got closer, and the booms came in droves. I didn't see any kids save for one small girl. I saw five adults drinking beer and barbequing hot dogs in their driveway. I thought it was strange to barbeque hotdogs in the front yard—that was a backyard thing to do. But there was a strange omen about these people.

I crept closer and kneeled down in the street and watched. One of the adults, with a beer in hand, knelt down and lit a string of black cats. He stepped back just in time before they went off like a series of gunshots—pop, pop, pop—the others howled in laughter. I laughed too in spite of myself.

Then I heard a bang, but it wasn't a firework. The screen door to the front of the house banged open and what materialized was a kid my age, my size with a bundle of fireworks. His eyes, like a wild nocturnal animal, gravitated to mine—at that moment time ceased to exist, the noise of the world was silenced. It was brief but real. Then he spoke and the world's torque began again.

"You want me get more? You want me get more?"

I nodded vigorously. "Yes, yes," I shouted.

The boy ran back into the house and emerged a moment later with an even larger armful. I ran up to him and helped with what I could. The adults didn't seem a bit surprised that some neighborhood kid had suddenly appeared within their ranks. I was handed a soda and the boy and I began lighting fireworks.

"My parents call me Christopher Clark, but I like Chris or Conan," he said. I was mesmerized—if anything, I was looking at myself. He was a skinny, brown-haired boy, same height, and we both had bright, blue eyes.

"I'm Orville James McFadden," I said. "But I'm just Orville."

"Like the popcorn."

"Yeah, I guess."

From that moment on, we couldn't be separated. He showed me the inimitable Legend of Zelda and Final Fantasy on the Nintendo, and I showed him all the great secret hiding spots in the neighborhood—the hidden passageways under the bushes and trees just like in The Legend of Zelda video game. He introduced me to G.I. Joe action figures, and I showed him how to properly turn a stick into a sword. He showed me how to build a tree house, and I showed him how to build a fort using blankets, furniture, and National Geographic Magazines.

The night before my eighth birthday, there was a massive thunder storm. The neighborhood youth had assembled to play an all-night game session. This particular night marked the first time Chris and I were allowed to play night games with the older kids.

"Alright, we have six teams of two," said Brian, a thirteen-year old boy who was the unofficial leader of the neighborhood. "Here are the ground rules for the novices." Brian was a soccer player and dribbled so incredibly fast that he could be up and down the field without having to pass along to his team members. But that was not his way. He was an intelligent and devout Christian who had learned to share. He had an aura of leadership and respectability I wanted to possess—he could quell any quarrel and make friends with anyone, and I wanted to prove to him tonight I had what it took to be a part of their night game gang.

"Front yards only—you can use the side yards, but no back yards. Also, you have to stay within the neighborhood. The boundaries are Mr. Scott's yard all the way to Mrs. Davis's yard. That's big enough with twelve. Third rule is that you have to be tagged to be it. Just because you see someone, movement or anything, doesn't mean they are it. You have to be tagged. And, I think that's everything."

"And no crying," said the biggest kid. "And newcomers are it first."

"No, just like normal. Rock, paper, scissors. Please choose a representative and square off."

Chris and I looked at each other. "Do you want to do it?" I asked him.

"Ah, I guess so," he said.

So Chris squared off with another boy and won two out of three.

"Good because I have the best, best, best hiding spot in the whole world," I said.

"Where is it?" he asked.

"I'll show you, but we shouldn't go there right away. We'll let the other guys go their ways first."

A team of girls end up being it first. Brian's backyard was where they had to count. If we heard the creaky wooden door squeak open, we knew we only had seconds to find a hiding place.

"Hey, you need help finding a spot?" Brian asked me.

"Thanks, but I'm going to try one I already know first," I said.

"I like it," Brian said. "Alright, see you later—or maybe not." He scampered off through some trees and was gone.

"So, where're we going?" Chris asked.

"Mrs. Henry's yard," I said.

"Everyone's going to use her yard," Chris said.

"But they'll never find us."

Chris and I ran furtively down the street toward Mrs. Henry's yard. We slipped in through the side because I didn't want to be seen entering. I didn't want the most secretive hiding spot to be known by anyone. I had found it the year before when I was out collecting bugs. I was looking for walking sticks and had climbed into one of the large juniper bushes when I fell into a small crevice. When I peered upwards, I only saw green foliage. I had lifted my head and could see that I was parallel with the street. All I would have to do is duck down and nobody could see me, even with a flashlight. It was there I was taking Chris.

I climbed in first and found my bearings. Chris climbed in after me. It was snug, but we both fit. We peered our heads up to the surface of the street. All was quiet. This was it. We had made it. This was our first night game session and it was going perfectly.

We waited there in the dark silence for about ten minutes, but ten minutes seemed an eon to an eight-year old.

"I'm kind of bored," Chris said.

"Really? How come?"

"Nothing's happening."

"They're out there somewhere," I whispered.

"Maybe the game is over," Chris whispered back.

"It just started," I said. "Be quiet. I hear something."

We both heard footsteps on the road. They were moving quickly, but skillfully like an assassin on a rooftop. Then they stopped. Chris and I looked out above our hole and saw the sneakers of one of the girls. She was so close to us, maybe five feet away.

"Mary," she whispered. Another girl came up to her. "I heard voices coming from somewhere around here." They started thrashing around the nearby bushes. I gave a hard look to Chris; if the girls found us, the secret spot would be revealed. And, even worse, we would be the laughing stock of the neighborhood. The girls moved quickly from bush to bush; but they only checked the surfaces. They quickly looked under trees and shrubs and finally moved up the street.

"You're lucky," I said.

"Whatever. It's more fun when they're close anyway."

A few moments later, we heard a rustle and then footsteps followed by a scream and then laughter.

"You're it," Mary said.

The two boys must have been hiding somewhere near us. They passed us by on the street grumbling about being found by two girls and went to count in Brian's backyard.

The game ended with Chris and I never being found,

our hiding spot secure for future use, and a congratulations from Brian for surviving our first night.

"Some of the boys thought you guys went home early," Brian said. "They couldn't find you so they thought you were pansies and went home. I didn't think so."

***

After our session, I went into the cafeteria to have lunch, which consisted of a wheat roll, tomato soup, saltine crackers, honeydew melon, green beans, and chocolate milk. I took my tray and sat down at a table. I looked around me. There were a few other patients in the room: a red-haired, rough-looking guy stared straight ahead and ate his food mechanically, a skinny, darker skinned boy about eighteen or nineteen wearing blue pajamas sat with an older, balding nervous-looking man, a large black man sat at the same table as the red-haired man reading a newspaper, and at my table was a large woman with stringy brown and gray hair. She looked over at me.

"You must be new," she said. "Normally, we can pick our own lunch, well, dinner and breakfast too, and we can get snacks out of that refrigerator over there." She pointed to a small refrigerator in the corner of the room. "I can tell you're new because nobody orders the tomato soup."

"Ah, I see," I said. I wasn't sure if it was a good idea to talk to the other patients, but she seemed harmless enough.

"We're not supposed to ask, but what did you do to get here?" she said.

"Ah, I had sort of a rough go," I said.

"Okay, okay. Me too. I've tried to commit suicide three times, but I like it here. The nurses are nice, and the food is good. Yes, things outside are pretty unhappy. Well, you know. Oh, I'm sorry. I'm Janice. Nice to meet you. What's your name?"

25

"Orville."

"Oh, just like the popcorn. You're famous you know. Well, it's a pleasure to meet you. So, I'm not sure if they've told you or not, but sometimes they just let us roam around like sheep, but we have classes here during the day when we aren't talking to the doctors. The classes are nice enough too. They really help sometimes."

"What kinds of classes?" I asked.

"Oh, you know, getting help classes. Like how to find housing, how to cope. They use that word a lot here— cope. It rhymes with hope so they use them a lot in the same sentence. I like it. Anyway, the classes help us find ways to make it outside. You know, in the real world. Some people here really listen to them, but others don't..." she said, whispering that last part.

"How long have you been here?" I asked.

"Oh, I've been here off and on for a few years now. I like it here. The nurses are nice, and the food is good. I like the classes too."

After lunch, I asked one of the staff nurses if I could see a schedule of the classes. I saw that there were classes on getting housing, dealing with stress, coping with struggles, finding information on jobs, everything someone would need to know out in the real world. The real world—it seemed so far away. I looked around again. The ward was an egg with a walking track. There were various rooms, some classrooms, some bedrooms, and some lounge rooms, and a few offices. The nurse's station and the elevator to the other parts of the hospital were at the tip of the egg. The ward felt miniscule and cramped. A few days in here, someone could really go insane. But I looked in at the lunch table and figured they were all probably insane anyway, at least to a degree. I looked at the schedule again. There weren't any classes for another hour so I decided to walk around the egg and get some exercise.

I walked twice around when I came across the skinny boy and the nervous-looking man just sitting down at one

26

of the side tables in the walkway with a deck of cards. I stopped at their table.

"Oh hello, I'm Peter," said the nervous looking man. "You must be new. How do you like it so far?"

"It's okay I guess," I said.

"Yes, it's quite nice I think. Please, sit down and play cards with us."

I sat down opposite the skinny boy. He looked at me with a wide grin on his face, but said nothing.

"This is Juan. He's shy and doesn't say much," Peter said. Peter had enough stubble on his face to suggest he hadn't shaved for a few days, and whenever he spoke, his nose twitched and his eyes blinked quickly. It was hard for me to look at him when he was talking. "So, what do you like to play?" Peter's voice was so soft I could have mistaken him for a woman.

"How about Rummy?" I said.

"Oh yes. I love Rummy, but I don't think Juan knows how to play. Do you know how to play Juan?"

Juan shook his head slowly.

"Could you, perhaps, explain the rules to Juan?" Peter asked. "I'm not good at that sort of thing."

I took the deck of cards and shuffled them out evenly to the three of us and explained the rules to Juan and Peter (who didn't seem to know how to play after all). We played a few hands, and I had nearly doubled both their scores.

"Oh, you're good at cards. Out there I would call you a card shark, but in here, we don't have any money to play with," Peter said.

"Oh, no, my mom taught me this game. She's much better than me. I'm no shark," I said.

"And a good liar too—not liar, I apologize, fibber—little white lies. Very good," he said, patting my knee with his hand. I slid my chair away instinctively. I looked at Juan who smiled back like this was all a big jolly joke. I looked at Peter who was trying now to shuffle the cards himself. We played a few more hands before I won the game, and then I said I wanted to go check out some of the classes.

"Well, we'll certainly practice while you're gone so that next time we play, we can be much, much better," Peter said.

I got up and left. When I turned back, Peter was explaining something to Juan, but what startled me was that Peter's hand was now on Juan's thigh, and Juan was no longer smiling.

Chapter 3

In the spring of 1989, Chris and I found ourselves in an old, magical forest of Christmas trees. The oldest tree had been there since 1976—the year my parents had purchased our house. My mother hated the idea of buying dead trees and tossing them to the inferno; so we bought potted ones and planted them every two years in the yard. A forest had arisen.

Beyond the backyard was a canyon, a boy's dream. There was no fence shielding the long sledding runs save a row of juniper trees. We overlooked it through the webbing of prickly leaves, our very own magical wardrobe. There were pockets of trees stretching for three entire neighborhoods, and there was an old tree house that had been built some years back at the bottom of the high slope. At the foot were long stretches of apple orchards.

"Let's go down into the canyon," Chris said.

"But my dad and uncle are building the garage," I said. "I want to watch."

My father was a professional pool player, sticking mostly to tournaments in the western half of the United States, but when he did venture east, our family would set out on a road trip together to watch him play, which is how I saw most of the United States (from the back seat of the car), but mostly he went alone. My father wanted to open a billiards hall in the backyard with the garage. At first it would be small, six to eight tables, and then he had plans to expand it once it got going. The concrete had been poured and the frame built, and now my uncle and my father were working on the roof. I watched and helped out as much as I could, but mostly Chris and I played while my father set out to work.

My mother was barbequing chicken just as life was about to change. My uncle and father wanted a break and went to get some beer. My uncle was a large, burly man who dwarfed my father, but he always said my father was one of the toughest men he had ever known. I believed it too. My dad was small in stature, weighing only 150 pounds or so, but he had done some boxing in his younger days and built quite a name for himself in the pool halls. He didn't talk about it much, but my mother told me they had had to run out of the boxing club once after he had pummeled a man.

My uncle came back carrying something in his hand. I couldn't make it out from the distance, but it looked like some sort of glove.

"Orville, over here," he said. The sweet smell of BBQ chicken permeated the air, and my hunger suddenly flared up. He handed me the thing. My father came over and didn't look surprised to see me carrying it. He had a subtle smile on his face. "I thought it was high time the kid got one of these," my uncle said.

My father handed my uncle a beer and went into the house only to come out moments later with an old, weathered glove of his own. I looked down at my new mitt, signed by Kirk Gibson, made by Wilson.

"Well, put it on," my father said.

I put the glove on; it felt good in my hand. I squeezed it a few times; it was a little stiff, but not too bad. Chris said nothing. Neither of us had ever expressed any interest in playing baseball, and the thought actually scared me a little. I had seen it played on television, and it looked dangerous.

"Well, how does it feel?" My uncle asked.

"It feels good," I said.

"I bet it does," my uncle said, taking a ball out of his back pocket. "Brand new." He threw the ball to my father who caught it easily.

My father told me to watch the ball into the mitt. We squared off a short distance, and he threw the ball to me softly at first. I caught it, and threw it back to him. My father look at my uncle, and my uncle looked at my father knowingly; his eyebrows raised just enough to indicate they were thinking the same thing. I felt like I was performing some ritual of fate, as if my entire life hinged on this moment—the hands of fate were weaving my future.

Chris watched as my father and I moved farther and farther back, throwing the ball back and forth with ease. If I could have stayed in that moment forever, I would have. The look on my father's face when he was throwing the ball to me was the happiest I had ever seen him. It was filled with pride and nostalgia—here was his son, his likeness, doing with me what his father had done with him, and he looked at me as his father had looked at him.

"He's a natural," my uncle said. "Just like you were."

"I suppose we need to buy a bat and a few balls," my father said.

Tryouts were later that spring. I convinced Chris to tryout with me. When we arrived, there was already a large group of boys mulling about. I recognized one kid from my elementary school class. The coach was a heavyset man, but with soft eyes and a big smile. He tried to lighten the nervousness by telling jokes, but nobody laughed—we were too busy surveying the kids circled together. There were some big kids there and my stomach felt like tiny butterflies were flying in through a tube and darting to and fro along the large, walled organ. Chris seemed fine because he didn't really want to make the team anyway. But the inside of my baseball glove was wet with sweat as the coach watched us play catch. Chris and I had been playing catch all spring so I knew how hard to throw it to him, but I also wanted to impress the coach so I was throwing a little harder than usual, and he kept missing it. I threw it at his chest like I had been taught, but he skirted to the side and tried to catch it at an angle, but it kept going passed his glove.

"Sorry," I shouted to him.

"Nice throw," the coach said as he walked by.

After we played catch, we were divided into two

groups. The first group would hit, and the second group would catch fly balls. I was in the second group, and my father offered to hit the balls. He had played baseball when he was young too and had been a natural, but somewhere along the line, he had stopped playing. I didn't know the details, but I had heard stories from my uncle about how great he had been. He had a good arm and had power in his swing. He sent the fly balls soaring up into the sky. The other kids around me had trouble catching them, but I was used to them by now and caught every one that was hit to me.

"How do you catch those?" asked one of the kids.

"I don't know," I said. And I didn't know. But when the ball was hit, I followed it with my eyes and ran to the spot I knew it was going. After that, it was simply squeezing it just like when playing catch. It seemed easy. There wasn't much to it I thought.

When it was time to hit, I passed Chris as the groups changed positions.

"How'd you hit?"

"I didn't," he said. "I missed."

After hitting, the coach had us run the bases. Chris and I were both quick so we both did well at this. Once we had finished, we were called over and were told that we would be getting calls later that night.

"I wouldn't worry about it," my father said while driving us home. "You did great. And you too Chris."

"Thanks Mr. McFadden, but baseball's not really my thing," Chris said.

The call came just after eight o'clock. The coach said he was excited to welcome me to the team and that practice started later that week.

When I hung up the phone, I ran downstairs where my dad was playing pool. "Dad, dad! I made the team. I made the team."

"I think this calls for ice cream," my mother said.

"Yes—can we go to Baskin Robbins?"

"Anywhere you want."

It was early summer, and the season was nearly over. We had done well, on the brink of making the playoffs if we could win out. I had been a surprise power hitter despite my scrawniness, and had had two inside-the-park home runs.

It was a hot Saturday morning, and the skies were blue and clear, perfect baseball weather. We were down by a run, and I had struck out twice already. But I found myself in an inevitable situation: the tying run was on second after hitting a double with two outs, and I was on deck with the nine-hole hitter batting.

Please get out; please get out. Was that me or the demon that had tunneled deep down into my mind and pervaded it with dangerously subtle thoughts?

You will strike out, said fear. You will fail.

The first pitch was a ball, high. The second swung on and fouled past the first base line. The third was low and in the dirt. Then a swing and a miss—two balls and two strikes. The fifth pitch was again low and in the dirt—a full count.

"Please strike out; please strike out," I muttered.

The next pitch was swung on and fouled into the catcher's glove, but the catcher dropped it. And then the payoff pitch...ball four. I slowly walked toward the batter's box with my head down. Don't strike out. Don't strike out. Don't strike out. I dug into the dirt with my cleats. I looked down at coach who clapped his hands. The first pitch—strike one on the outside corner. The second pitch, I swung on and hit a line drive diving toward the right field line—I made a few steps when it was called foul, just an inch or two off the white chalk. That could have been it. That would have done it. That would have scored the runs we needed to take the lead. Two inches had decided my fate. I had two strikes. I was going to strike out. It was inevitable. The next pitch came. I thought it looked outside, but it caught the corner and was called strike three. I hung my head and headed back into the dugout. I

33

had had three at bats and three strike outs, and my father watched from the stands.

Our last chance came in the bottom of the sixth inning. We were still down by one run with two outs. There was a runner on third when it was my turn to bat. It seemed inevitable that the same situation featured itself.

"Orville," coach said, calling me over from the third base line.

I walked from the batter's box to where he was standing.

"You've had a rough go today huh?"

"Yeah..."

"How do you feel?"

"I don't know," I said, tears beginning to swell in my eyes.

"What do you think? Do you want a pinch hitter?"

I nodded my head. Coach called time and had a pinch hitter hit for me. I trudged my way back into the dugout without looking at my father. The pinch hitter struck out.

After the game, my father and I walked towards the car. Coach caught up with us just as I was sitting down in the passenger seat.

"What you did today Orville took a lot of guts," coach said. "I want you to have the game ball." He handed me the ball and walked away.

My father sat for a moment without starting the car.

"Orville, what you did today didn't take a lot of guts. You gave up a chance to make up for the other at bats. Who cares if you struck out three times before that? It was a new at bat. A hit would have won the game, but instead you put the bat in the hands of someone who didn't have as good a chance of getting a hit. You should never back down from opportunity even if you're scared."

***

"What happened that day?" Dr. Fields asked.

"I failed because..."

"Because of what?"

"Because...I was scared of failing. My entire baseball career I didn't focus on getting hits, but on not striking."

I went back to my room and lay down on the bed. It was three o'clock in the afternoon. I didn't feel like going to any classes. I just wanted to sleep. But I couldn't sleep. My entire baseball career was centered on not striking out. I wasted all the talent I had. I had the gifts: a strong arm, a quick bat, speed, baseball smarts, but I was a head case. Nobody defeated me more than myself. I was my own worst pitcher. Stars are born. How do those same stars diminish their light?—they do it themselves. I did it to myself. No one else—I diminished my own light through fear. I did it every time I went up to bat. I did it with the thoughts and words 'don't strike out'. Those words were the perfect pitch. And I did it every time. And in my family's eyes, I was just a gifted ball player not playing to his potential. And it was because I struck myself out.

I wanted something to eat. I got out of bed and went into the kitchen. A few of the patients were in there eating snacks. I watched as they slowly spooned out their Jello and stared at their peanut butter sandwiches, mesmerized by them. What the hell was I doing in this place?

Peter and Juan came in with a deck of cards.

"Ah, we were looking for you. I thought you might be in class, but here you are. Do you want to play rummy?" Peter asked.

"Sure, let's play," I said.

35

Chapter 4

"Lands of enchantment—the elements provide ample opportunity to imagine. Have you ever noticed in movies, when desired, the most astounding magical effects come from nature? Concrete just isn't fantastical enough. No—trees, mountains, fog—those are mysterious things...or can be, but cities are not—they might be scary or exciting, but not mysterious."

"Why do you think that is?"

"Because we build cities; we know their intricacies. The things we build have no magic. But we're only beginning to fathom the natural world."

***

Chris had an underground pool in his backyard and we cannon balled in from the sides.

"Have you ever played water demon?" Chris asked.

No.

"The legend says there's an ancient demon that comes up from the bottoms of swamps and lakes and sucks people down into its mouth."

"Like the Loch Ness monster," I said.

"But very, very evil."

We played water demon until we were hungry and then after lunch we played a game Chris dubbed Gruesome. We were marines, and we had to investigate and fight off an alien invasion that came from underground. Many marines perished. An average day in the world of Chris and Orville.

On a sweltering day in late August, my father took Chris and me fishing near the convergence of the Snake and Columbia Rivers, just outside Sacajawea State Park.

"The best place to fish is where the two rivers meet," my father said.

"Why?" Chris asked.

"Because the Columbia River is slightly warmer than the Snake so the fish want to go from the cold into the warm. And our worms will be there when they do."

We packed up our gear. Chris and I both had rustic tackle boxes filled with things we really didn't know how to use: plastic-looking fish with rusty hooks, metal weights of various sizes and shapes, extra fishing line, big bobbers and little bobbers, small, gummy-looking things that looked like grubs, and other strange nameless entities that had seemingly opaque uses. Inevitably, on these fishing trips, Chris and I would cast our lures into the water, and then after a few minutes scamper off to explore on our own the land around while my father drank Olympia and watched the poles.

We piled into my father's brand new Chevrolet pickup.

"Nice truck," Chris said.

"Never buy a Ford," my father said.

"It's true," I said. I didn't know why one should never buy a Ford, but if my father thought Fords were bad, then that was enough for me.

We stopped at a local convenience store and bought some worms that came in circular Styrofoam containers packed with soil. We drove through Pasco and out past the railroad tracks.

"You can drive all day in Pasco and never see a white person," my father said.

We had been driving for a while when we pulled off onto a narrow dirt road. We drove down that for a while until we came to a small cliff overlooking the two great rivers. I saw the contrast easily between the greenish Snake River and the dark blue Columbia. My father parked the truck and we hauled our gear down a sandy pathway.

"Watch your step," my father said. "It'll be wet down near the river."

Chris and I waded through the watery passage of pussy willows. Our shoes suctioned down into the water and mud—plop, plop, plop—we continued on through the tall grasses. My father stopped, turned to the two of us and smiled a mischievous and knowing smile, eyes alit and bright. He spread the grasses aside dramatically and there was a small shore with a sandy little beach and a log that we could sit on as we cast our lures out into the river. The water was sparkling blue, glistening in the sun's rays. It was like opening a door to a new world.

"Wow, this place is great," Chris said.

"I've been coming to this very spot for years," my father said. "I don't think anyone else knows about it."

We set down our tackle boxes and my father took Chris's pole and fished for a worm from the Styrofoam container.

"Do you know how to put the worm on the hook?"

"Uh, yeah, I think I remember," Chris said. Chris took the pole from my father and the worm, and while steadying the pole on his shoulder, he took the head of the worm and squeezed it onto the hook. The worm's blood trickled down Chris's finger, but the worm was attached.

I took my pole and dug for a worm in the soft soil. It started wiggling around on the palm of my hand, and I didn't like the feel of its slimy body, but I wasn't going to let my father see that so I steadied the pole just like Chris had, and I grabbed the hook and forced the worm onto it—a bit too hard as the hook jabbed into my forefinger.

"Shit," I said.

"What'd you say?" my father asked.

"What? You say it all the time," I said.

"Fine, this one time, but don't say it again and definitely don't say it around your mother."

"Say what?" I said.

"Good." My father took a band aid out from his tackle box and wrapped it around my finger. "Okay, you guys are ready to cast off. Here, let me show you how." My father took Chris's pole and flipped the spinner and held the line down with his forefinger. "Now, always check behind you before flinging your line back." He looked behind him to make sure there was no grass or trees impeding his cast and brought the pole back and whipped it forward letting go of the line just as the hook flew over his head. The cast was a good one, and it went a ways out into the water, the bobber bobbing happily in the dark blue. He handed the pole back to Chris.

"You want to try?" he said to me.

"Sure," I said. I took the pole, set the spinner, and held the line. I looked behind me just like he did and brought my pole back. I then swung it forward and let the line go—a successful cast. Chris and I held onto the poles for a short while waiting for the bobber to start bobbing, but nothing happened. My father set up his pole and cast it out. He then opened the ice chest he brought and took out a beer. He handed a soda to Chris and one to me. We three drank and watched our poles.

After about ten minutes and a few more casts, nothing seemed to be biting. Chris set his pole down between a circle of rocks and stretched. I did the same. My father looked over at us.

"It hasn't even been fifteen minutes," he said.

"What? We're just stretching," I said.

"Be careful," my father said.

"Okay," I said and Chris and I crawled up the sandy incline to go exploring.

Chris found a wooden stick and picked it up. I looked around until I found one too.

"I'm Conan," Chris said.

"You're always Conan," I said.

"So?"

"Be someone different."

"No, I want to be Conan."

39

"Fine, then I'm Link."

"You're always Link," Chris said.

"So?"

We walked around until we found the patch of trees we had gone through to get to the secret fishing hole. There, we looked around for significant treasure that may have been dropped—a chest of gold, silver coins, a wallet stuffed with cash—nothing could be found so we moved on. We walked up a small sand dune and stopped when a giant desert beetle slowly crawled across the hot sand in front of us. We watched it for a moment, deciding whether to kill or not to kill. Chris and I looked at each other and simultaneously put our thumbs up. We stepped slowly over the beetle and it stuck its back straight up into the air as a warning. We crested the hill. We stopped. I heard a distinctive sound. No more than six feet away was a giant rattlesnake rattling furiously, and just beyond it was another, baby rattlesnake.

"Shit," Chris said.

"Don't move," I said.

"Call your dad," Chris said.

"Yeah...dad," I yelped. "Dad, come here."

"What?" We heard his voice far down near the river.

"Come here—quickly."

My father came running up the sand dune with his .22 rifle. He came up behind us and saw what we were looking at.

"Okay, step back slowly," he said, taking the gun's safety off. We both stepped behind him, and the rattlesnakes coiled up in anger and fear. My father aimed and shot at the mother, blowing her head right off. The baby rattlesnake slithered quickly off into the brush.

"That...was...awesome," Chris said.

"True," I said.

***

"The introduction to sudden death is shocking and fear inducing, but it's nothing like the introduction to sex and desire," I said.

"Which is potentially more scarring," Dr. Fields said.

***

It was an inauspicious night for the unthinkable. Chris and I were playing Nintendo with a 14-year old girl named Rachel who had recently moved into the neighborhood. She told us she normally wouldn't be seen with 12-year olds, but the circumstances favored us—her being new and all. "We can only *play* if you do what I say." "Sure, fine, yeah," we said in unison. My father was out shooting pool and my mother was sleeping on the couch with an empty bottle of red wine on the nightstand. She had bought pizza and coke for our Friday night sleepover and left us to the typical small town suburban action of finding our own entertainment.

"Have you ever played truth or dare?" Rachel asked. No.

"Let's play. It's more fun than Mario World."

"How do you play?" I said.

"Easy. If someone dares you to do something, you have to do it or you lose. Or if someone says truth, you have to tell them a secret, a good secret—not something stupid like what your favorite color is. If you lose, you have to leave the room, and the winner gets whatever *she* wants. So let's play. Chris, you go first."

Chris and I looked at each other. What could we do?— she was older, cute, and the first girl that we had ever really talked to.

"Okay...Orville, truth. Do you think Rachel is cute?"

I didn't dare look at Rachel, but I felt her burning gaze upon me like the sun through a magnifying glass on a poor, hapless ant. My face turned a deep crimson and I

41

suffocated on my own words. I didn't like this game. "Ah...geez Chris...ah, yeah, so what? So do you."

"My turn," Rachel said, unaffected and unabashedly. "Orville—truth. Have you ever kissed a girl?"

"No," I said. "Geez, why are you guys picking on me?"

"It's part of the game. Your turn."

"Okay, Chris—dare. I dare you to kiss Rachel."

They looked at each other and Rachel giggled. Chris shrugged his shoulders and leaned in and gave Rachel a peck on the lips. I couldn't believe it. I had never seen Chris even talk to a girl before. "That was easy. My turn," Chris said. He seemed to be enjoying himself. "Rachel, I dare you to kiss Orville with tongue."

She wouldn't possibly...what if she did though? What would I do? What if she was disgusted? I didn't even know how to do it. I didn't know if I wanted to know.

"Orville," she started. "Come here Orville." My legs proved indomitable against my own resistance to crawl my way over to her. I found my heart racing to an unyielding tempo—something in the realm of drums beating on top of the sacrificial Tenochtitlan temple. Rachel turned my head toward hers. How much older she looked than me. Her short brown hair had been crimped just that day and she wore makeup on her face, even lipstick—so fashionable, so chic. "Close your eyes," she said. I closed them. Then I felt soft lips upon mine, but I didn't know what to do. "Open your mouth Orville." I opened it a bit and suddenly felt her wet, slimy tongue touching mine. And I was lost in the moment. Then, just as quickly, it was over. I opened my eyes and looked about me. Chris was cracking up and Rachel simply leaned back against the dresser. My first kiss was done and the moment was already moving on.

"My turn. Chris and Orville, I dare you to take your shirts off." We had been swimming all day and I had had my shirt off the entire time so I didn't think that it was going to be strange at all, but it did feel strange to take it off in my little bedroom while she looked on. I took it off and set it next to my bed. I felt Rachel look at me again and I crossed my arms.

"You're so shy," she said.

When it was my turn again, I asked Chris something about truth, but I couldn't even remember what he said or what I asked. I felt completely uncomfortable sitting there half naked in the black spandex shorts I had worn swimming. I looked down upon my body—the baby fat around my stomach rolled up into what looked like two fatty rolls of bread dough, and I couldn't see even an ounce of muscle. My chest hadn't started to harden up and it looked like my pectorals were inverted. I felt miniscule.

Then Chris dared the unthinkable and the awkwardness was compounded. Rachel mused for a moment and then shrugged her shoulders. She got up, took her shirt off and then quickly pulled down her shorts and underwear. She was completely naked and just inches away from me. Then she started dancing, and I saw something I had never seen before, and it wasn't even where I thought it was supposed to be. Her two, small round bubbles of breasts jiggled as she danced and I found myself mesmerized by them—I wanted to touch them and squeeze them. Rachel then promptly sat back down with her legs crossed. She looked right at me, but I couldn't stop staring at the little tuft of hair that had grown around what I considered Antarctica and the strange little opening that lay beneath it.

"Orville," she said. "I dare you to touch me."

The motions of time in relation to thought and awareness were moving too quickly to stop, and the air seemed like a discombobulating haze of fateful soup pouring down upon my head. I reached over and touched her just above the knee. She then took my hand and slid it slowly down along her thigh, and I felt the spandex shorts inch upward, and suddenly everything felt so good.

My father came home shortly after, and Rachel went home. Chris was spending the night, but I left him in my bedroom while I went into the bathroom. I locked the door. I laid down on the cold tile and thought of Rachel dancing around naked, and I thought of touching her and how good it felt. And I felt my hips swiveling slowly in circles upon the cold tile.

Touch yourself, touch yourself, said the great concubine.

I found my hand reaching down and rubbing the spandex, and it felt good. I thought of Rachel and putting my finger in her, and then something explosive happened. I thought I had peed myself. I took off the spandex shorts and found I was covered in a white, gooey liquid. I quickly took some tissue paper and wiped it away, but it was extremely difficult. I flushed what I could down the toilet. Then I heard my mother crying downstairs.

***

"I thought it was because of what I had just done," I said. "It was perfect, or rather imperfect timing. Everything was bewildering at that moment. That night I kept moving from one experience to the next without time to think clearly about any of them. It was all impulse."

"Why was your mother really crying?"

***

I put my shorts back on despite their stickiness and crept along the hallway. I met Chris there and we both crawled along until we got to the top of the stairs. My mother and father were downstairs, and my mother was sitting on the couch with her hands to her face.

"What did you do?" she asked my father. "Who is she?"

"She's nobody," my father said. "Nothing happened."

My father looked up at us with dull eyes and for the first time I saw something I hadn't seen before. "Orville, go back to your room. Your mother and I are talking."

44

***

Dr. Fields sat next to me on the couch, which I appreciated—it felt like we were having a conversation rather than a psychiatric appointment. These sessions were nothing like the movie scenes within nicely decorated offices with plaques and credentials on the walls, with bookcases carrying large voluminous books with increasingly difficult names to pronounce, with elongated brown leather couches. No—this was the nitty-gritty psychology that real life required.

"Tell me first about your father."

"My dad was a great man. He was...everything I wanted to become. He was athletic, intelligent, charming, adventurous, loving, a fantastic pool player, once a great baseball player, he was attractive. He was my hero really."

"He was flirtatious too," Dr. Fields said.

"Yes, he was also flirtatious," I said.

"Did you know that then?"

"No, no. I was blind to it. My dad had demons—he was all these great things put into one person, but he was still human. Very human. My mom told me about the cheating after I got married."

"How did that information make you feel about your father?"

"I don't know...I still see him as this great man. I understand demons; I understand *his* demons...." I stared at the white walls of the little room. His demons were my demons. Everything my father was, I was. I saw it now. I had become my father. "Boys want to become their fathers whether they know it or not."

Chapter 5

"When we're professional, we'll be surrounded by money and women," Clint said.

"Where'd you hear that?" I said.

"Everyone knows this."

"I'm going to play for New York," Brett said.

"Yankees blow. Boston baby," Clint said.

"Mariners all the way," I said.

"The Mariners are horrible," Brett said.

The three of us stood in a corner outside of Mrs. Smith's classroom. I was the starting center fielder for the seventh grade A team and had adjusted well to the larger fields—three-hundred-fifty-foot plus fences, ninety-foot bases, a sixty-foot, six-inch (elevated) pitching mound, and now we were able to use big barreled bats and metal cleats. I had been nervous about the changes; I had heard of star Little League players not adjusting well and whittling out.

It had been no surprise what was tucked away under the tree that year—a brand new, big barreled, white TPX baseball bat with a pro cap at the end. My father and I had gone to the middle school's baseball field and he had pitched to me from the mound (I couldn't wait to try it out despite the frigid temperature), which seemed massive compared to the Little League mounds that were only forty six feet away and basically flat. It seemed as if he had been pitching from second base, but I had liked it because I could see the ball for a longer stretch of time. It felt like I could sit there and wait all day. But, the TPX was a full eight ounces heavier than the bat I had used just a few months ago so I had had some work to do before spring.

A trio of slender girls wearing black leggings and skirts rounded the corner of the hallway and walked straight toward us. We shut up immediately and Clint leaned back against the lockers, Brett crossed his arms, and I felt awkward and out of place so I leaned against the wall and tried to follow suit.

The tallest slender girl in the middle was named Jennifer Baxter. Her black leggings hugged her legs to the point I thought that they were a part of her skin; I couldn't look away from them, but she didn't even look in my direction. The other two girls were cute, but Jennifer Baxter stopped you dead in your tracks. She had an older sister in ninth grade who showed her how to apply makeup flawlessly and to walk with a purpose so that boys would notice. And we noticed.

They stopped directly in front of us. Jennifer's two friends twitched excitedly, but Jennifer stood with her hands on her hips in complete confidence. She tilted her head slightly to the side when she talked.

"Hey guys," Jennifer said.

"What's up Jennifer?" Clint said.

Clint and Brett chatted with Jennifer flawlessly, a skill I marveled at—where did they learn it?—I was awkwardly left off to the side against the wall, and I felt the burning heat of embarrassment warming my cheeks. I couldn't stay still and kept changing positions, which finally drew the look of the girl next to me, but she didn't smile and quickly turned away when I managed to look her in the eye.

"We're coming to your game today," Jennifer said.

"Good. We like to have an audience when we destroy somebody," Brett said.

"You'd better because I don't want to waste my time."

Jennifer's two friends feigned confidence and tried to scowl at us the way Jennifer could, but they were just as nervous to be around us as I was to be around them. They kept changing their stances I was sure they practiced in a mirror at home, but didn't say a word.

"Hey Orville."

That voice. Not now.

Chris and two of his lackeys came up to me. Jennifer and the rest of the gang stopped talking immediately and turned toward me as if surprised I was there (and perhaps even more surprised that somebody addressed me rather than them). Chris was a little taller than me now, but was extremely thin, almost deathly I thought; he hadn't begun growing into his father's body. His two friends were identical twins with red, curly hair and glasses. One wore a tie-dye shirt with blue jeans, and the other wore a black shirt with a raccoon on it.

"Are we going to finish Avengers tonight?" Chris asked.

"What's Avengers?" Jennifer said.

"It's just a game," I said. I shuffled Chris quickly down the hall away from Clint, Brett, and the girls. Jennifer watched as I shooed them away for a moment.

"I have a game tonight," I said.

"What about afterwards?" Chris asked.

"Maybe. I'll call you," I said.

"Who are those girls?"

"The tall one is Jennifer Baxter," I said. "I don't know the names of the other girls."

"They look like bitches," Chris said.

"They're okay," I said.

"Do you want us to come to your game?"

"No, it's going to be boring."

"Okay, call me when you get home."

They walked away and I went back to the group.

"So what's Avengers?" Jennifer asked.

"It's a video game," I said.

"Sounds stupid," Jennifer said.

"Yeah, it kind of is," I said.

She promptly turned her back to me and continued talking to Brett and Clint.

"Don't suck tonight," she said and walked away with the other girls.

Tonight would have to be my night.

I called Chris after the game. We had won 7 to 6 against our most hated rival, Highlands. I had hit a home run and the game winning single, and Jennifer Baxter and her two cute cronies had watched it all. I was indulgent in the aftermath of glory. If I had had money, I would have given it away. If I had been 21 years old, I would have bought the entire bar a drink. Instead, I met Chris at the top of the canyon wall in high spirits, ready to conquer the world.

"Where did we leave off?" I asked jovially.

"Yeah, yeah, sweet. We were just about to go into Solkanar the Swamp King's swamp," Chris said.

We picked up the wooden sticks that magically turned into swords as soon as our golden hands touched them, and we cascaded down the slope into the canyon, swords raised, screaming our war cries into the night. It was there our greatest adventure was taking place, heavily influenced by the new card game, Magic: The Gathering. We called ourselves The Avengers.

The Avengers – Cast

Dakkon Blackblade played by Orville McFadden
Ihsan's Shade played by Orville McFadden
Chandler played by Orville McFadden
Tor Wauki played by Orville McFadden

Marhault Elsdragon played by Christopher Clark
Veldrane of Sengir played by Christopher Clark
Joven played by Christopher Clark
The Dragon Summoner played by Christopher Clark

Lim-Dul, the Necromancer, played by imaginary monster
Solkanar the Swamp King, played by imaginary monster
Miscellaneous monsters, played by imaginary monsters

We traveled stealthily through the muck-filled swamp, trying to keep the clanking of our armor to a minimum—a group of heroes out to destroy the Necromancer, the evil Lim-Dul. His reign of terror had swept through the land; his horde of evil minions had ravaged the innocent. All who had tried to destroy him before had been vanquished by his devilish subjects and his evil magic. We were the land's last hope. We were, The Avengers!

We traveled deep into the vast swampland.

"I've heard this swamp is the home of Sol'kanar the Swamp King," Marhault Elsdragon said.

"We must make our way through it," Dakkon Blackblade said.

We stepped into the murky green and black water with trepidation. We knew that the dead made this swamp their home. Yet all was still. The only sound was the swishing of our boots through the watery depths. Silently, bats flew overhead. But where there were bats, there were vampires. We knew it was just a matter of time before the blood coursing through our veins was made known to the wraiths and creatures that fed on the living.

"Quiet, I think I hear something," Veldrane of Sengir said.

"I didn't hear anything but all the racket you're making," Chandler said.

"You're one to talk loud mouth," Joven said.

"Joven, you couldn't...wait—Bog Wraith," Chandler screamed.

And out of the muck came a soulless wraith—all the shadows under the bright moon materialized into this evil being. The wraith let out a screeching scream and flew toward us. Its touch was death. It stretched out its hand towards Marhault's throat when Ihsan's Shade slashed at it with his black sword. The wraith's hand turned to smoke and its piercing scream cut into our minds. At the sight of the blood, the wraith went insane and started slashing with its other hand at our throats, desperately wanting to turn our bodies cold so that it could feed. Just as the ghostly hand was about to squeeze the life out of Chandler who had fallen over a log in the swamp,

Veldrane of Sengir slashed with his mighty sword from the wraiths head down to its black body and it was split in two.

"It's about time," Chandler said. "That was too close."

"I should have waited just a second more," Veldrane said.

The party traveled on, more alert than before. One wraith was only the beginning. Sol'kanar the Swamp King knew all that happened within his swamp—he knew we were coming. It was only a matter of time before the news of that wraith's death traveled throughout the swamp. We only hoped that our legendary deeds preceded us and that the swamp creatures would fear our swords. But their hunger was a maddening force.

"Uh oh," Joven said.

"I second that," Chandler said.

Descending down upon the party was a horde of vampires, but not just any vampires—Sengir vampires. The Baron Sengir's horde of bloodthirsty undead were flying directly toward us with mouths agape and fangs protruding.

"Veldrane, you know how to fight them best—what do we do?"

Veldrane of Sengir once swore allegiance to the Baron, but betrayed him when the Baron had killed Veldrane's love, Rashka the Slayer (the best vampire hunter in the world). And now Vedrane wanted his revenge.

"They are fast and show no mercy. Cut off their heads."

And then it was an all out battle as the Sengir vampires attacked mercilessly from all angles. Dakkon's sword cut through them two at a time—Ihsan's Shade split their oily, bloody bodies in half—Joven tossed his knives relentlessly into their hearts—Chandler knifed them from behind. The blood spilled was the blood of all the innocent people the vampires had drank up. Their screams as they sank into the muck were deafening. The warriors fought on, slashing and slicing until all the vampires had perished. Once again, Sol'kanar the Swamp King was thwarted.

Our swords became walking sticks once again as a car passed us on the roadway. Two teenagers slashing about with sticks might be seen as strange to some.

"That was awesome," I said.

"Yeah, we took down a horde of Sengir Vampires—I was thinking when we fight Sol'kanar, we shouldn't kill him. I really like him," Chris said.

"Okay, we'll just fight him to a standoff or something."

The warriors rested briefly before moving on. They took some mana out of their pockets to eat so they would be ready for the next battle, whenever it came. They trudged on without incident until they came to a large half circle of skeleton trees. A figure approached them silently out of the shadows.

"What's that?" Chandler said.

"That must be Sol'kanar," Marhault Elsdragon whispered.

Sol'kanar the Swamp King approached them slowly— he was the scariest looking beast they had ever laid eyes upon: his body was of pure black and green muscle and he carried a huge bone cane with spikes on both ends. His head was covered in horns and his black hair flowed down to his shoulders. His teeth were like those of a vampire and his eyes flashed a cruel yellow. He came alone.

"To ever escape this swamp, you must defeat me," he bellowed with a deep, frightening, thunderous voice.

"We don't want to fight you—our battle is with Lim Dul," Dakkon Blackblade said.

"Your battle is with me," Sol'kanar thundered. And he raised his two gruesome arms in the air and all around the warriors, pinkish oozes seemingly seeped up from the swamp. Their bodies oozed with the flesh of their victims.

One touch from their slimy hands meant death. They looked as if they constantly were melting away, but the slime and ooze never stopped flowing. Their eye sockets were slits with nothing behind them.

"Abominations," Veldrane cried.

"Don't let them touch you," Ihsan's Shade said.

And the abominations flanked the warriors and Sol'kanar with his spiked bone club sprang upon them with such quickness and speed, they were forced to retreat back.

"It's now or never," Chandler screamed.

"Attack," Joven said, hurling his knives into the abominations' pink bodies.

The warriors cut down the horde of abominations as they were slow and fleshy, but Sol'kanar was anything but—he attacked quickly with his club and moved from one warrior to the next. He suddenly attacked and struck Marhault across the body—Marhault fell quickly and two abominations oozed their way to feed on his flesh, but then Dakkon Blackblade, whose power was as vast as the plains flew into a rage and crashed his sword into one abomination, felling it instantly, and then with a jumping stroke, his sword came down upon the other abomination's head, crushing it into his body. He helped Marhault up who for a moment had to egress from the battle.

Chandler was the first to get a hit on Sol'kanar as he knifed him in the back. Sol'kanar swung around and crashed his bone club into Chandler's arm, which made Chandler fly across the swamp. Sol'kanar went to finish the job, but Joven threaded his body with knives—his blood, a blackish, green ooze, poured out. Veldrane then leaped in and cut Sol'kanar's hand off with a slash of his great sword. Sol'kanar knew he was overwhelmed. He sunk down into the swamp and left the abominations to die. The battle was won.

They came to the edge of the swamp and emerged out victoriously, but the jubilation was short-lived as they saw an army of Ironclaw Orcs lined up for battle. Normally, Ironclaw Orcs were cowards and would run at the hint of danger, but something was keeping them in their ranks. The warriors stepped out of the swamp onto the battle field and surveyed what was holding the orcs captive. They saw *him*—a craw giant leading this charge. The orcs wouldn't dare run away with a craw giant there—the craw giant would destroy any who ran and his power was boosted when there were more attacking him. It would go into a sort of frenzy and his body would actually bulk up in the middle of the battle so that his strength was unparalleled. There was nothing the warriors could do but attack. Luckily, the orcs were not skilled in fighting. But the craw giant was and with six warriors attacking him at one time, his strength would be immense.

The six descended upon the enemy. The orcs must have felt confident that the warriors were going to retreat because their eyes lit up in surprise and were having trouble getting their weapons ready. Instead, the warriors crashed into their ranks and hacked away their lives. The craw giant was pacing back and forth, agitated. He began attacking the orcs himself in an attempt to reach Dakkon and Veldrane. A craw giant cannot help but jump into the fray.

The craw giant crashed down finally and the orcs retreated to form a circle around the six. They were trapped and would have to battle the craw giant and watch their backs from the cowardly orcs at the same time. A craw giant's skin is like rock, his strength like a volcano. He uses no weapons but his fists, but they are deadly. One strike could crush an armored man to bits. His white eyes glowed intensely—this giant wanted to battle and crush any under his massive foot. Nothing stood between Lim Dul's castle but this craw giant and the orc horde—they had to succeed.

Dakkon Blackblade attacked first, his sword alit with flame and struck down hard on the giant's shoulder to no avail. Quickly before the giant could crush Dakkon,

Veldrane of Sengir struck the giant on the underside of his ribcage, but his sword merely bounced off the giant's rocky skin. Chandler was sneaking around the giant to try and slice open his Achilles heel while Joven was rapidly tossing knives toward the giant's eyes. The craw giant swung his great body around and his fist smashed into Marhault Elsdragon's right leg—the sound of cracking bone and sinew being torn ripped across the field—the giant went to crush Marhault with his foot, but Ihsan's Shade with a mighty bellow, thrust his sword into the spine of the giant. Blood. Blood seeped out of the giant as he fell to his knees. The Dragon Summoner then called forth the ancient dragon Nicole Boles to battle the giant and Dakkon pounced on him and started hacking at the giant's thick legs, slicing and dicing until the giant could no longer get up. Joven and Chandler made sure no orcs attacked, but their attempts were unwarranted because the orcs were already fleeing from the fight. Then, with a great thrust, Dakkon Blackblade crushed his sword down upon the giant's chest. They had never heard such a howl of pain as Nicole Boles chomped away his head—his life was extinguished.

The battle was won. Only Lim Dul the Necromancer's fortress was left.

Unfortunately, it was time to go home—the epic battle would have to wait another day. We began walking back toward Chris's house. Our plan was to have an all-nighter. First we needed food, which would consist of corn dogs and ice cream bars. Then we would play Final Fantasy 2 on the Super Nintendo until morning.

Chapter 6

"By the time I was 13, I had forgotten what intense, sudden pain of loss felt like. All was well in the life of Orville McFadden—baseball and girls and school."
"What happened to change this?"
"I was reminded."

***

Brown hills and green irrigated fields drifted slowly by as I looked out from the car window at the golden lines whizzing by like thinly stretched rays of sunlight. I attempted to count each strip in my head, but gave up past twenty as the numbers began getting too long and my brain's computations weren't quick enough.

Light brown hills, speckled with sagebrush under blue skies—round mounds to other worlds and treasures with pockets of thick trees and pools of reflection were my childhood. I twitched excitedly at a knoll not seen before because of what could lie on the other side—there is always a glimmer of hope on the other side. My world was Hyrule wherein under a bush or within a cracked wall, I could find a goblin to give me thirty gold pieces if I kept his home a secret to everyone.

As all young adventures in the deserts of eastern Washington, I had begun the arduous task of digging a hole to China. Of course I told my father I was digging for worms, which he always allowed. A hole to China is a quest for something greater. Like the journey to the center of the earth, a hole dug is symbolic of its true purposes.

In the summer of 95', we went on a cross country trip to Raleigh-Durham, North Carolina for the thirteen-year old Babe Ruth World Series. It was scorching hot and dry as

56

an oven. My father drove, smoking cigarettes and drinking coca-cola. He wore faded blue jeans with small holes at the kneecaps, a striped baseball t-shirt, a mesh Slat's Jr. baseball cap, and aviators. I looked over at him. That was the image I would always remember him by—one arm on the wheel, one on the windowsill, an open coke can between his legs, cigarette in his mouth. My mother had found a black-and-white picture of him when he was eight-years old and had shown it to me. I was amazed at how similar we looked. I held the photo in my hand and looked at it as if I were looking into a time-warped mirror.

We drove with the windows down, the wind crashing into our faces. We talked of baseball and pool, of Wolfenstein 3D and computers. My father and I had a healthy competition going on with the Nazi destroying, Hitler toppling computer game Wolfenstein 3D. The scorecard was simply based on points—for most treasure found, secrets found, and Nazis killed—surprisingly, my father was winning thus far.

"Dad, do you remember that girl I met?" I said.

"Ah, well, refresh me, will you?" he said.

"The sister of the friend of Chris," I said.

"Ah, okay—I think I remember."

"Anyway, she's an artist—she paints. I saw one of her paintings. It was amazing."

My father didn't say anything for a while. The highway hummed by, and I waited for some kind of response. I wasn't sure I wanted to talk about her just yet, but the words sort of came out of their own accord.

"So you like her," he said.

"I don't know. I just said she was a painter."

My father snorted.

"C'mon dad, I'm being serious here," I said.

"What kind of paintings does she paint?"

"Right now she's doing landscapes, but she told me that she hates landscapes and still life because she said that they are tacky and don't represent good painting. She wants to move into sur—sur...oh what was the word she used?"

"Surreal?"

"Yeah, that's what it was. Surreal paintings like...oh, some painter she likes...cow something from Mexico."

"She sounds serious."

"Yeah, I know. And she's only 13. I feel funny around her. She has this smile," I said, leaning back against the seat, sighing purposefully for effect just as Aladdin did when speaking of Jasmin.

"Oh boy," my father said.

"Yeah, I know."

"Yeah, I know too. When a girl has that smile, that laugh, that way of making you feel funny all over, you tingle, right? Yeah, I know too."

"Exactly. That's exactly what I mean," I said.

"Do we need to have that talk?"

"Dad, c'mon—be serious for once," I said.

"Yeah, well, I do remember what it was like at your age—hormones racing, heart pounding, sweaty hands."

"Geez, I can't talk to you about anything," I said.

He snorted again. "Okay, sorry. So what're you going to do?"

"That—I don't know."

We crossed over into Idaho from Oregon and stopped for lunch in a small town diner. My father ordered a BLT, and I had a Philly cheese steak sandwich with fries. Being around my father, I felt like I was hanging out with my best friend—not like Chris best friend, but something different, something even more special. I could tell that it was the beginning of something wonderful—not that it had not been special before, but just different. We had crossed that invisible line when a father becomes more than protector and guide, but a buddy of the first degree. I was at the height of the age, my thoughts filled with girls and baseball, trying to edge myself higher and higher within the right circles and yet fighting the conundrum of maintaining what I thought was truly most valuable in life—being oneself (but without knowing who that self was). But with my father, everything was okay. I could be me; my father was sanctuary.

He craved driving above all things, and that first night we slept in a Motel 6 in a small town on the border of Idaho and Utah. This was a treat as most nights we would stay at a KOA campground in either a tent or the camper. We had a late dinner at McDonald's—a Happy Meal for me and a Big Mac meal for him. Then, we went back to the hotel, played one game of Uno and then promptly fell asleep.

The next day, we drove through Salt Lake City just to see the Great Salt Lake and then on through the rest of Utah until we crossed the border into Colorado and came to the dense, opaque Colorado River. We spent half an hour finding the perfect spot. There was a section around a bend in the river with a group of trees providing shade over a small pool of relatively stagnant water. My father enjoyed fly fishing just as much as reel fishing so we took off our shoes, rolled up our pants, and waded into the water and aimed for the stream that flowed into the little pool. The water felt frigid, but it was so hot that summer, it felt refreshing against my skin. He showed me how to cast and let the fly float down stream to simulate a captured insect. The river was empty save for us, and I felt a part of it. I didn't care if I caught anything. I listened to the water rush by, over the rocks, and heard the birds chirping in the trees along the banks. And I knew I was in heaven. I didn't even want to go exploring as I normally would have if Chris were there: we could have really created an adventure game here, without the fear of being caught by the cool kids.

"Dad, do you ever think about Abby?" I asked.

"Yeah, I do," he said after sending out another cast.

"What do you think about?"

"Oh," he said. "I think about what she might've been like, that sort of thing."

"Me too. I don't really remember her all that much," I said.

He sent out another cast. "I'll never forget her."

I couldn't remember my sister, only vague images and words she may or may not have said. But I would never forget that night. I would never forget the horror on my grandmother's face, but I couldn't remember my sister's face at all. I could only see the blood, her blood.

My father had caught a good-sized Rainbow Trout, and he packed it up in a cooler with ice and we drove for a few hours before finding a campground to sleep. My father grilled the fish and sprinkled it with lemon juice and salt. We ate canned beans and melted marshmallows and chocolate on gram crackers for dessert. It felt good to eat something real, something we had worked at getting. We went straight to bed after dinner as being in the sun all day exhausted us.

The next day we spent making ground, only stopping for lunch and coffee. We ate a quick dinner and were in Missouri by nightfall. The next morning, we woke up early, had a quick breakfast of omelets with salt and pepper and sausage, and were on the road by eight-thirty.

"Dad, do you believe in God?" I asked.

"It's a bit early for God don't you think?" he said. "I've only had two sips of coke."

"C'mon dad, be serious," I said.

My father sighed and didn't answer for a moment. "Well, I think something is out there," he said.

"But you don't believe in God like Christians do?"

"Well, I don't know really," he said. "I believe in something. I just don't know what that something is. I think there is something mysterious about this world, but I can't put my finger on it so-to-speak." He laughed. "And I doubt I ever will."

"Well, what do you think happens after you die?" I asked.

"Jesus, who have you been talking to?" he said.

"Just curious," I said.

"I don't know what happens after death. I'm sure something does. It would be a big waste if something didn't."

"I think heaven is where you play all day with your friends and family, and everything you ever wanted to exist, does," I said.

"Well, I think I'd go to a place like that. What would you want to exist?"

"Well, like Link and monsters from Final Fantasy, but they would be friendly."

"Well, that's probably the way it is then. Heaven is probably whatever you want it to be," he said.

The next couple of days we drove through parts of Illinois, Kentucky, and Tennessee and finally arrived in Raleigh-Durham, North Carolina. I met up with the baseball team the night we arrived at a fast-food joint called Hardee's. We were a jolly bunch, talking of the trip—all the other players and their families flew, but my father loved driving and wanted to spend the extra time with me.

We played the first game to start the tournament against Minnesota. Our host families drove us to the field—I was staying with Clint and Brett. When we arrived at the stadium, we jumped out of our host family's van with our gear and stood enthrallingly looking up at the magnificent stadium. It was the home of the Raleigh-Durham Bulls, a triple-A minor league team for the Cleveland Indians. Spectators and parents of both teams were filing away into the stadium. Each player had received a guest pass with their names imprinted. I looked down at mine: Orville James McFadden.

"This is where it begins boys," Clint said.

"Fame and fortune. Fame and mother-fucking-fortune," Brett said.

The field was massive with wooden bleacher seats and a large overhang that provided enough shade to cover them. The infield was beautifully manicured with sharply cut dark green grass and freshly raked dirt around the bases and positions. Maintenance personnel were out watering the field to keep any dust down. I surveyed the outfield where I would make my home. The grass had been cut short, professionally, and I was sure a ball hit in the gap would continue rolling to the wall.

"Can't let one get by me here," I said.

"You could hit one out of here," Clint said.

"I swing for singles," I said.

Our other teammates had arrived and we gathered our gear and headed towards the third base dugout. We took a run from pole to pole to warm up and then stretched and began throwing. We were well conditioned against heat but the humidity even at nine in the morning was demanding. We could see the Minnesotan ball players across the field doing just as we were doing. They had some tall players, and I felt a pang of nervousness—those must be their pitchers I thought. After warm-ups, we performed a perfect infield/outfield. When Minnesota took the field, we took one knee outside the dugout and scrutinized any weaknesses. They were pretty solid.

The game began after the singing of our national anthem, and they took an early one run lead. In the bottom of the inning, we batted a straight one, two, three-out inning. Brett pitched a great second inning allowing no hits or runs. Clint batted first in the bottom half of the inning and hit a single to left field. I followed. I watched the pitcher wind up—he was big and threw hard. That pang returned deep in my gut. He was tall and intimidating with a snarl of confidence on his face.

I stepped into the batter's box. He threw me a curve ball first pitch, which I hit hard up the middle, but he moved quickly, caught the ball on a short hop, threw to second for one, and the short-stop quickly threw to first, but I was fast out of the box and had made it safely just in time. The next pitch, I stole second. Then, the next batter hit a line drive single up the middle, and I rounded third without slowing. There was a throw at home. I hook slid around the catcher to tie the game at one.

We won in seven grueling innings: 2 - 1.

My father met me for lunch after our team meeting. We ate at Hardee's since we didn't have them on the west coast. I had a huge steak burger and fries with a strawberry smoothie.

"You played great today," my father said.

"Not really. I struck out and grounded into a double play almost," I said.

"But you hit the ball hard, stole a base, and scored one of only two runs," he said. "They had tough pitching."

"Well, anyway, I'm glad you came," I said.

"You think I would miss this?" he said. "How many world series tournaments do you get?"

"Hopefully this is the first of many," I said.

The next game, we took an early 3 - 0 lead against Connecticut. We were playing a night game, and I felt like a professional baseball player. I had never before played a night game, and the lights were difficult to adjust to. Before the game, I had practiced catching fly balls. It was difficult to judge the ball accurately. First step always back—first step always back.

We were still up three to zero through four innings. We were cruising along. Then, in the bottom of the fourth, they loaded the bases with only one out. The next batter hit a line drive to shallow left center. I had a good jump on the ball, but it was far enough away I thought I might have had to dive. It was an outfielder's nightmare—to dive and potentially create a worse situation by letting the ball go behind me or to let it drop in for a single.

I dove.

The ball fell into my mitt, but my chest and mitt hit the ground hard, and the ball popped out and skidded off deeper into left field. All three runs scored to tie the game. I looked at the scoreboard: an error was registered.

"Fuck. God fucking damn it. You fucking suck Orville. God fucking damn it," I screamed into my mitt, the burning tears sliding down the sides of my face.

They scored eight runs that inning, and the final score of the game was 8 - 3.

I didn't say a word at dinner that night with the host family. I ate the food, and afterwards I simply wanted to go to bed.

"That was a tough play dude," Clint said.

"Especially with the lights," Brett agreed.

"It doesn't matter. I should have caught that ball," I said. "If the ball hits the mitt, it should be caught."

"Who cares anyway?" Brett said. "We like to play with pressure anyway."

Instead of going to bed, we took the host family's four-wheelers out around the neighborhood. We zoomed in and around the streets, and the wind rushing against my face allowed me to momentarily forget the play. When I crawled into bed later, I noticed I had been bit five or six times by mosquitoes. I itched all night before finally falling asleep amidst the snores of Brett and Clint.

The next day, I went to my father's hotel room and listened to the game on the radio and every few minutes, I went into the bathroom and puked. I had a fever, my stomach ached, and I couldn't keep anything down.

"You reckon it's those mosquito bites?" my father asked.

"Yes," I groaned.

The radio announcer announced we won the game 4 - 0 against Louisiana and would be playing again that night.

"Why would they have two games for you guys in one day? I came here to watch you play," my father said.

"I don't know. It sucks," I said. But truly I was relieved. I wouldn't have the chance to mess up any more games, and we could still win.

The next game was against Florida. They were undefeated and had dispatched the previous three opponents with relative ease. I was able to watch from the dugout, but didn't feel well-enough to play. I could only watch as the game closed with Florida up 5 - 1. And just like that, our dreams of winning the Babe Ruth 13-Year Old World Series were over. We were heading back home.

After the game, I said my goodbyes to our host family, and then went to my father's hotel to check out. When I walked into the room, he was on the phone. The conversation was brief and he didn't say much, and when he hung up the phone, he stared at the wall for a short time.

"Who was it?" I asked.

"It was your mother. Sorry, she couldn't talk long."

I have found you again, death said.

We packed up the truck and were off for the long haul home. My father drove in silence. My own thoughts were preoccupied: I saw that fly ball land in my glove and bounce out over and over again. I wondered if that would not have happened, we would have won that game. I wondered if we would have won the tournament. I was just a charade, a fake. Somehow all the coaches who had put their faith in me were blinded by the magic spells I must have cast on them. The miles flew by in a blur. On the way home, one doesn't care to take time.

"Son, I'm not sure how to tell you this," my father started to say.

I looked over at him, and his face was serious, and he had tears in his eyes. I thought of mother—they would split at last. The end had come. All those suspicions were true. He had done something with another woman and she finally had enough of it.

"Chris was killed in a boating accident."

Nothing is real when you're away from home. Everything is just an act in a play. I heard the words, but they were just that, words. Even the tears I shed moments later were simply a natural physical reaction, like getting hit in the nose. I didn't want them to come—they simply appeared perhaps because of my father's soft spoken voice as he uttered those words, *Chris was killed....* Or perhaps because I didn't want to seem cruel, but what was a boating accident on the river, what did that look like?—feel like? I didn't know.

You are now in my icy grasp, said death.

Chapter 7

The water was cool, and my teeth chattered incessantly as I waited for the boat to circle around. I watched the inner tube bounce erratically against the water and wondered how far I had been flung. I had hit the water hard, on my side, and it felt like plunging through a large block of cement. I was only under for a second or so, but I opened my eyes to a dark underworld. The luminescent green light shined into this world of darkness, and I reached toward that light with all my might. I quickly scissor kicked my legs to swim forever upwards. Finally, my head emerged into the light, into the air, and I took a deep, exhilarating breath.

I treaded water impatiently, fearing the slimy eels sliding against my legs and going under again. I was not wearing a life jacket. The boat came nearer to me, and I saw Chris and Sage on the edge laughing.

"That was awesome," Chris said.

I climbed up the staircase aside the boat as it rocked side-to-side. This was the part I feared most—being sucked under and swept away into the dark abyss.

"That was a nice run," Phil, Chris's dad, said.

Sage strapped on a life preserver. "I'm going to out do you. I probably won't fall off all afternoon," she said matter-of-factly.

I stared at her dumbfounded. No girl I had ever known had talked that way—such confidence, such feistiness. She stepped toward the inner tube, her back to us. Chris and I both watched her slim body maneuver down into the black, circular rubber tube—her swimsuit tight against her body and the curvature of her backside perfectly shaped in a sloping arch like a banana. She was the sister of Chris's friend and we all knew she was untouchable because of that. But, it seemed my relationship with her had begun inevitably morphing into something more; I felt the cross over of that singular line of trust never meant to be crossed. A boy had to choose what he valued most.

She had been, just one year ago, a flat chest, explosively dramatic girl of thirteen—a girl we kept around as an additional player for night games or when playing Magic: The Gathering. But now, now she was a tall, blonde-haired beauty with emerging breasts too full to pass over, with a wet swimming suit that snuggled closely against her developing body. I couldn't take my eyes off her. Chris somehow seemed impervious, but every so often, his eyes glanced towards her furtively.

We looked across the boat at each other, into each other's eyes, and for a moment, just a moment, I recognized the animalistic fierceness of Man on the hunt. He, too, must have felt something. I looked out toward the water at the girl bouncing along in the inner tube. Was she worth it? Did I have a choice?

A sudden lurch. A large barge was cruising parallel to our boat off in the distance, and the waves it generated were the biggest and most dangerous. The tube bounced high into the air, and Sage's little body flew straight up away from the tube and came crashing down against the hard water. My heart pounded heavily against my chest cavity.

"Do you see her?" I screamed into the wind. "Is she okay?"

"I see her Orville," Phil said. "If I didn't know better," he said.

"Whatever," I said, my face burning red.

Sage climbed back into the boat, her body dripping and glistening in the sun.

"Shut up," she said with a finger pointed at me. "I don't want to hear it. You didn't have to go through the barge gauntlet like I did."

"I wouldn't dream of saying anything," I said. "I'm actually surprised you lasted as long as you did. I'm surprised you got on the inner tube at all really."

Sage launched her little body at me, her eyes alit with feigned rage. She began swinging erratically, hitting me in the arms—her little punches hurt, and I backed away laughing. Chris strapped on his life vest and got into the inner tube.

"I don't know if I should leave you two alone up there," he said.

"Don't worry," Phil said. "I'll keep on eye on them." He looked at me with his eyebrows cocked. I glanced furtively at Sage to see what her face said. She looked at me with the eyes of a deep, 14-year old and shrugged her shoulders. I didn't know what it meant, but I smiled sheepishly and looked away—then back at her as I was prone to do—she was still looking right into me. I knew at that moment our destinies were somehow entwined. I felt something so strong, something like a voice, telling me that this girl would forever change my life.

Phil gave Chris the ride of his life. He maneuvered the boat left and right, and Chris held on for dear life. I looked out at his face—one moment it was stern determination, his eyebrows furrowed inwards, his facial muscles taut, and the next he was laughing deeply from his stomach, uncontrollably. It was that moment I took a mental picture of Chris, one that would forever cement itself in my mind.

Phil couldn't shake Chris as hard as he tried. Finally, he slowed the boat down, and Chris came on board with a look of smug exhilaration. He took off his life vest, didn't say a word, and sat down.

"Ahh...," he said. "I think...I might be a little tired. Not sure why though."

"You're a punk," I said.

"I just wanted to give you more time for smoochie, smoochie," he said.

That shut me up. For some reason, when Phil made jokes about the situation, they didn't affect me, but with Chris it was different. I didn't know if Chris liked the idea. He had been the one to introduce Sage to me via his red-haired twin friend. Maybe he liked her too.

We boated all day. The sun lit up the orange and yellow horizon when we decided to head home. We sped back to the boat launch. The air felt good as it dried off the water that splashed against our bodies. I sat next to Sage and across from Chris. He was staring out at the brown hills that paralleled the Snake River coastline. I looked at the tan leg resting against mine. I couldn't think of anything but how nice that touch was. Her touch made my heart beat to a beat I had never experienced before. It wasn't like the times with Rachel—nervousness and the uncanny fear of doing something prohibited.

We came up slowly to the boat launch. Phil left the engine running and got out to tie the boat against the dock.

"I'll get the truck," Phil said.

We waited in the boat until Phil's trailer came down into the water. Phil parked. "Chris, slowly take the boat up onto the trailer," Phil yelled.

Chris was that kind of kid, one who could ride a motorcycle, shoot a gun accurately, drive a boat onto a trailer at fourteen. I was not that kind of kid. So, I waited with Sage while Chris undid the ropes.

"The rope is wrapped around the engine," Chris said. He quickly jumped into the water and went under. He came back up a moment later. "Almost got it."

"Be careful," I said. He hadn't looked the same when he had emerged. He had looked slightly flushed, dizzy even. I went to the back of the boat and looked at the engine. It was smoky and the rope looked like it was still tangled. I couldn't see any movement in the dark, murky water except for the small waves gently rocking the boat. I only saw my pale reflection staring back up at me. I jumped up onto the dock. I looked at Sage who was pacing alongside the boat looking down into the water.

"He's been down there too long," she said.

"Phil," I yelled.

Phil got out of the truck and quickly came down to us.

"Chris went under to unwrap a rope that got stuck. He hasn't come up yet," I said.

"Turn off the engine," Phil yelled and dove into the water.

I jumped back into the boat and shut off the engine. The river was suddenly quiet. Sage and I waited for Chris to suddenly pop his head out of the water laughing at his extremely hilarious joke. But we waited for what seemed like hours and the tick-tock of the sun's clock ticked away. When there was a sudden splash, Sage and I both jumped, but it was only Phil. "Did he come up?" No. He took a deep breath and plunged back under. Sage and I paced along the dock looking down into the water. I wanted to jump in and help, but my body wouldn't do it. I willed myself to jump in, to find Chris, to save him, but I couldn't, and I knew I wouldn't. The water was dark and frightening.

Phil popped up again and went back down quickly. It went like this for a full hour before he came back onto the dock.

"We have to call the police," he whispered.

I found you and I'll never leave you again, death said.

I woke up, sweating in the darkness. It was early morning and I crept downstairs to get a glass of water. My father was reading in an easy chair in the corner. He looked up when he saw me and put his book down.

"Can't sleep either?" he said.

No.

He looked me over, noticing the sweat drying on my arms and face in the lamplight. "Same dream?"

"Yeah," I said.

I took a cup from the cupboard, filled it with tap water, and gulped it down. I put the glass next to the sink and sat down on the sofa next to the easy chair. It seemed I noticed every move I made, felt every touch sensorial.

The funeral was later that morning. His body had been found four days after the accident.

"Are you okay?" my father asked.

"I'm okay," I said.

Was I okay? How could one be okay after something like this? I didn't know what I was feeling. I sat very still on the couch trying to feel something, anything. But nothing made sense. Chris was my life; my father was my life. These were the men meant to guide me—Chris through fantasy, my father through reality. Chris was now gone. But where had he swam off to—some mysterious rest haven we always talked about?—an island in the open blue? Where, if anywhere? I couldn't imagine that Chris, my best friend, who just a few days ago was battling goblins and sorcerers in the orchards beyond our houses, was gone, existing somewhere out there. Where was this God who directed all things? Chris was alive...flesh and blood only a few days ago, but now...what now? There were never any answers, only questions.

My father and I sat in silence until we both finally fell asleep. It was light when my mother woke us from our slumber. She had fried some eggs and bacon, and we ate toast and fruit before getting dressed to go. I wore dark blue slacks and a black long-sleeved shirt. I looked ridiculous with a bowl hair cut, which was done with an actual bowl. The kids at school said I looked like Jim Carrey from Dumb and Dumber. I was fine with that I guess.

We three arrived at the church, and there were already quite a few people there. We took our seats in the middle pews. The casket was at the front, dark and closed. A picture of Chris smiling was framed and set in front of the casket. I looked into the eyes of that face and tried to remember all the things we had done together. The images passed through my mind as if on a panoramic screen: the adventure games, the video games, the night games, four square, octopus, the club we started to track down and record the movements of ghosts, the gun

72

battles and war games like Gruesome, the slumber parties, the pool parties and barbeques with his family, watching movies together and playing with our G.I. Joe action figures—even the nights with Rachel wherein we practiced kissing. I saw it all as a convoluted soup, images swirling around until out of sight and new images would arise to the top. No more memories were to be made. For seven years we were best friends and now all I had were images.

I looked at the faces around me, solemn and gloomy, and I looked at Chris's parents, Phil and Patricia, standing at the front of the church watching each face as they came in. But they weren't really watching. They were pleading—they were pleading for somebody to say or do something that would make sense of it all. Some word of an after life that felt true and sensible. Some secret knowledge that only a wise man on a mountaintop could know and give. But everyone was just as confused as the rest. Nobody knew what any of it meant. I could tell from the adults down to the children that a 14-year old boy drowning in a river had no answers. This was not part of the plan. And now Chris was in a casket next to them, bloated and looking like something out of one of our horror games, and I couldn't imagine how they must have felt. Phil stood tall and straight, determined not to cry as he perused the faces. Patty looked down, already tears welling in her eyes.

And yet I couldn't cry. I played video games, and when I tired of those because they were not the same, I played basketball with some of the neighbor kids—anything to get my mind off of Chris. And I thought of Sage. I didn't go into the canyon. I didn't go into the orchards.

I saw Sage on the other side of the church sitting with the red head twins. Her head was down and she was reading the pamphlet the Clarks had made about Chris. She wore a slim black dress and she had dyed her hair a dark blackish blue. What strange thoughts came even at a funeral. Sage was life. She was alive and full of life. I marveled at these thoughts. I had never looked at another

73

human being like I looked at her. And even in that church, even at the funeral of my best friend, I thought how I wanted to sit next to her, to comfort her in her loss. I wanted to touch her and be touched by her. I wanted to look into those eyes and have those eyes look right back into mine.

I turned away. Chris was in a casket, forever to be buried in a short while and I was thinking about spending time with Sage. But she was a distraction, and that's what I needed to get through this funeral without breaking down. So I glanced at her, but she was solemn, her eyes red, and I only thought of her sorrow, the pain of loss she must be feeling. Death had knocked on her door, and she seemed so fragile. But was she? Wasn't I the fragile one? Wasn't I the broken spirit who knew death intimately?

You shall know me fully, said death.

The time to approach the coffin had come. I walked slowly within the line, my parents behind me. I didn't look around—I didn't want to make eye contact with those faces surely watching me, the best friend. I looked straight into the black jacket of the man in front of me as I would during communion. The line moved slowly like a line for bread and clothes outside the Salvation Army. Phil and Patricia had many friends. When the line moved, we waddled like penguins, side-to-side in an uncanny rhythm. We were the drones that said: "Hello, I'm sorry for your loss. He was a good kid. Hello, I'm sorry for your loss. He was a good kid. Hello..." Chris deserved more than those words.

The man in front of me paid his respects. Suddenly, and I wasn't ready, it was my turn to approach. I first hugged Patricia, and she hugged me so tightly, I had trouble breathing. She kissed my forehead. I didn't know what to say to her so I just said sorry over and over.

"I'm sorry. I'm so sorry," I said into her breasts.

"I know. I know," she whispered into my dark brown hair. "Please still come around the house."

I went to Phil who tried unsuccessfully to smile at me. I wanted to tell him what Chris had meant to me, that a part of me drowned in that river too, but I couldn't say anything. And I'm not sure he wanted me to say anything, or needed me too. I went to him; I hugged him. I felt his warm body against mine. He was not my father, but he was my friend. Phil was a grownup version of Chris just as I was a younger version of James, my father. And yet I would never see Chris as I saw Phil. Chris would only always be a 14-year old boy...even when I was old and gray, Chris would be that same, smiling youth.

I went up to the coffin. I felt the eyes of the church on me, but I knew I would never have this moment again. I took a piece of paper out of my pocket; I had found a poem, On the Death of Friends in Childhood by Donald Justice.

"Chris," I started. "We shall not ever meet them bearded in heaven, nor sunning themselves among the bald of hell; if anywhere, in the deserted schoolyard at twilight, forming a ring, perhaps, or joining hands, in games whose very names we have forgotten. Come memory, let us seek them there in the shadows."

I set the poem on the coffin.

"I don't know what to say right now. Everything happened so suddenly. I guess I still can't believe it. I don't want to believe it. I'm sorry, Conan."

I couldn't fathom the emotions I was feeling. Some sickened me. Some confused me. Some scared me. I thought of all the faces out there looking at me, feeling sad for me, the one who was left behind, the best friend. I felt like a celebrity, like this was my moment of fame. I wanted everyone to send thoughts of love to me, the one most affected by this tragic accident. I thought of Sage. I wanted Sage to know how much I was suffering. I wanted Sage to notice me. I wanted Sage to watch me at that moment and have thoughts of love. I wanted to be comforted only by her; only she could comfort me because she understood what it was to be young and marred by death. This tragedy would bring us together. I thought of Chris and wondered what adventures he was going on in the next world.

After the funeral there was a brunch. Everyone was laughing at jokes Phil was telling. But I knew no one was laughing because they thought the jokes were funny. Maybe they were funny, but no one heard them for what they were, or were supposed to be. And Phil wasn't telling the jokes to evoke laughter. He wanted to think of anything other than his dead son being hoisted down into the ground. I found it hard to think of the dead at funerals. I ate the food and chit-chatted with the ones left behind.

After the brunch, we went home.

"Do you want to go to the batting cages?" my father asked.

"No," I said. "I'm going to go to the canyon."

I picked up one of the stick swords that Chris and I had left at the edge of the canyon, and I maneuvered down the dirt pathway. I swung the sword a few times, but nothing remotely fantastic came to me. I didn't imagine Magic: The Gathering characters, or Nintendo monsters, or anything. It wasn't the same. Without Chris, it meant nothing.

I threw the stick sword as far as I could down into the canyon. I plopped down into the dirt, my fancy clothes getting covered in brown dust, but I didn't care. I wanted to be dirty. I wanted to be young and dirty again without death and sorrow.

"Why God? How could you do this? He was my best friend, my only real friend..." and I took a deep breath and suddenly the floodgates opened to 14 years of tears. Great heaves and sobs; I didn't want to stop. Tears poured down my face and my hands as I clutched my head. "Why? Why?" I screamed into them. "He was my best friend. My best friend damn it. You can't exist, doing this, you can't exist. No loving god would do this. Or you hate me. You must hate me. Why do you hate me? He was my best friend...my best friend...and I'll never see him again..."

I got up. I looked to the top of the canyon, and my father was there watching down. He's all I have left now.

Chapter 8

"I didn't know how one should act, how one should feel. It was the most difficult time because I thought I should've felt only the utmost melancholy, but I felt the most extreme happiness at the same time. Love and melancholy. A paradox. It didn't fit into my life's schemas. I was 14 years old. How could I piece any kind of sanity from that? And the hits just kept on coming."

"What do you mean?"

"If I felt any kind of relief from sadness—or worse, if I felt happiness—then I would be hit with another blow, worse than the previous one."

***

The days were shortening as the trees changed their colors and shed their coats. The irrigation canals had dried up, leaving only cracked crust like that of the moon's surface. The apple orchards produced what would be the last remnants of fruit, and the farmers set out their portable smoke stack heaters. The fields were barren save the pumpkin and corn patches. The afternoons glowed golden as the sun set to sleep a deep sleep. The seasonal sea change had begun; we prepared for the onslaught of winter.

Sage's parents dropped the two of us off at the cinema around noon. I did what I only thought was right on a first date—I bought the tickets, a large popcorn, a large soda to share, Sour Patch Kids (my personal favorite), and Reese's Pieces. We found a seat in a corner of the back row. We heard the muffled whispers of the couples dotting the cinema and the sifting of hands through popcorn. I asked her about the intricacies of painting. She told me how still life was boring, about how abstract was difficult to pull off, and that she was getting into painting surreal reality. She spoke of a masterpiece, but I couldn't know what it was.

"I will discover this masterpiece if it's the last thing I do," I said.

"If you discover it, it *will* be the last thing you do."

"Is that a threat little girl?"

"Little girl? I believe I'm older than you."

"One week, but maturity wise..."

"Oh brother..."

The cinema went black, the whispers died, and the screen flashed. The dramatic change in my body's condition was astonishing—my hands began to perspire and I felt tense. I saw that other guys in the cinema had begun putting their arms around their girlfriends like clockwork as if a subliminal cue had been given from the previews on the screen. I had missed the cue. Did Sage want me to do the same? If I my put my arm around her and she didn't want me to, the entire movie would prove awkward. But she was here with me...but maybe only as friends. Free movie, free popcorn and candy...it did add up. Maybe I shouldn't...

Sage reached over and took my arm, leaned forward, and placed it around her shoulders. She snuggled down into my arm and put her hand on my upper leg. I didn't remember the previews, Titanic or something with that heartthrob Leo DiCaprio. Even when my arm went numb under the weight of Sage leaning against it, it didn't phase me. I knew from that moment on, like the two star-crossed lovers on the screen, fate had aligned the two of us.

I didn't even remember the movie. The credits rolled and people began exiting, but we sat still, happy to be able to spend those extra moments together before having to go back to our separate lives. But that was the moment that couples kissed, and I had never kissed anyone before—well, Rachel, but that didn't count since it wasn't real, not intentional. I didn't know what to do. Sage looked at me with those deep brown eyes—those eyes said everything, those lips, those sweet, ruby-red lips protruding slightly out, slightly parted, and I felt tense all over again. She whisked the few strands of hair out of her eyes.

My hand somehow moved upon its own volition and took her neck into it. And then as a slippery slope moves a ball, my hand moved toward hers and she closed her eyes, and I closed my eyes, and our lips met. Her lips were soft and sweet like peeled peaches and sugar. I had never felt something as wonderful as those lips, and in that moment, all my fears, all my memories melted away, and only Sage and that kiss were real. We were two beings floating in the nether sphere, in a warm, quiescent bath of light, two beings alive and it was as if all of civilization depended on our lives joining together. We were the future—we were the evolution of love.

We pulled away from each other and our eyes slowly opened. She smiled, and I smiled. We were sealed through a kiss. We were changed. And we left the cinema to a changed world, but it was a short lived moment. Our eyes squinted in the sun of the mid-afternoon light—I felt cheated of something, and it ruined the romantic moments of just a few short minutes ago. One should always leave a movie in the dark. We took the bus home to Sage's house.

"So, I guess we're official," I said.

"I guess so," she said.

"Good," I said. "Good."

"Yeah, you're a lucky guy," she said.

I kissed her again and then I walked the rest of the way home. It was strange and sickening to feel elated when just a couple months ago, my best friend had drowned. But I couldn't deny that a part of me had never been happier. Everything seemed new and fresh—even the air around me was alive with energy, the brown hills beyond in the distance were round and jolly, the trees bright orange and yellow, birds, birds, everywhere were birds chirping and dancing together in the soft breeze. Fall was a time for hearts to fall.

I rounded the corner around Mrs. Henry's yard, which had become a collage of oranges, browns, and yellows—only the junipers remained green and strong. I loved the neighborhood for its mystery and charm. Each yard was well manicured with pines, birch, black cottonwood trees, and juniper bushes. The houses were painted white, yellow, brown, violet; their trims green, red, and brown. I saw the three pines acting as rooks, silent protectors outside my own house. They had once been Christmas trees, planted by my father and mother some time ago. Now, they stood high and branched out almost to the point of touching each other.

We had a visitor. A green Volkswagen was parked in the driveway.

I approached the car from the side and looked in—there were a few bibles on the passenger seat as well as church literature and a copy of Luther's Large Catechism. I looked to the sky as a change was upon it—it was gray and misty, holding off the onslaught of rain that was to come from the west. An omen? I approached the house cautiously now, some foreboding welling up within. The house was plain, yellow with white trim, a face of sorts with a knobbed door and two elongated windows to the left and right, a white manual garage with a side storage shed next to the closest window, and my bedroom on the second level next to the room that had been my sister's. It was a house in all appearances the same as any other house on the block, but it was marred by something. I couldn't quite put my finger on it, but I felt that something was not right.

I opened the front door and saw Pastor Givens sitting on the couch next to my mother who had her hands spread across her face—I saw her red-webbed eyes through wet fingers.

"Okay, who died?" I asked.

"Your dad," she whispered.

"Oh."

***

"I can't for the life of me think why I said that. It was a joke, and yet, at the same time it wasn't a joke. It was what first came into my little head and I said it. Why would someone react that way in that situation? Everything hinted toward death. My mother was crying. The pastor was there."

"It seems to have been a natural defense mechanism," Dr. Fields said. "You had recently gone through the death of your best friend, and suddenly you were falling in love for the first time. There's a range of emotion going on there—and for a young man as you were, those emotions probably didn't make a lot of sense. So when you came home just after being with your girlfriend, you came home to a situation that couldn't be possible. And yet, it was very real."

***

I crept upstairs, stepping on my toes to make as little sound as possible, to my room and laid down on the bed. I wanted to empty my mind, devoid of thought, but I couldn't stop thinking. What did this all mean? This couldn't be real. There was some sort of mistake. Where was Sage? What was she doing? Where was my father? What was he doing? What would become of me? Would Sage and I get married? What the fuck did this all mean? Goddamn it, what the hell was this thing called life? This couldn't be real...this couldn't be real.

I got up, looked quickly around me, wanted to find some sort of bearing to where I was. I couldn't focus on anything. I saw colors and things, but I had no idea what they were. Then I saw an orange glow come from somewhere in the back of my room. I went to it. I grabbed it. I picked it up. It was a basketball. I went to my window, opened it savagely, and jumped out. I hit the ground with my knees, bent and rolled. I had done it a thousand times as a trick to show off to the neighborhood kids, but this time, I wanted to run away, far away to where things were living, not dying. I ran, ran, ran to Sage's house. I didn't stop until I was outside her bedroom window out of breath. I knocked. She came to it.

"Hi," she said.

"You want to play basketball?" I panted.

"Well, I don't know. I was going to paint..." she said. "Did you run all the way here?"

"Of course," I said. "I wanted to see you."

"I suppose if you want to lose, we can play."

We played in her neighbor's driveway. Neither of us were very good, but we didn't care. We played 21 and horse.

"You're lucky I'm shorter than you or you wouldn't have a chance," she said.

"Ha, I've been toiling with you this whole time," I said. "You want to see the Jordan in me? Okay, here it comes." I faked left, went right, passed her with my tongue hanging out, and sped to the hoop. But just before I jumped for the lay up, I slipped and fell onto the concrete. My elbows hit first, and I rolled into the grass and feigned unconsciousness.

"Ouch," I moaned.

"Which Jordan was that? Michael or his lesser known and less talented brother Dufus?" she laughed.

"Ouch," I moaned.

"Oh, do you need a nurse?" she said.

"Yes," I said.

She came over to me, rolled me over and kissed my elbows. "Is that better?"

"No," I said.

"Where does it hurt?"

"My lips," I said.

She kissed my lips.

"You always make me feel better," I said.

"So you couldn't get enough of me. You had to see me again."

"Something like that."

"Something like that or that was exactly it?"

"My dad died."

"What? What're you talking about? How?"

"I don't know," I whispered.

James McFadden broke as Gail watched, drink in hand, sipping slowly, her red lipstick imprinting its mark, her red nails tapping incessantly against the glass. She didn't taste the alcohol so much as felt it coursing through her. She peered above the rim furtively as if to see what lay just beyond it. There is very little talk playing pool. There doesn't need to be. It was like old lovers conversing with touches, shared cigarettes, and the clinking of glasses. Gail watched James glide alongside the pool table as a professional moves with grace and finesse, the brilliance of fluid movements. He ran through the table without pause before Gail could finish her drink.

"Will he or won't he," Gail whispered into the last of the ice cubes in her glass. "He loves me. He loves me not." She set the glass down quickly on the bar table, and it rattled to a stop, a sound James found especially satisfying, and he looked her way and smiled, just before he broke—nothing fell. Gail didn't move. James went and sat on a barstool next to her and peered at the table as if he were surprised nothing had fallen or to see if he was mistaken and a ball had suddenly decided, as if from its own volition to muster its energy and fall into a hole. Gail jerked up.

"I didn't know you could miss," she said while walking towards the table. And she turned back towards James and flashed him a smile, her eyes alit with the confidence and mischief of a forty-something, single woman in a short skirt and push-up bra. The effect was instantaneous.

The smile was returned with one of boyish innocence—
the mark of James McFadden.

"No woman could resist that smile," Gail said.

"I certainly hope not," James said.

Gail threw James on the bed; Gail threw me on the
bed. She tugged off his briefs; she tugged off my boxers.
We lay on the bed, flat and stiff as a board, our arms to
our sides, and our legs straight out, our faces looking
toward the heavens. White, white, we were white.

Gail looked from one to the other. She sat down on
my thighs, and I felt her black panties beneath her skirt.
She took off her shirt and bra and her breasts looked like
Spectacle Rock on Death Mountain. She placed my
hands on her breasts, and I let out a deep gasp.

"Calm down," she whispered.

I was breathing hard as she inched her way up my
thighs and on top of me.

"Just look into my eyes," Gail said.

I did.

James McFadden lay next to me, immobile, as I took
hold of Gail's hips, and in his eyes were all the
contradictions of the soul: his lust, his sorrow, his ecstasy,
his love for another, his power, pain, suffering, his
failures, his triumph, his disgust of himself, his desire for
her body, his appreciation of friendship, his greed of
flesh, his want of conquering women, his love for his son
and wife, his memories.

He was all these things and more as his heart gave out
and he breathed his last. And Gail was gone, and he lay
on the bed, naked in wet, soiled sheets, his eyes open,
blank, turned toward heaven. And I, looking through his
lens, zoomed out and faded to black.

I awoke in my room to the blue light of early morning.
My father had died of a heart attack while playing pool.
Gail had said he had looked pale, like a ghost even and
had slid off his barstool during one of the games. He had
said nothing; there were no famous last words or heroics.
He simply died.

The funeral was held at the church. The family sat together on one side while friends of my father sat on the other. If it had been a wedding, it would have been a grand display of loving friendship, but it was a sorrowful display of the ones left behind to grieve a great man. People kept coming and coming through the wood doors. His friends came from work, from the pool halls, from Oregon where he grew up.

Our pastor took to the altar and the church fell silent.

"James Herbert McFadden walked into rooms and strangers became his friends, as is evident by the number of people in this church—more than any Sunday service. The McFadden family has said James himself would laugh at this fact. James was a man of many talents and he had many interests. If he was not playing pool, he was building a pool hall in the backyard. If he was not watching baseball, he was playing it with his son. He enjoyed the challenges of conquering puzzles—computers, he was especially good with computers. He loved card games, and I have been told he always won and yet always played fair, a fact hard to believe, but true. James made this world a more exciting place. His energy for life was such that he affected all those around him. His loss of life is our loss. But he is in heaven now, playing cards with the angels, and winning too I'll bet. It's a difficult task to sum up who and what a person is so the McFadden family has asked me to share a story that highlights James McFadden's personhood:

James loved to drive. He was always driving to pool tournaments, with his family on long road trips—James felt as comfortable behind a wheel as he did in a pool hall. When Orville and Abby were very young, James decided to pack the car and with his family in tack and the car full of gas, they left to take a road trip to Texas. Three days of travel through Oregon, Utah, Arizona, and New Mexico, with few stops along the way, they arrived in Dallas, Texas. They arrived, they ate dinner at the Hard Rock Café, and then...they drove home. That was it—a

86

drive to Texas to eat dinner. James' life was never about the destination, but the journey."

My father's friends paid their respects. Our family lined up for our final look at the man we all loved. I approached the open casket under the eyes of my family and my father's friends. I felt strange as if this were simply a ritual I had to perform every now and then. It was to become routine, that my entire life was going to be walking to a casket, open or closed, to say a final farewell. And then at last it would be my own.

My father was dressed in a light green shirt and blue jeans—he would never have agreed on a suit. He laid serenely, his eyes closed as if he were only in a deep sleep. His hands, those capable hands, rested across his belly as if he were praying. I looked down at him, my eyes dry. I felt the heat from the lamps and the eyes of the people. I lay my hand down upon his chest. I felt no rise and fall, and yet he was there, before me, and something told me everything was fine, he was fine, I was fine.

"I miss you," I whispered. "I love you."

***

"What makes a man great Orville?" Dr. Fields asked.

"I don't know," I muttered. I didn't feel like talking anymore. I sighed. "I guess I thought of my father as a great man because he was larger than life. He always seemed magical—he could enchant an entire room wherein people would flock to him to hear whatever he was saying, crowds would actually watch him play pool whenever he played. And whatever he put his mind to, he was great at it."

"And this makes a great man?" Dr. Fields asked.

"I don't know. He seemed great to me, but I guess I was just really getting to know him. Maybe it wouldn't have been like that when I was older. I'll never know."

"What do you mean?"

"Well, he wasn't really home all that much. Most nights, every night really, he went out to play pool with his friends. I think since I was getting older, maybe I was more interesting to him. We started spending more time together. And then he was suddenly gone. My best friend and my father—gone. What does it mean to lose a father, a friend...a sister and grandmother so violently? What does any of it mean? I had reached my threshold for death."

"Your threshold for death."

"I think somewhere in my brain, my subconscious, I had had enough. I couldn't handle any more deaths. I think I feared...I feared that everyone I loved and have ever loved would die, and they would die because I loved them. It's like some cosmic punishment—since I was born, my fate has been fear and death."

"Do you still believe that?"

"I don't know," I said. "Sometimes I feel everything that happens to me has been leading up to the moment of my own demise. And I've tried to fight against it every step of the way. But then it won, and sure enough, here I am, after jumping off a bridge."

"But here you are. Perhaps you have won—a battle, a deciding battle. Now what are you going to do with that victory?"

"Hmm...I don't know if I 've won. How can you be so sure?"

"You mention fate. You talk about fate a lot. Let's follow this line of thinking then. If your life has been fated to fear all and fail, then that moment at the bridge was the accumulation of all that fear and failure. Well, what happened? You lived. You lived and now you have a chance to figure it all out, to discover what now lies ahead. You are the one who now makes your life what it will be. Fear, fate have had their chance, and now that you conquered them, you have won that battle, you have a new life ahead of you."

"It doesn't seem like I've conquered anything."

"But here you are alive with the knowledge of your past. You've won a deciding battle. Now, tell me about Sage."

Chapter 9

My body molded itself into the warm comforter on Sage's fore poster. My eyes dozed from turkey and mashed potatoes, a glass of champagne, and chocolate cake. Sage's parents had left to attend a friend's party, and because it was New Year's Eve, I was allowed to stay until after midnight. Her room was without time, enchanted with magic, a portal to escape the constraints of real life: surreal paintings hung delicately on the walls, a string of bright blue Christmas lights magically lit the small room creating an air of comfort and happiness, and Sage, beautiful Sage lying next to me breathing softly into my ear already drawn toward her sweet mouth. My eyes lingered on an oak bookshelf in the corner—how many lands lived in those words, how many worlds apart we were in this room.

"If I could, I'd never leave this room," I said.

"Because of me?" Sage asked.

"Because of everything. When I'm in here, the real world is no more. When I'm in here, I feel that everything will be okay."

"Everything will be okay," she said.

She snuggled into me, and the sweet smell of vanilla wafted soothingly into my nostrils. With her arm draped over my chest and her legs entwined with mine, we began to drift away into that blissful slumber that only lovers, alone and without haste, could fall into. I didn't fully understand how I felt at that moment in time. There was nothing I wanted more than to forever sleep with Sage at my side. I loved her. I fell in love with her the moment I saw her. That much I knew to be true. I felt it in every fiber of my being. She was my life, my entire life there in that time. I felt that without her, I would perish in the black, darkness of this world.

"We can't sleep," she whispered.

"I know," I said drowsily. "We can't ever let this night end."

"Let's get up and make root beer floats," she suggested.

"And leave this warmth?"

"I promise we can come back to it," she said.

We went into the kitchen and took out root beer from the jumbo refrigerator and vanilla ice cream from the equally large freezer. Sage's family firmly believed in buying in bulk and every other Saturday, they, together, as a family outing went to Costco for a few hours. I had accompanied them on one of these excursions, my first time in Costco, and felt like the kid in the candy store. My eyes, large and round, went from aisle to aisle, wanting to buy everything because everything came wrapped in large bundles of boxes or came in large tin cans. I envisioned myself in world four in Super Mario 3, the land of giants. I was in the land of bulk foods.

We made the floats and stood across from each other sipping on them. I saw how much she had prepared beforehand in the bright lights of the kitchen—she had put on red lipstick, black mascara, a black skirt and a peachy long-sleeved shirt. She had dyed her hair black as well, and I loved how it contrasted with her pale skin. I was simply average in her presence.

"Do you want to watch a movie?" she asked.

"Yes," I said.

We finished off our floats and went back into her room rejuvenated and feeling the happiness of the night and the promise of a new year. She set up the VCR, put in Ghost, and we leaned against the pillows against the wall. We wrapped ourselves up in the bed covers and I put my arm around her as she snuggled back into me. All was well.

I thought about the ways in which I would sacrifice myself for her: if we were walking along the road, I would walk on the outside so if a car veered off, it would hit me and not her, or if we were accosted by thugs, I would jump in front of the bullet. I thought of countless ways I could sacrifice everything for her—given the chance I would do it unfailingly.

"I love you," I whispered. There, I had said it.

She looked up into my eyes alit with blue light and adjusted herself to straddle my lap. She leaned in and kissed me slowly and fully on the lips. I had never felt anything like it before—upon telling her I loved her, it made me love her even more. There was nothing I wouldn't do for this girl. She pulled away from me and gripped the bottom of her shirt and pulled it above and over her head. She unclasped her bra and threw it off the bed. I rubbed my hands slowly over her soft flesh, and I knew I was touching an angelic being. She kissed me again and then jumped quickly off the bed. She unzipped her skirt.

"Do you want me to?"

I nodded.

She wiggled her way out of it. She stood in front of me, naked save for the soft, purple panties she had worn just for me. She was the most beautiful creature I had ever seen. She climbed back on the bed, and with her tiny body in my hands, I held onto her without any intention of ever letting go.

At 11:50 pm, the alarm clock went off—we had set it so that we could take a quick nap. She stirred slowly, tiredly under the covers. I ran my hand down her back and over her panties and thought there was never a better feeling than the contrast between soft flesh and satin.

"Come on," she said. "We have to get up. It's almost New Year's Day."

"Only if you don't put your clothes on," I said.

"So you like what you see?"

"It's okay," I said.

"You're bad," she said. "I'll put a shirt on. My parents said we could have a glass of champagne with orange juice. It's called a mimosa."

We went into the kitchen, and she made the drinks.

"Not yet," she said. "Ten..." We counted down until the clock struck 12 am.

"Happy New Year!" we screamed. We drank our mimosas and kissed our first kiss of 1997.

I hurried into the school after the bus dropped me off so I was not seen anywhere near the big, yellow, horror of punishment and all that was not cool. A large group of the other sophomores were standing with their backpacks on against the wall where they always stood before and after school talking about what party they went to that weekend or the latest gossip of which I was never involved in. I didn't see Sage there.

"Hey Orville, what's up?" one of the guys said.

"Not much," I said.

I stopped at the wall, on the edge of the small crowd gathered there. I felt as a leper perhaps does, a part of society, but as an outcast. I had nothing to say to these people and yet there I was standing with them, not a crucial piece, but an insignificant pawn. But I liked to be seen there as-well-as anyone else. At that moment, high school was what seemed the most important and significant part of life and there was nothing beyond that could rival it. It was pitiable that I could not look past high school as the true beginning—high school was the end all, and if you did not achieve stardom there, you could safely assume you would lead a miserable existence for eternity. I believed that. But I knew I was not one of these people no matter how hard I tried. And there was no fighting fate.

"Happy birthday." I turned around and secretly thanked the stars I had someone to talk to rather than lingering awkwardly against the wall. Sage's smiling face lit mine up considerably. "16 now. You're old," she said.

"You turned 16 last week," I said.

"Posh," she said, then leaned closer to me. "I have a surprise for you tonight."

"What is it?"

93

"It's a s-u-r-p-r-i-s-e," she said. "Geez, I'm not going to give it up that easily."

You haven't given it up at all.

"So, see you tonight right?" she said.

"Of course," I said.

"Okay, I have to go to class," she said and skipped happily down the hall.

"And there she goes—the virgin and his virgin lover," Clint said. An understatement at best.

Clint and Brett came up next to me at the wall. "How long have you been with her now? Two years?"

"About that," I said.

"And you really haven't slept with her?" Clint asked.

"You really think he hasn't slept with her?" Brett said. "He's probably just not telling us."

"I would hope so," Clint said. "Because why would you stay with her? She's hot, but c'mon, Mindy Halverson is hot, and she puts out. And she's looking at you right now."

Mindy Halverson: tall, brunette, athletic build but with a well developed bust never seen before on a 16-year old girl. I looked at her chatting with two hens, but then quickly turned away.

"I would stick it in her so fast," Clint said.

"You would stick it into anything," Brett said.

"No, no, Denise the beast was a drunken mistake," he said. "But she can suck a mean one. Dude, even Brett is getting more out of Stacy fucking McCalister after two months than you are after two years. That's a bad track record. You're going to go to college with a lot of kissing experience, and you're going to cream yourself just by looking at all the hot bitches there. And they don't like that."

"And why do you care again?" I said.

"Because real friends look out for one another," he said. "There's a party this weekend and Mindy will no doubt be there itching for a romp in the hay with Orville

94

James McFadden. You should come and just try it out. Sage will get the picture."

"Even if you don't sleep with Mindy, you should come just to get your face known," Brett said.

"True, you're like the shy, mysterious guy, but that doesn't hold up for too long," Clint said.

"Fine, I'll come," I said.

"Fuck yeah, it's about time," Brett said. "You'll have to learn to drink beer though."

"We're going to get you fucked up. You're going to be banging Mindy Halverson all night. I'll give you some tips."

"Oh yeah, like what?" I asked.

"Like don't just go straight in for the kill. You want to sort of do a rotation," Clint said.

"What do you mean?" I asked.

"Like, you should be hitting her thigh on the side and then her thigh on the other side," Brett said. "Like this." Brett swiveled his hips around, paused at the left. "Nickel, dime, quarter."

"Dollar twenty-five baby," Clint said. "Dollar twenty-five."

Sage took me to a fancy restaurant down by the river. She carried a mysteriously wrapped package under her arm, which she kept saying was nothing special.

"Your dress looks beautiful," the hostess said to her. She wore an emerald green dress that pulled in the chest and waist and cut off at the knees.

"I told you," I whispered to her. "You'll learn someday I'm always right."

"Posh," she scoffed. "You'd be lost without me."

We sat down to a table overlooking the Columbia River. It glowed as the sun made its way down behind the earth. The sky looked like the inside of a giant pink balloon, and only the cross flights of the magpies tore into it. Sage and I watched the fading sun in silence.

"Sometimes I wish I was a bird so I could fly off in the distance wherever and whenever I wanted to," I said.

"You'd be shot by a farmer within a week," Sage said. "Probably by Clint."

"No, I'd be a bird, but with the intelligence of a human."

"Then you'd be bored."

"Fine, I won't be a bird."

The server game round and we ordered; then Sage brought out the wrapped package. "I want you to open it now," she said. "Come sit by me." I moved beside her and opened the package slowly because we were in a restaurant and didn't want to draw attention to ourselves. Inside was a book, a photo album. I opened it to the first page. There was a picture of Sage and me when we had first met, when she had tried to submerge me in Chris's pool. We had been thirteen years old. Above the picture was an inscription: Memories of a Forever Growing Love.

"It's amazing," I said.

"Keep looking," she said.

I looked through each page filled with the pictures of the two of us at various times in the three years we had known each other. At the middle of the book was an empty page with an inscription: Orville's 16th Birthday – A First for many things to come.

"That sounds, what's the word...apocalyptic," I said.

Sage giggled. "I hope it's not apocalyptic."

"I mean, futuristic—wait, not futuristic," I said.

"You mean ambiguous," Sage said.

After dinner, we drove to my house.

"Is your mom home?" Sage asked.

"I don't think so," I said.

I opened the door, yelled for my mother and was given no response. Sage carried a small white bag in with her. We went up to my room. She opened the little bag and took out four small candles and placed them around the room; she then lit them with a lighter she always carried (just in case). She closed the bedroom. She un-strapped

96

her dress and squeezed out of it. She wore navy blue satin panties and a matching bra. She unclasped her bra, let it fall, and then she climbed on the bed. I quickly took my shirt off and pulled my jeans down. She climbed on top me, and began rubbing against my pelvis. She leaned down and whispered in my ear. "I love you."

I couldn't breath. It was too much: her on top of me, rubbing against me, loving me, loving me. I couldn't take it all in. She slid my boxers off and pulled her panties down. We were both naked, and my hands were all over her; our breathing was rapid and heavy, and I felt an immense warmth—I felt that my entire body was in my penis, and I was submerged in a warm oily bubble bath. Within ten seconds, my body convulsed uncontrollably and was like a shotgun firing shells at nearby pheasants.

"Well, that was..." Sage began.

"Sorry, I couldn't stop..." I breathed.

"No, it felt good, just faster than expected," she said. "But it was the first time."

Suddenly the thought occurred to me what I had just done.

"Shit, I wasn't wearing..."

"I've been on birth control for three weeks now," she said. "Of course this was planned. I do think of everything."

"I love you," I said.

"I know."

When Sage went home, I went to the garage in the backyard. I felt like a new man. I felt like I had finally achieved something in my life, that a new life was opening itself up to me. I kept going back to what had just happened—I visualized Sage's naked body on top of me. I visualized my penis sliding into her, as brief as it had been. It was the most beautiful thing I had ever seen.

"Now I won't be pestered anymore by the guys at least," I said into the silence. My voice seemed to echo throughout the garage. I looked about myself. No one was there with the bright white lights humming above. I sneezed from the dust. There were six pool tables in the garage, equal distance away from each other in two rows of three. An unfinished bar was at the back, and wood counters lined the walls.

I saw my father and my uncle there now, sanding the wood and applying finish. I sat on one of the barstools and remembered all the nights I had come out to watch my father work. Most nights I found him shooting pool instead of working though.

"Got to test the tables," he would say.

"You're always testing the tables."

"Well, if I keep missing, the table must not be set up correctly."

The garage was empty, but I found myself going out there at night. I felt him there. I only felt him there.

"I miss you. Sometimes I wonder if you'd be proud of me. I wish you could see Sage now. I wish you could see us together. This is the woman I'm going to marry. And I'm never going to be able to talk to you about it. You'll never be able to see what I become. I don't know. I just miss you. You just disappeared so quickly—I was just getting to know you. Sometimes I feel my fate is death. Sometimes I feel I'm supposed to suffer. What am I supposed to learn? Or am I meant to lose everything and then simply die myself? You're gone. I only have Sage left."

The garage was quiet save for the humming of the overhead lights.

"Sometimes I feel I'm the antagonist in a Shakespeare tragedy, and I'm meant to die tragically."

I will take away everything you ever love, said death.

Chapter 10

We formed a crescent moon around the coaches, taking a knee. There were a mismatch of uniforms, and I was surprised at how many sixteen-year olds were there pining for the couple of spots open. They could have my place for all I cared—this was my last season, and I was only trying out because everyone expected it of me.

"There's a lot of folks here today, more than the first week," one of the coaches said. "We'll split into three groups—pitchers with Coach Bartlett, batting in the cages with Coach Stevenson, and infield, outfield with me."

I was sent to the batting cages with most of the sixteen-year olds, which I didn't understand since I had played legion ball the last two summers and was a lock to make the team. The sixteen-year olds were chatting incessantly about whatever was going on in their lives. I stood off to the side of one of the cages, alone, swinging my bat—I watched the hitters take pitches, but I couldn't help but feel I was being ostracized, sent with the sixteen-year olds as punishment for missing the first weekend of tryouts. The coaches didn't even look in my direction as if I were an unfamiliar or worse, a liability.

I hit with the sixteen-year olds and took infield, outfield with them as well. Afterwards, the entire squad got together and played a simulated game. We were divided into two teams. Clint and Brett were both on my team and I felt I had paid my penance and was once again an insider—Brett pitched an easy one, two, three first inning with two fly outs and a strike out. There was no doubt he was on the team. The guy was the hardest working baseball player I had ever known. He truly loved the game. In the gym, he worked mostly on legs whereas most guys worked their upper bodies out of vanity. Brett had a vision though. He knew what he needed to do to succeed. He went on long distance runs after games and was always driving his teammates to be the best they possibly could.

I stepped up to the plate for my first at bat. I didn't recognize the young kid who was pitching.

"C'mon McFadden, let's go," Brett yelled. He was fired up—he treated every situation as a live game. "This is it. Let's get it done."

On the third pitch, the kid threw one belt-high and right over the plate; I hit a deep fly ball to left center field. I began to trot to first base. I had seen this many times before—it was gone.

"You never know," the first base coach said. "Better get going."

"I know," I muttered to him as I passed. The ball sailed over the fence.

"That a baby, that a baby McFadden," Brett shouted, greeting me at the plate. He was more excited than I was.

After the game, we had conditioning. It was a hot day, and we sweated profusely through our jerseys. Looking at all the guys standing around, I realized it felt good to be with them. Those guys really wanted to be there, and their passion was motivating. I felt ashamed to be amongst them, almost as a spy would amongst comrades. And especially as I was taking one of their spots on the roster. The young guys especially had so much potential; a senior legion season at sixteen would give them invaluable experience.

After conditioning, the coaches conferred together with their notes in the dugout. The guys stood around bullshitting with each other. The sixteen-year olds scarcely said a word—their fates were being discussed, one after another. The coaches came back over after fifteen minutes. They separated the guys into two groups. I watched in horror as the group I was amongst consisted mostly of the sixteen-year olds and some of the guys I was surprised were there at all. I was called over first.

"Hey Orville, are you surprised?"

"I'm a little surprised," I said. "I don't really understand."

"Orville, you missed this year's first tryouts because you weren't sure you wanted to play. Last year you did the same thing. Your heart doesn't really seem to be in it. We have some guys here who really want to be here. You haven't shown us you wanted to be here."

I walked to my car, opened the door, and got inside. I sat there in silence watching the other members who got cut walk to their cars with downcast eyes. The sixteen-year olds were chipper though as they knew they were still going to play for the junior legion team. But for me? My baseball career was suddenly and swiftly over. It was true; my heart wasn't in it, but I still felt this wasn't right. This didn't just happen. It was over. It was all over. My baseball career had just ended.

"What do you want to do tonight?"

"I don't know. What do you want to do tonight?" How many times had we had this conversation?

"There's a show at The Rift. We could do that."

The Rift was a show box downtown where local bands could play, and admission on Thursday nights was for anyone under twenty-one years old. It was loud, obnoxious, and smelled of body odor and nachos, which they sold there for two dollars. It was also a haven for the delinquents and dropouts. And I told her that.

"Hey old man, it was only a suggestion," Sage said.

"The twins want to play four-player Goldeneye," I said. "Do you want to?"

"Yeah, I guess. There's nothing better to do," I said.

"Wow, you're going to be fun tonight," she said.

"What? There isn't is there?"

"Fine, I'll come over then," she said.

Sage showed up ten minutes later. She walked through the front door, which had become custom.

"There's no point in knocking. I'd rather hear the door open and know it was you than hear a knock and not know who it was," my mother had said. "Especially late at night."

Sage wore the baggy black sweats that track team members were given and a gray shirt.

"You planning on going to bed?" I asked.

"Is this how it's going to be all night?"

"I'm sorry. I'm just pissed about the try outs," I said.

"But now we'll have the whole summer together," she said.

"I'll probably have to get a job," I said.

"Maybe we'll get one together."

"Maybe we will."

"Where's your mom?"

"Getting pizza."

"How much time do we have before she comes home and the twins get here?"

"I don't know—half an hour maybe."

"I could cheer you up in less than half an hour."

"I don't think we have time," I said.

"We have time," she said, coming closer to me. She kissed me hard, biting into my lips—she tasted of dill pickles, which she liked to eat one by one out of the jar. We laid down on the heap of blankets I had set up in front of the Nintendo. She took my shirt off and unbuttoned my jeans—yet I felt no tingle and I worried she would discover this. I pulled her into me and kissed her, and our breathing deepened. I took her shirt off and cupped her black-laced breasts. I slid her sweats off and moved my hand slowly from the back of her leg to where the outline of her panties began, and I finally felt that twitching tingle that meant I still found her sexy. I focused on sliding my hand along the smooth satin to the small of her back, back and forth. She slid my jeans and boxers off and unclasped her bra. She slid off of me to take her panties off.

"Leave them on," I whispered.

"Why? They get in the way," she said.

Just fuck her and be done with her, said the great concubine.

102

"Never mind," I said. "Come here."

She slid them off the rest of the way and came to me. Her body felt good, and I focused on watching myself slide in and out of her.

After we finished, I slid off her and went up into my room. I stood in front of the long mirror that was against the wall. I looked at myself, naked, hair on my legs, my stomach and arms, stubble on my face. What an ugly thing you are. I looked at my visage, stern and hard, my eyes narrowed to slits. I looked at my pelvis, my penis. What an ugly thing you are—the hair, the penis, wet with semen and whatever—it was disgusting.

"Cover it up," I said into the mirror. I wiped myself off and put on fresh boxers and felt a little better. I went back downstairs and found Sage lying on the blankets, naked still. The female body was no different: her breasts were hanging lumps of flesh, her pelvis a cavernous ravine, smelling of sweat, dark and ugly. Cover it up. Put something on.

"You'd better dress," I said. "They'll all be here soon."

"Just give me a moment," she said. "Come lay next to me."

"Sage, we don't have time," I insisted.

"Fine," she groaned and moved to put her clothes back on.

The twins came over just before my mother showed up. My mother brought two large pizzas and cokes, and I was thankful for the twin's company. Something was changing inside of me, and I didn't understand it. I couldn't look at Sage without thinking something negative. I didn't even like to be around her. And there was no one to talk to about it.

The graduation ceremony lasted at least three hours as we had 375 students graduating. I walked with Clint and Brett and Sage walked with the twins.

"You're going to the graduation party tonight, right?" Brett asked me.

"Of course," I said.

"Is Sage going with you?" Clint asked.

"No, I was hoping I'd go with you guys," I said.

"Fuck yeah man," Clint said. "Drive to my place. We'll pre-funk this bitch to high heaven."

I met the guys later in the evening. They both sported backwards baseball caps, blue jeans, white long-sleeved shirts, Fossil watches, and at least four squirts of cologne, Ralph Lauren Polo Sport—I owned the same bottle. They both opened the door to Clint's country home with a beer in their hands.

"What did I walk into? Were you guys about to kiss?" I said.

"Oh more than that," Clint said. "Two hot single guys."

"You need to shotgun two beers," Brett said. "To catch up." He tossed me two Budweiser beers. I cracked them both open and double-fisted.

"Oh, tonight's going to be a good night," I said.

"Yup, three single guys out on the prowl," Clint said.

"Yup, I'm single tonight," I said.

"You guys broke up?" Brett asked.

"No—but she won't be there. We had dinner together before coming here."

"Bullshit," Clint said. "You fucked her before coming here."

"A man's got to do what a man's got to do," I said, tossing one of the empty beer cans in the trash. I shook my head from the dizziness. "Oh, that was fast."

We left for Denise the Beast's house at 9:30. Her parents owned a farmhouse just outside of town, and they had said we could throw the graduation party in the barn. When we pulled up in Clint's truck, there were already quite a few people milling around drinking beer. The trucks were lined side-by-side—Ford, Chevy, Dodge—along the long dirt road that led up to the farmhouse.

104

We jumped out of the truck feeling good from the Budweiser. Two guys were drinking together at the end of the road.

"Oh, the party's started now. The crazies are here," one guy said.

"You guys the watch dogs?" Brett asked.

"Yup, got your passes?" the other guy said.

Clint lifted the case of Budweiser. "Yup, right here."

"You may enter."

The barn's wood floors had been swept up, and all the cows had been let out into the pasture. The wooden pens were still intact, but they served as transparent rooms people could go in and out of. The barn was full of people, and I at once saw Mindy Halverson. I remembered what I had said about being single to the guys and instantly regretted it. I also regretted being there. I always felt like this when first coming to a party. Before the party, there would be high hopes that it would be amazing, that this and this would happen, that it would be epic—girls would dance topless on tables, I would meet my dream girl, and we would kiss at the stroke of midnight. But these things never happened.

What did happen was drinking and occasionally, the intentional eyes of one who wanted to do things to you, the susceptible, you, the one person who had held out for four years. Mindy Halverson was looking across the room right at me. Her hazel eyes flashed like sparkling emeralds across a sea of voices.

"Wow, would you look at that?" Clint said.

"Danger there McFadden," Brett said.

It was the three of us looking at Mindy and the two hens who were attached to her like leeches, sucking from her all the knowledge she could give about sex, makeup, drinking, and dressing. The three looked identical as the three of us did.

"Tell you what—I'll sleep with Mindy if you both take a hen," I joked.

"I'll take both hens at the same time if you sleep with Mindy," Clint said.

"Not what I wanted to hear," I said.

"Give it a few more beers," Brett said.

The barn was equipped with a loud stereo system that bumped out Tupac and Biggie Smalls, and there was a large ice chest filled with beer in one of the cow pens, a freezer filled with wine coolers and orange juice for the Vodka drinkers. The dancing that goes along in a barn during a party starts out innocent enough. One or two guys, usually the class clowns, start moving to the music, together. People stand around and watch and drink until enough alcohol has been consumed, and it usually takes one fat girl to get on the dance floor to get all the other girls on the dance floor. And that's what happened here.

I drank a few screwdrivers and made my warm body get out on the dance floor. The room spun happily around, and the dancing felt good. I looked around. I couldn't see Mindy anywhere.

What are you looking for, the great concubine said.

"Looking for somebody," Mindy said.

"Oh, hi," I said, taking a deep sip of the screwdriver.

"God, I needed to get away from Matt. He's all over me," Mindy said. "Shit, dance with me—he's there again."

Matt had just come in through the barn door, his head wagging around as he searched for Mindy. He was a big, farm boy oaf—Lenny came to mind. He wore Carhartt overalls and a tight white shirt that his beer-filled gut hung just out of. I noticed then my hands were around Mindy's tight hips.

"I can see why you wanted to get away," I said. Mindy smelled of cheap perfume, but it was a nice relief from the stench of cows, which could never be eradicated completely.

"Where's Sage?"

"No esta aqui."

"You've never been this close to me before."

"You're the one thing that smells good in this barn."

106

"Well, let's get out of this barn then."

I wanted to say no. I wanted to just say right then that Sage was still my girlfriend, that I thought she was beautiful and if things were different...but my hands were around her hips, and her tan, hard stomach pressed against mine, and going outside didn't mean anything. It was hot, it smelled, and Matt the pervert was lingering around like a goddamn giant mosquito.

Take her outside and fuck her, the great concubine said.

We went outside.

The night air was cool, and it felt good against our faces. We went to the side of the barn where the hay bales were kept. The bales were lit up by overhead lamps and briefly, I thought of the manger. But only briefly as Mindy pulled my hand along the hay—we were like two drunken school kids, tripping and falling, laughing, giggling as if we had stolen the cookies out of the cookie jar and were eating them as quickly as we could to get rid of the evidence. We ran to the end of the hay bales. We suddenly stopped and before anything could be said, Mindy Pulled me close into her and kissed me.

She tasted of sweetened orange juice and her perfume clouded my senses, and I kissed her back hard, without any inhibitions.

"I've wanted this..." she said.

Sage drifted out of my mind in a plume of faint smoke. She was blocked by alcohol, by Mindy, and by desire for freedom. I had been with Sage for so long, I forgot what it felt like to be free. Mindy felt free. Her body felt new and free and good in my hands.

She unzipped my pants. "Here?" I said. "Let's go over there."

"No, here. Now," she insisted. She pulled down my jeans and boxers, and I stood there like a lightning rod in my white shirt.

I unzipped her jeans and pulled them down. I turned her around. She wore a sexy black thong, which I moved to the side. This was the kind of girl I wanted: a girl with a black thong on during sex with her jeans wrapped around her ankles bending over a hay bale. It was over quickly, and I wiped myself off with some straws of hay.

We opened the barn door and I caught the eyes of Clint, and I smiled involuntarily like just before the punch line in a joke I was telling and thought hilariously funny. Mindy went to the hens, and I went to Clint and Brett as two people do after doing awkward things up against a hay bale and seeing each other in ways only two people well acquainted should see each other. We didn't catch each other's eyes the rest of the night.

"You have a good chat?" Brett asked.

"If you didn't at least bang her..." Clint began.

"I turned her around and gave it to her," I said.

"What?" Clint screamed.

"Shut up," I said. "Fuck dude."

"Seriously, though, you fucked Mindy Halverson—where?" Clint said.

"Over a hay bale," I said.

"You fucked Mindy Halverson over a hay bale...wow," Clint said. "You, my friend, have achieved super star status."

I had achieved nothing. I had lost something great. In five minutes, I had destroyed four years of a loving relationship. I had fucked everything away in five minutes, less than five minutes, against a hay bale. Was it simply a way to end things? My love had waned, but even if that was true, there was something left, wasn't there? And when I thought of Sage, when I thought of everything we had done together, when I thought of her giving herself to me in the greatest expression of love, I realized what a terrible mistake had been made. I should have ended it long ago.

We sat on a bench in her front yard. The sun's glow died behind the dark hills to the south. I held her hand and tried to say the words that needed to be said. But she sat stoically and beautifully next to me in silence, waiting.

We faced the hills, and I knew she was thinking about what was beyond them. If I could just get through this moment, a new life was beyond them, a life at the University of Washington filled with the promises of guiltless sex and raging parties.

"You want to breakup," she said.

"I love you, but..."

"You love me? Then why are you doing this?" I let go of her hand. "What? You thought I would simply say okay, goodbye, have a nice life?"

"No," I said.

"You're breaking my heart."

"I'm sorry. I just..."

"Tell me one thing. Please tell me the truth. Did you sleep with Mindy Halverson?"

Did she know? Of course she would know. Tell her yes. Tell her everything. But I couldn't.

"No—I'd never do that to you," I said.

"Then why? What is it?"

"Everything I have ever loved has been taken from me," I said.

"Well, I'm sure to live a long life then."

***

"And that was it?" Dr. Fields asked.

"Yes. We broke up and I went off to the University of Washington. She went to art school in New York, and I never heard much from her after that. I think she got married, but I'm not sure."

"Do you think you did the right thing—breaking up with her?"

"I've asked myself that many times. At the time, it seemed right. But now I'm not so sure. She was an amazing woman...is. I think about those times nostalgically. I wonder what happened to her."

"Did she ever find out about Mindy?"

109

"I don't know. Probably, but I regret not telling her the truth then and there."

"Why didn't you?"

"Because I was a coward...am a coward. My entire high school experience was of cowardice. I couldn't say no to Mindy either. But I wanted to. Yes, a part of me wanted to sleep with her but that was simply because I wanted something new. I guess I was a little bored. But truly I didn't want to because how I felt afterwards was too much. The guilt weighed too much. In a way, I didn't deserve Sage at all. She was too good. I had begun to go down the spiraling staircase to hell. Lies and cowardice. I was way down before I knew I had even begun. It didn't stop with Sage. I lied and cheated my way through university too...with women I mean. But instead of being with girls for four years, my relationships usually lasted two months or less. I couldn't keep any before I wanted to move onto the next one."

"Tell me about Hadley," Dr. Fields said.

Part II
Chapter 11

Kitchen – A glass, oval table, centered. Stacks of books next to pantry against back wall. White drawers; white cupboards; linoleum flooring, white with blue detailed flowers. Countertop, turquoise with CD player, toaster, microwave, 13-inch television. Oven, refrigerator, next to countertop. Ikea painting on wall opposite refrigerator. Chandelier, centered, hanging from ceiling.

The kitchen was something of a jack-of-all-trades, if that could be said for a room in a house—a room in which many things happened, but none spectacular. Hadley only dined at the table if there was nothing interesting on the television, which for someone with her interests, was a rare occasion. For me, the kitchen was a sort of study. I liked to pace around the table reading while sipping on red wine. I kept scripts in a drawer so if there was a spark of ambition, I could take one or two out and practice monologues—all the kitchens a stage. During the summer, I could drink beer and watch baseball since I had no claiming rights to the television in the living room.

Kitchen – I placed each delicate plate and bowl on the table with care. With each clank and clink, Hadley looked over quickly.

"If you break those..." she said.

"I know. I know. I just like to watch your beautiful blonde hair sway to the side every time you turn around like you're in a shampoo commercial."

"Did you really just say that?"

"I think so."

"You're a dork."

Settings for four: plate, knife at 3 o'clock, fork next to knife, one inch away, spoon at 9 o'clock, napkin, folded neatly across plate, salad bowl at 10 o'clock, two inches from plate, wine goblet at 1 o'clock, two inches from plate. Space for entrée, large salad bowl, plate with garlic bread, center table. I stepped back and admired my meticulous work.

"Your mother would be proud," Hadley said and kissed me on the cheek.

"No, something's missing," I said. I quickly left the room and came back a moment later. "Flowers. For you. Pike's Place Market."

"Oh honey they're perfect."

"You're perfect," I said.

"I know," she said. "You're so lucky."

"And it smells amazing in here—lasagna is officially your signature dish."

"Yes, made with love."

"Oh yes, cheese, sauce and a big helping of love," I said.

"Don't you remember *Como agua para chocolate?*" she asked me as she glided from countertop to cupboard like a lithe wood nymph.

"Ah, refresh me again," I said.

"Nothing made without love will nourish. C'mon husband. When we have girly movie night, you need to start paying more attention. I don't just watch those movies with you because I like to cry. Geez," she said.

"I'll try harder. I promise."

"You better."

"Ah...what's the name of the alien with the laser on his shoulder and he self-destructs when Arnold Schwarzenegger is closing in on him?"

"What're you even talking about?"

"Yeah...you don't think I watch manly movie night with you just to cuddle, do you?"

"Ah...that's because when I'm snuggling with you, I only think about you. You can't expect me to pay attention to anything else?"

"Oh the lies. The lies," I said.

"Now, be a good boy and go change your clothes for dinner. They should be here any minute."

Bedroom – Bare, white walls. Queen bed, unmade, centered with a stuffed bear in between two pillows. Underwear, nurse scrubs, socks and undershirts spread throughout room. Night stand next to bed with an old lamp. Piles of magazines—*Elle, Nintendo Power, Good Housekeeping, Vanity fair*—in various corners. Books on floor—Hemingway to Danielle Steel—and a stack of CDs next to nightstand. Closet open with many empty plastic hangers. Jeans and a white-collared shirt laid out on the bed.

Bedroom – I changed quickly and dusted off a black dinner jacket that had traveled from one closet to another over the years.

Kitchen – Hadley was taking the lasagna out of the oven. It sizzled and bubbled in the hot glass container.

"I knew I married you for a reason," I said.

"Lasagna?—is that the only reason?"

"I'm sure I could find more—if I dug deep."

There was a pounding at the front door.

"The Stevensons have arrived," I said in my best English accent. "The Stevensons."

"Now Orville, you remember what we talked about? Please pretend to be friends with him," Hadley said. "At least for tonight."

"My best acting gig yet—unpaid and unnoticed," I said.

"I notice."

Living Room – Cream-colored couch against wall, loveseat at right angle next to couch, large coffee table in front, bookshelf against wall next to couch, desk with computer next to bookshelf, television set with television, DVDs, CDs, and stereo against wall opposite couch.

Living Room – I opened the door to a tall, stoutly, lightly bearded man in black slacks and a gray V-neck sweater hugging his midsection. Standing next to him was his lovely wife in a light blue sequin dress and a jacket to cover her shoulders.

"Russ, Wanda, welcome to our humble abode," I said, letting them in.

113

Russ held up a six pack of Coors Light. "We'd better open these straight away," he said.

"Truer words have never been spoken," I said.

Kitchen – "I present you the Stevensons," I said, bowing to Hadley.

"Oh brother. Hi," she said to Wanda, giving her a hug. "You look gorgeous."

"So do you. Your dress is beautiful," Wanda said.

Hadley wore a plum Betine dress and copper necklace. "My husband took me to Anthropologie for my birthday last week."

"Russ would never take me to Anthropologie," Wanda said. "You're lucky."

I looked at Russ standing oafishly off to the side of the table with his shoulders hunched over staring intently at the beer in his hand. He suddenly perked up as if a switch had been turned upwards on his back. "Well, the girls are off to the races," he said. "Let's drink."

This lasagna is amazing I heard Wanda say from across the table.

"Sealed the ad deal with Komo 4 and played golf with the bosses afterwards. Shot an eighty-nine too," Russ said.

"Another beer?" I asked.

"Keep it coming," he said.

"Honey, will you open another bottle of wine too while you're up," Hadley said.

"Those are beautiful glasses," Wanda said.

"A wedding gift from...from..."

"My Uncle Jim and Aunt Marta," Hadley said. "Honey, don't strain yourself with details."

I smiled at Wanda.

"I see your roles are clearly defined," Wanda said.

"It really works nicely," I said.

"Well, I see you put those plates to good use," Russ said, indicating the plates and bowls on the table. "Can't for the life of me see what you see in them."

Wanda rolled her eyes heavenward. "He has no taste. They're gorgeous."

I opened the wine and poured for the ladies and some for myself, gave a beer to Russ.

Living Room – I put on some Dylan.

Kitchen – I sat back down, suddenly struck by a strange thought—I was in rapid metamorphosis mode—before my very eyes, I was becoming Domesticated Slug Man. My life: slow nights at home (on my nights off) and dinner with married couples, idle conversation or watching television or movies, walks in the morning only to think about the perpetual boredom of it all, working in the evenings into the night, coming home and doing it all again the next day. Domesticated Slug Man strikes again!

This was marriage? This *was* marriage: a perpetually slow death. There was a time, just a few months ago, when I was striving to be an actor. An actor—movies, sets, stages, costumes, makeup, lines, late night practices, shows, cameras. A *Mid Summer Night's Dream* slipping away into the darkness. I hadn't looked at a script in months, not seriously; I hadn't even looked at what plays were being auditioned for.

"Honey, will you pass the garlic bread?"

Pass the garlic bread? The garlic bread. My life now was lasagna and garlic bread. I was young and had succumbed to the way of the buffalo: practically extinct. Pass the garlic bread indeed.

I looked over at Hadley and for the briefest moment, I saw not the woman I loved and married, but the shackles to dreams, a bondage to domesticated slavery. I was being transformed by the very woman I loved. Where had her dreams gone? Was I taking them from her too? Or were these it? Was it something else? Was it her or was it marriage as the institutional destroyer of dreams? I looked at her, her beautiful face and saw the face of an old woman dying anonymously in the night, a woman loved, but unknown to the world. And across from her was me, a man who was born, who went to work, who had kids,

115

who grew old, who died, a man who could only say his greatest accomplishment was to create two new human beings. And weren't there enough of those around?

I passed the garlic bread to Hadley.

"Well, Bush is taking his second term by the horns I'd say," Russ said.

"So Orville, Hadley tells me you're trying to be an actor," Wanda said.

"Not trying very hard," I said.

"I enjoy a movie just like anybody else, but really, actors are pretty much worthless," Russ said.

"Well, if you're interested," Wanda said. "I have a friend who opened up a theatre recently and is casting her first play. I think the auditions are in a few weeks, but the cast will be small she said, but she may need some help with ushering and things like that if you didn't get a part. It could be a nice in."

"Really? Yeah...I mean that would be great," I said.

"Sure, I'll talk to her tomorrow." Wanda smiled at me, her eyes twinkling a touch more in the chandelier light.

We spoke of sports and politics, our jobs. Russ did something in advertising and Wanda worked with Hadley at the hospital. But I found myself thinking of the theatre and stealing glances at Wanda. How strange it was to sit at a dinner table and discuss things like grownups. It felt like a murder mystery, a whodunit dinner. Wanda, the mischievous home wrecker and her idiot husband; Orville, the passionate artist and his naïve wife. A murder will be committed. How had I envisioned marriage as a kid?—we would talk of literature and politics, theatre and revolutions, drink wine and steal glances at our wives, take them to bed after our guests had left. Frida Kahlo and Diego Rivera type dinner parties. I envisioned candlelight with red wine, good friends, evening gowns and tuxedos, sex and music. That was what marriage was supposed to be like.

"NASCAR guys use more muscle groups than baseball players any day," Russ said. "How is it you can get paid twenty-five million dollars a year and be fat, out-of-shape, and do five minutes of work each day? I mean, some of these guys don't even play defense. They're designated hitters," he added with contempt. "That shouldn't even be a paid position. These guys get like four at-bats a night, five minutes of work, and get paid that much. Pisses me off man. I work day in and day out and don't get shit like that."

I finished with the dishes. "You want a beer or something?"

"Yeah, what do you have?"

"Pike's Kilt Lifter," I said.

"Ah, you're into that micro brew stuff," he said.

"So you want one or not?"

"You want to head down to play pool or something?" he said. "The girls are going to be gabbing away awhile."

I looked at Hadley. "Yeah, get out of here. We need girl time."

"Man, you *shouldn't* even ask," Russ said.

The pool hall was tucked in a side street off First Avenue under an inconspicuous brick building. After a sloping decline and down some stairs, two men stood smoking together. Any minute now men with Tommy guns would storm out of the bar in a blaze of bullets or some coked out junkie would be tossed out and left to die in the alleyway. It looked like that kind of place.

Pool Hall – Shadowed exterior with six pool tables lit by hanging fixtures above. Bar on left hand side with bar stools cemented in the flooring. Dimly-lit dance floor in right hand corner next to rest rooms and pool tables.

Pool Hall – Inside, a woman with black hair wearing a green dress greeted us perfunctorily as she leaned against the bar countertop. I heard the clink of glasses in the darkness and then a man would emerge, take a shot, and then retreat back into the shadows. I had no idea how many people were at this place.

"Lovely place," I said.

117

"You find a table. What do you want to drink?"

"Gin tonic please."

I took the nearest table to the dance floor. I took a stick from the wall rack and put it on the table and rolled it left to right like my father had taught me. The end of the stick jumped with each roll; it wasn't straight. I tried another with the same result. I stayed with that one. I racked the balls.

"Dollar a game then?" Russ asked, handing me the drink.

"No, I don't like to just give money away," I said.

"It's just a dollar," he said and leaned down to break. He reared his stick back and shot it through like an ancient cannon. The balls spread out all along the table. Two balls dropped. I stood in the shadows while he made short work of the easy shots. He missed a tough bank shot on the seven ball, and I approached the table. I shot at the nine ball, and it missed the hole by a few inches. "Ouch," he said.

"I usually play my best pool after two beers," I said.

"What do you want?" he said. "I'm buying."

"Whatever you're having," I said.

Russ went to the bar to get the drinks when a woman stepped out of the shadows like a will-o-the-wisp. For a brief moment, I couldn't tell that she was a woman at all—she appeared so suddenly, like an apparition or shadow—her face was white, her long hair black, and she wore deep red lipstick. She wore a tight, long-sleeved, low-cut black shirt and a white skirt. I simply stood there, holding my pool stick. The time seemed to stop, the bar silenced.

Then she spoke, "Do you guys want to play doubles? My friend's in the little girls' room."

"I'm sure we do," I said, instinctively taking the wedding ring off my finger and slipping it into my pocket. Russ came back with the drinks—he never wore his ring anyway. The woman's friend, too, came out of the shadows. She was a bit shorter, but dressed similar.

118

"I guess I should've brought back four," he said, handing me a beer. "Good work," he whispered to me.

Russ broke and nothing fell. When it was my turn to shoot, I lined up my shot, but then the woman in the white skirt came over and came up behind me. She gripped my left arm tightly and held my right arm with hers. I thought this was something that only happened in the movies. Her breasts fell against my back and I stiffened up.

"Calm down. Hold the stick loosely here," she said, indicating my left hand. "And tightly here for stability. And bring it closer to your hips. Focus on where you want to hit the ball." I did so and shot. It went in. I turned around. She shrugged her shoulders and smiled.

"Well, next round's on me. What'll it be ladies?" Russ said.

"Long Island." "Whiskey."

"Orville, come help me carry," Russ said. I leaned my pool stick against the table and walked over to Russ. "Dude, you want to take the taller one back to my truck? She's been eyeing you all game man. Or we could take them both to a one-hour motel."

"I don't know..."

Take her out to the truck Orville, said the great concubine.

I looked over at the women playing pool. The one in the white skirt was leaning over the edge, one leg on the floor, the other over the side of the table.

What's under that skirt? You want to find out. You want to run your hands slowly up there. You want to know you still can, said the great concubine.

We could take these girls home tonight, I thought. Where would we go?—to Russ's place?—a motel? A quick rendezvous before going home. I could take her outside and just lift her up against the wall. Why not? It's just sex. We don't even know their names and they don't know ours. Hadley would never know. It wouldn't be betrayal because it's just sex. It's not love. It's one time. It's like playing softball or tennis with a female friend. Oh, you play tennis...let's play sometime. Oh, you play sex...let's play sometime. The only reason you wouldn't tell Hadley is because she wouldn't understand that. She doesn't think like that. And what's sex? It's two people doing what people do. Big deal.

But you can't do that. You won't do that.

You're a coward. You couldn't have that if you wanted to, said fear.

Take her. She's practically begging for it, said the great concubine.

What would you do with her? Recite a monologue? She wants to fuck, not listen to poetry, said fear.

"Ah, it can't happen tonight," I said. "The girls are waiting for us."

We played for an hour or so before the women had to go home.

"So, can I call you sometime?" I said to the white-skirted woman.

"Oh...well...actually we're up from San Fran, only here tonight, so..."

"Oh yeah, no problem. Okay, well...thanks for the games."

"Yeah...sure."

After they left, Russ brought over another beer. "Don't worry about it. They were old anyway. Bar wenches. So you and Hadley have been married how long?"

"Four months now," I said.

"You're in that phase then—why the hell did I do this— that sort of thing," Russ said.

"I don't know. Everything seems fine," I said.

"From the way you looked at that woman tonight, I would guess everything's not fine. Dude, it's okay. We all go through it. There's an easy solution man."

"What's that?"

Russ shrugged his stout shoulders. "Sex—with other women. You love your wife right?—of course, but we're men man—naturally we want to have sex with as many women as we can. We want to know we still have what it takes. It's totally natural. What's not natural is sleeping with one woman your entire life. I can't think of anything less natural."

"Yeah, but I think we have to make sacrifices too if we want to raise a family, have commitment, that sort of thing. Don't you think?"

"Sure, I mean, I love my wife," he said. "But man, sex with one woman for your entire life. C'mon. It's not meant to be like that. That's just stupid, especially when sex doesn't have to be an emotional connection and all that shit. Why can't it just be a release sometimes too? You know?"

"So you sleep around a lot then," I said.

"I don't just sleep around." He paused before saying, "Dude, I have to know you can keep a secret."

Oh here it comes. The great revelation: Russ and his midnight runs to various women throughout the city.

"Sure, of course," I said.

"I joined an online sex club," he said, shrugging. "But this one's different because it's only for married people."

"Really?" I said.

"Yeah. I mean, these people still love their spouses. They just want a little excitement in their lives sometimes. It's just sex. Why does it have to be more than that?"

"I don't know. Don't you think sex is better with someone you're connected to?"

"Yeah, sure, but that's the sex you do with your wife man. Not the sex you do with a stranger. It's fucking. And it's fucking amazing. You chit-chat a little, but none of that bullshit you would on a first date, and then you meet in a safe place—never at your house or anything. And then you fuck. That's it. You fuck. You have screen names so you never even have to know the person's name. It's easy. It's fast. And it's not even cheating because it's just sex. No emotional connection whatsoever."

"Man, I don't know..."I said.

"Well, no big deal dude. I'll give you the website information. Sign up if you want to. You can do a free trial too where you can send email, but you can't check emails in return unless you sign up."

Bedroom - I lay in bed that night thinking about what Russ had said to me. Hadley's warm body snuggled closely into mine, her soft leg wrapped over me, and her head rested on my chest. She breathed softly, contently, securely. I was her husband, the man she loved and devoted her entire life to. And she was my wife. My wife? What a strange thought. I'm twenty-four years old and have a wife. I can hardly say it to my friends without laughing. How absurd it sounds off my tongue. Hi, nice to meet you—this is my wife Hadley. Is this my future now? Boring dinners with people I hardly care about and television afterwards?

Chapter 12

Bedroom - A rare, warm October morning, the sky being a milky rice soup with clumping thin clouds prompted Hadley to get up, to get dressed, and to drag me cockeyed to the garden. "We're real grownups now husband. We...wait for it...have a garden." She wanted tomatoes, tulips, daffodils, peppers, spinach, cucumbers, pumpkins—anything that could grow. "No roses though. I'll let you buy me those." "What about potatoes?" I grumbled. "QFC is down the street husband."

Garden - The weeds had infested every crevice of earth, every niche between pumpkins. It was a small scale city of crabgrass, shot weed, and dock weed littered with tiny inhabitants working towards a commonality—to gorge on the large, orange pumpkins, bringers of civilization, sustenance and livelihood for pill bugs, slugs, and myriad dangerous killers. I watched Hadley struggle to dig down into the hard earth and uproot a massive crabgrass weed. She looked at me.

"Are you just going to stand there?"

"I was just thinking you're at your sexiest in holey jeans and a white shirt," I said.

"And I think you're at your sexiest when you're digging up weeds," she said, handing me the shovel. "I'll get the small ones."

A halcyon morning, quiet streets, sleeping dogs, a fine Saturday. I took a deep breath, the clean, fresh air cooling my throat and lungs. Working alongside Hadley felt good, like we were building something together. Hadley wiped the sweat from her forehead. "This is hard work husband. How about I make sandwiches?"

"I would love a sandwich my sweet little pumpkin," I said.

"Oh brother..."

Yard work (like doing dishes, taking a shower or a walk) allows time to organize those rapid, sporadic thoughts that bombard the mind during times of strife, to ponder the life to come and reflect on the life already gone.

It had been a short screen pass. I caught it, ran to my left, juked a few defenders, went to my right, and plowed into a tackle, was in the midst of being taken down when...I saw white, pulsing stars shining bright, my eyes squinting as if seeing for the first time. I heard a cacophony of voices, but it was all gibberish, an ungodly vernacular, discordant and muddled. I was in limbo.

"Am I dead?" I groaned. I opened my eyes wide and saw before me an angelic face, brightly lit with flowing golden hair and gleaming hazel eyes. She was the most beautiful creature I had ever seen.

"You've had a concussion," the angel sung.

"Yes, please," I said. I didn't know what it meant, but it sounded fantastic.

"You don't understand. You *have* a concussion."

"And what is your name sweet angel?"

"Oh brother..."

I came round moments later and realized I was still alive and in a hospital room. Then, I remembered I had been playing football and got tackled. The word 'concussion' rang in my head. Who had said that? That angelic nurse clad in white singing beautiful, harmonious music. And then I heard soft steps come to my door and she, the angel herself, came in a moment later.

"Your friends are here in the waiting room. They said you were playing football without helmets and you got tackled hard from behind. Not very smart, huh?"

"Hmm...no, but I did get to meet you," I said. "Although, you still haven't told me your name."

"And what is your name sweet angel?" she said. "Is that your go to line?"

"Hmm...yeah, sometimes, yeah," I said. "On rare occasions."

"Like when you get a concussion."

"Ah, yup, that's one time it is," I said.

"Hadley St. Claire."

"It sounds heavenly," I said. "I'm Orville James McFadden. Have you ever been to Bleu Bistro on Capitol Hill?"

"No, why?"

"We should probably go," I said.

She laughed and I promptly fell in love with the two dimples that appeared at the sides of her mouth. "First my name and now dinner?"

Backyard – Hadley and I sat on the porch together eating the sandwiches.

"Do you still love me?" Hadley asked.

"Hmm, tough question," I said.

"You better because you're stuck with me."

"Do you still love me?"

Hadley puckered up her face. "I probably could've done better, but you were charming at first. I probably should've waited a little longer."

"That's why I had to act quickly," I said.

"You sure you don't mind if I keep my name? I can still change it," Hadley said.

"No; no. You cannot change it. Your name is perfect. Everything's in a name. I will never make it as an actor because my name's too bland. It's boring. McFadden—it sounds like I came straight from the farm. I'll have to change it if I ever want to do any serious acting."

"You're weird...okay, back to work loafer, back to work," Hadley said.

"First, the restroom," I said.

Kitchen – I put the plates in the sink. I looked out the window and saw Hadley inspecting the garden. I watched her. What a mother she would make. What a wife she was. She was perfect. Why did these thoughts come to me?—the world passing by. Each day I gardened, each night I waited tables, the world passed me by. There must be something more than this.

Living Room – I went to the computer and signed into the account I had set up.

Messages(1)—click.

Hi, thanks for the message. I'm interested in meeting with you tonight if you can make it. Let's meet somewhere open first to see if we like each other. Can you meet me at Cherry Street Coffee in Bell Town at 8 o'clock? Hope to hear from you soon ☺ Sammyslove36@gmail.com

I leaned back in the chair and took a deep breath. What a strange thing: cyberspace messaging. It didn't feel real. Somewhere out there, in the real world, was a woman who wrote this message. But to me, she was just words on a screen, not real—not disastrous. But, this was the deciding moment.

Are you finally going to enjoy life, said the great concubine.

It's just coffee, just a little adventure, *just*. Simply go, simply converse, simply leave. It's nothing more than coffee. Curiosity killed the cat...well, boredom killed everything else. One finger moved, then another:

Hi Sammy, good to hear from you too. 8 o'clock sounds good. See you then. Baseballnut1982@hotmail.com

I logged out, switched web pages.

Garden – I put gloves on and picked up the large shovel.

"Do you think there's enough room for squash too?" she asked.

"Anything you want."

Bathroom – I dressed in jeans and a gray silk cashmere sweater. Hadley was in the living room reading Nick Hornby. I spiked up my hair with jell and looked in the mirror. Who was it that stared back? It was the face of a liar, of a man who took everything from the ones he loved and gave back only enough to keep them hanging on.

"What're you doing?"

It's just coffee you coward, said fear.

126

First coffee; then what? What do you need to prove? What are you looking for?

She's what you're looking for—adventure, love, said the great concubine.

"It's just coffee," I said. "You haven't even seen her face; she's probably ugly."

"Who are you talking to husband?" Hadley yelled from the living room.

Living room – I kissed Hadley on the forehead. "I always talk to myself. You should know that by now."

"I'm beginning to think you're crazy," Hadley said.

"And yet I still love you very much," I said.

She stopped reading and looked at me with those gorgeous hazel eyes. "I know. And I love you sweet husband. Have fun with Jack tonight. Hmm, you smell good. Dolce and Gabbana? You have to leave right now, right now?"

"Yeah, I'm already late," I said.

"Fine. Jack can have you all to himself tonight."

I bent down and kissed her on the lips—the kiss of betrayal. Kissing your wife before meeting with another woman is an invisible poison that creeps through the lips into the veins unnoticed and makes its way to the heart and mind wherein it attacks and attacks until it whittles the soul dead.

Leave and get on with it, said the great concubine.

I left.

Car – I drove Hadley's Honda through the rain and felt my apprehensive heart beat quicken as thick raindrops splattered on the windshield and the coffee shop loomed. My hands slipped against the steering wheel from perspiration and I rubbed them together to calm myself. I took deep breaths. Everything would be fine.

You're playing a role. It's just a sex scene. Don't fail the audition, said fear.

"I can do this. It's a scene. Play the part and then leave. Have fun with it. You're both here for the same thing," I whispered. "Why am I whispering? C'mon Orville—this is what you want."

I didn't think of Hadley. I thought about how I would touch her, a woman I didn't know at all, how I would kiss her. What would I say to her? Maybe I won't have to say anything. It's just coffee. It might not even go that route; I hope it doesn't go that route. It would be so much easier if we just met for coffee and she said she couldn't go through with it.

You're a fucking coward. Do it, said fear.

Cherry Street Café – A typical café.

Cherry Street Café – I ordered a tall vanilla latte and sat at a table near a window. I glanced furtively at the three other people sitting at three other tables. There was a man with a laptop, a teenage girl on her cell phone, and a professionally dressed woman reading a magazine article. Could that be her? The picture of the woman had been from her neck down: she had been in a short, black skirt and buttoned up white shirt. I couldn't get her breasts out of my mind—that's what I was looking for, a woman with ample breasts. The woman reading the magazine didn't raise her head when a customer walked in—it was not her.

I sipped my coffee and my legs shook underneath the table. Those same damn butterflies I got playing baseball were swarming and fluttering within my stomach. My hands felt cold against my skin. Why was I so nervous? You have to be in control here. It would be just like it was with Hadley.

Goddamn it Orville—it's just sex, said fear.

The door opened and a chill swept through the shop. I looked up and saw a woman in a black dress. She looked vaguely familiar. "Oh shit," I muttered. It was Wanda. She looked around the shop and when we made eye contact, she looked surprised and then slightly annoyed.

"Hi Orville—wasn't expecting to see you here. Are you heading to work?"

"No, I'm meeting a friend of mine here, from university," I said. "What's up with you? Are you meeting Russ?"

"Oh no," she said, shaking her head quickly. "I'm meeting a new co-worker."

"Oh, does Hadley know him...her?"

"No, no, different department."

"Okay," I said.

"Yeah, well I'm going to order some coffee," she said.

"Well, have a good night."

"Yeah, you too."

I should just leave. If Wanda sees me with another woman, she will certainly tell Hadley. What would I say? I could say Jack's friend met up with us too. I could say lots of things. Wanda ordered coffee from the barista and sat down on the other side of the shop. We briefly made eye contact again and she smiled. What a gorgeous woman.

The time ticked by and my nerves slowly calmed themselves—Sammy wasn't going to show up. I would give her five more minutes. I looked at Wanda. She had finished her coffee and was getting up to leave. She separated the lid from the cup and placed them in their marked recycling bins.

"Your university friend hasn't shown up yet huh?"

"No, no co-worker either huh?"

"No...can I sit down?" she said.

"Yeah, sure," I said.

"Orville...you're not meeting a friend, are you? Orville, are you *baseball nut?*"

"You're *Sammy?*"

Wanda closed her eyes and leaned her head back against the wall. "I'm an idiot," she said. "What're you even doing here?"

"I don't know...why are you here?"

"Oh c'mon, you know Russ," she scoffed. "But what're you doing? Hadley's perfect. How could you do this to her?"

"What? Nothing's happened. We didn't do anything."

129

"How many times have you done this?" she asked accusingly.

"I've never done this before. Have you? Does Russ know about this?"

"No, he doesn't. And I want to keep it that way. God, I can't believe you're cheating on Hadley," she said.

"I'm not cheating on Hadley. I haven't cheated on Hadley. Anyway, you're doing the same thing," I said.

"That's the only reason I'm *not* going to tell Hadley," she said. "This is so embarrassing. We just leave and forget this happened."

Car – I drove home in silence. I couldn't get Wanda out of my head. I couldn't get that black dress out of my head. I wanted to run my hands over it, over her.

Why didn't you suggest going somewhere, said fear.

She would have gotten a drink with you. She needed a drink, said the great concubine.

I was caught up in my own confusion—why didn't I ask her? She was dressed up. She was there for a reason. She was obviously looking for something too. Why couldn't we have had our little rendezvous?

Bedroom – I undressed and lied down next to Hadley.

"You're back early," she said, snuggling into my body.

"Jack ended up having to work. I met him there and had a drink with him, then came home."

"Okay, good night husband."

"Goodnight."

Chapter 13

My eyes opened.

Bedroom – Drip, drip, drip the rain against the pane went. Drip, drip, drip the trickle of poison went—into my eyes, my ears, my mouth and nose, permeating through my skin, quelling sensations—what's left but a phantom you cannot see, cannot hear, taste, smell or touch. Love's assassin—lonely, dissenting thoughts. Alone in bed, Thanksgiving morning, the assassin dominated my mind.

I stared at the white ceiling, and in that stillness and quietude, dark thoughts floated freely and I snatched at them. What did it mean to be in love?—to love someone? What was sacrifice—to give your life to her, to devote your time to her, to continuously think about her and buy flowers unexpectedly, to sleep with her and whisper in her ear that she was the sexiest woman on earth, to give her children, to grow old with her? How was I expected to do these things? We only get one life. At the age of 24, I'm expected to give my entire life to one person? Impossible. But I chose this...did I choose this? How can I be so sure? It happened so quickly. Did I consciously know what I was doing? Do we ever know?

Wanda. Wanda in a black dress. I wanted Wanda. One glimpse of Wanda opened Pandora's little black box; but was there any *Hope* in there?

Men are animals, nothing more. We have dreams and purposes, which may separate us from some of the more brutish beasts, but when it comes down to it, we are animals. We have natural instincts. Meet woman, spread seed, move on. We are not meant to live in houses. Houses represent responsibility and permanence—slave dwellings to the rampaging beasts of sexuality within our beings. How could we give ourselves to the same woman day in and day out? It goes against everything our bodies tell us, our minds tell us. It's the sad truth. Our minds, my mind, wants her to be there for me when I come home after a raucous night of drinking, come home from work, be there for me when I want to sleep with her, when I want someone to talk to. But my body wants freedom, freedom to choose again and again and again. A relationship of convenience. Sex—every man wants the feel of a woman underneath him, on top of him, beside him, the feel of her shaking, sweaty body against his is something men crave at night after a few drinks. Nature. When seeing a woman from across the street, in the grocery store, in a pool hall, at the gym, everywhere there were sexual conquests that needed to be undertaken. Men want to conquer.

Conquer, the great concubine said.

I needed it. I needed that power of possession—victory over another in the most satisfying and revealing way. To take a woman from behind, against a wall, to meet a woman at a bar and take her home that very night and feel nothing but animalistic desire to fuck—that, was what I wanted.

But Hadley St. Claire, sweet Hadley St. Claire, was not to be conquered. She was one to be loved. I stared at a blank white ceiling, listening to the still house. I could not do the very thing I said I would do the rest of my life: to love her, to keep her, in sickness and in health, to sacrifice my life to her.

Bathroom – The warm water felt good against my skin as it trickled the gloom away. Stop brooding; no more thoughts. Tell yourself you love her in that special way. Feel the warm water wash away the poisonous thoughts of the night.

The bathroom door opened, and the steam was sucked away, and I felt cold.

"Honey," said a voice. Whose voice was that? "Honey," it said again. It sounded unnatural, something echoing from a great distance, from the past perhaps. But it was me who was far away.

"Yes?" Was that me? Did I just say that?

"When you get out of the shower, could you make the pumpkin pie?"

A pumpkin pie? Ah, yes...the duties of Domesticated Slug Man: the man brought out of the wild, thrown into a life of routine, and ultimately despairing at the trivialities of a life achieving nothing. A pumpkin pie.

"One pumpkin pie coming right up," I said.

"Thanks, you're the best," Hadley said.

"Yeah, I feel that way too."

"Are you okay?"

"Yeah, I just woke up on the wrong side of the bed."

"Well, snap out of it because today is Thanksgiving, and think of all the yummy food we'll be eating soon."

I had been making the Thanksgiving pumpkin pie since I was a little boy. Although all I really did was mix eggs, flour, sugar, cinnamon, a touch of salt, evaporated milk, ginger, butter, and pumpkin pie mix (from a can) in a bowl and pour the concoction into the pie pan. But at least I had finally learned how to make the crust myself.

Bellingham – The rain was swept away and gave way to the sun and an allure of warmth. Evergreens twinkled with the melting of the morning dew, and the snow-tipped Olympic Mountains glistened from across the Puget Sound. Hadley's father owned a bookstore, and her mom was a nurse at St. Joseph Hospital. Hadley's younger brother wasn't going to make it out this year as he was a senior at Emerson College in Boston and had decided to spend the holiday with friends in Maine.

We parked in front of her parent's vintage blue two-story house. The paint had been slightly chipping off for a few years, but I thought the house was beautiful. It was on a little hill surrounded by thick green trees overlooking Western Washington University. We walked up the stone steps quickly as a chilly wind came up upon our backs. Hadley had made a fruit salad with oranges, grapes, bananas, walnuts, and apples in a lake of whipping cream. I brought the pumpkin pie.

Foot of Stairs – We stepped inside through the front door and a delicious waft of turkey and stuffing rushed into our nostrils.

Dining Room – A large table with a smorgasbord of black olives, celery with peanut butter and cream cheese, cranberry sauce cut into thin slices, buttery rolls cut through the middle, mashed potatoes with thick, brown gravy in a side dish, an assortment of fruits and nuts, stuffing, and a great turkey right down the center. Heavy oak chairs were placed in front of expensive china.

"You're just in time," Sue yelled from the kitchen. "Mitchell has been foraging the table. I've had to keep adding things so it wasn't all gone." Hadley's mother wiped her hands off with a rag and came through the kitchen saloon doors to Hadley and gave her a hug. "Happy Thanksgiving. My God Hadley, have you lost weight again?" She turned to me with the face of a woman happy as if her own son had come home for the holidays from a far off place. "Happy Thanksgiving dear," she said, hugging me. "I love you both so much."

Kitchen – Square kitchen with dark cabinets and drawers, refrigerator, microwave, oven, pantry, a small table tucked away in a corner with papers and various things on it.

Kitchen – I put the pumpkin pie in the refrigerator (cold pumpkin pie was the best pumpkin pie).

Dining Room – Hadley's dad came into the dining room from the hallway. "Well, it's about time. Let's get this show on the road."

"Nice to see you too dad," Hadley said.

"Okay, okay," he said, hugging Hadley. "Let's eat."

I filled my plate with a healthy helping of turkey, mashed potatoes, a roll, and off to the side along by itself, cranberry sauce (it was okay for browns and whites to touch, but anything with color like cranberry sauce or green beans had to have their own space). I had the olives in a dish next to my plate for easy pickings and Hadley's fruit salad in a small bowl. I was set.

"So what news?" Mitchell asked, scooping up a large portion of mashed potatoes and plunking it down upon his plate.

"Well, Orville is going to get back into acting—did you know Wanda has a friend who runs a theatre? He's going to audition or at least try and work their production of *Tape*," Hadley said.

"Oh, that should be fun. What's it about?" Sue said.

"High school friends getting back together after 10 years or so. There's only three people in the entire play."

"Well, there's a production of *Hamlet* being done here in Bellingham. You should audition for that as well. You'd make a great Hamlet," Sue said.

"Oh, I doubt I'd ever be Hamlet," I said. "A lot of actors go for that role. Tough odds."

"Didn't you do *Hamlet* in college?" Mitchell said. "You were one of those two quacks—Fitzgerald and Guildstood, right?"

"Rosencrantz and Guildenstern you mean," I said.

"Yeah, those two chaps."

"Don't you own a bookstore?" I asked.

"Last time I checked."

"And you don't know who Rosencrantz and Guildenstern are?"

"Why? Are they dead?"

"Oh brother..." Hadley said.

"He's been saving these up all week," Sue said. "And I've had to listen to it."

"Honey, we're not modeling our marriage after my parent's," Hadley said, taking another roll from the bowl.

"Below the belt," Mitchell said.

"Just kidding—mom, these rolls are to die for."

"Well, I'm glad you like them."

"So, Jenny broke up with John again," Hadley said.

"Oh, what happened this time?" Sue said.

135

"John just doesn't get it. He cheated on her again. She found out because he didn't sign out of his email account, and she went to use the computer and saw an email from this other girl John has been seeing. I can't believe it."

"Oh no. Did she move out? What're they going to do with the place?" Sue said.

"Not sure. I don't know what's wrong with him though. He just can't seem to get anything together. He never finished his degree; he's constantly ruining his relationships," Hadley said.

"That's why you don't move in with each other so soon," Mitchell said.

"It's too bad too because Jenny was so good for him, a real nice girl," Sue said.

"And he leaves for Iraq in less than a month too. He's not going to do well over there without Jenny's support," Hadley said.

"He'll probably want your support," Mitchell said, eyeing Hadley.

"He has my support, but there's only so much I can do for him," Hadley said.

John Thatcher, Hadley's childhood friend and first boyfriend. Did he cheat on her too? What was it he had said to me?—it had been during our wedding reception.

St. Claire's Backyard – A red carpeted walkway over green grass from front yard through fence on side of house to backyard. Large pavilion tents setup with white tables and chairs underneath. Catered food in rows on patio behind house. A bar setup in corner of yard. Space for dancing in front of tents.

Red Carpet – Sarah Marshall strolled in wearing an elegant, pleaded, marine blue evening gown with one strap over her fair shoulders. She wore a single, yellow bangle on her right wrist—the same yellow bangle I had given her when we had been dating. I remembered when I had first met her. There had been a house party near the end of my freshman year at university. I was exhaustedly drunk and had stumbled into the restroom. Sarah was there, crying over something. She had worn a red bangle on her wrist then. "Your bangle matches the color of your eyes," I said. "You know it's called a bangle?" she sobbed. We had dated for four months before I let her slip away.

"Sarah," I smiled. "I'm so happy you could make it."

"Congratulations," she said. "To both of you—you look amazing together."

"Thank you very much," Hadley said. "Your dress is gorgeous."

You didn't even sleep with her, said the great concubine. And look now at that sleek backside as she walks away, those hips, those thighs.

What had gone wrong? It was her friends: I couldn't stand her friends. They were egoists. They thought they owned the world merely for being brought into it. They poisoned her mind against me. I spoke blue collared bullshit to their white collared wit. And she chose them over me. No—I pushed her away somehow. I pushed her away because I always felt inferior to her because of those friends. And now she's here in a sexy dress, single and waiting for her own Mr. Right. Perhaps he's here. Perhaps it was me at one time. Not anymore.

"Congratulations Mr. McFadden."

Hannah Crowley: sweet, beautiful, Hannah Crowley. She came like a Pegasus on a silver cloud, swiftly and silently in a gorgeous silver strapless dress. She was tall and slender with high cheek bones and a strong jaw and had the piercing eyes of a fortune teller.

"You're very lucky Mr. McFadden," Hannah said, turning to Hadley. "To have a gorgeous wife. Congratulations Hadley. You look radiant."

"I like your friends Orville," Hadley said. "Thank you very much."

"And you look stunning too Hannah," I said.

"What? In this old thing," she smiled.

You fucked up that night. All she wanted, all she needed was for you to take her clothes off and fuck her, said the great concubine.

She walked away from me into the throng of people standing at the bar. It had been after a friend's dinner party, sometime in my junior year. We had had a lot of wine and had suddenly begun wrestling on the living room floor. She knew I had been watching her every step that night, but I had been dating someone. So she flaunted her presence with a black skirt and low-cut shirt, with those piercing eyes that challenged my conviction.

We went back to my college house and slipped in unnoticed. We clambered up the stairs unbuttoning our clothes. We made it through the darkness and into my room. She fumbled with the zipper on my jeans as the moon's light penetrated into the room through the skylight above, and she stood in the moon's glow. We stood there in that pale silver light naked if but for a moment contemplating what it was we were doing.

I kissed her neck, and she leaned her head back and sighed. I kissed her warm body, her stomach, her thighs. She lay down on the bed. I stood and stared at that most beautiful sight, that which man wanted most, what I wanted most: a beautiful woman giving her most precious gift.

Spread those legs and conquer her with your thrusts, said the great concubine.

I came down to her, kissing her calves and thighs. I slid up next to her, kissing her lips, her neck.

"Is everything okay?" she asked.

"I don't get it; I don't understand...I think I drank too much wine," I said.

"Oh...if you're going to take a girl back to your place, you can't drink so much," she said.

What the fuck was wrong? How is it possible to desire somebody, to fulfill your conquistador goals and suddenly, as if struck by lightening, your machinery, your whole being shuts down?

One pitiful failure after another, never to opportune again, said fear.

Megan McDonald had come in quietly wearing red earrings that matched her lipstick and a black, sultry, nearly sheer dress. She had colored her hair black, and her skin was pale. She didn't look at me, but went first to Hadley and said her congratulations. She turned to me.

"You've finally found someone who'll put up with you," she said.

"I believe I have," I said.

"Well, congratulations."

"I like your hair black."

"You liked it any color," she said.

"M & M," I said.

"I don't believe you can call me that anymore."

"No, I suppose not."

She was the last girlfriend I had had just before Hadley, my senior year at university. We had dated four months, and I had been in love with her. I had wanted to marry her. But she hadn't been ready for marriage, and even worse, she refused still to have sex with me. I had wanted to sleep with her above anyone else. I had wanted her to give herself to me in love. She didn't.

But she was here now at my wedding. They all were. Somehow I had managed to keep them as friends, perhaps as a reminder of my past failures. But not anymore. Not with Hadley. She was the one—the one I truly loved and would be with the rest of my life.

You'll die with your regrets, said death.

"Oh my God," Hadley screamed and wrapped her arms around a cowboy, a tall man wearing jeans with a massive belt buckle and a tucked-in white shirt. "You weren't at the wedding so I didn't think you were going to make it."

"You know how I like to make an appearance," the man said, his voice low and strong. "I wouldn't miss this for the world."

I felt a sudden slight burning sensation in my arms and legs as Hadley's face lit up upon seeing this man. She forgot I was there as she and the man continued talking. Some other guests had begun lining up waiting to greet the newlyweds.

"Orville, this is my oldest friend, John," Hadley said. "We grew up together."

"Nice to meet you. Hadley has told me loads about you," I said.

"I hope not everything. I thought you'd be taller," John said. I shrugged, not knowing what to say to that. "Just playing bro. It's just Hadley never dated short guys."

"He's not short," Hadley said. "It's just you're so tall. You should meet some of Orville's friends—they're quite the lookers—and single too."

"Just my type," John said. "Of course, you're the most beautiful woman here."

"But not single," I said.

"You're the lucky one here," John said.

"Yeah, I know," I said.

Once all the guests had arrived and were happily seated and properly fed, Hadley became a skilled hostess—she flitted around the room from guest to guest asking them about their lives, skillfully turning the conversations to revolve around them rather than her. She knew as well as I did that people were genuinely happy when talking about themselves. Her humbleness amazed me. Her blonde curls hardly had time to settle before she was onto the next guest chatting away.

As per usual, the more alcohol consumed, the more people began letting themselves go on to the dance floor—from old men to young maidens, the floor was ripe with swinging bodies in tuxedos and dresses. I went over to get a drink from the bar.

"It's a nice wedding reception," John said.

"Yeah, it's turning out well," I said, sipping the gin and tonic.

"Look, I don't know you that well at all, but I know Hadley very well. She's my best friend, and I would do anything for her."

"Okay," I said. The stink of alcohol was thick.

"I've watched you all night and you've hardly even talked to Hadley. You've spent the entire night talking and dancing with those girls. I don't know if they are ex-girlfriends, best friends, or what, but I want you to know that Hadley's the one now. I hope to God you're up to the challenge."

"I haven't seen my friends for a long time," I said evenly.

"I hope that's the case. I never want to hear Hadley's hurt in any way...look, I don't want to start off on a bad foot, but Hadley's my best friend. I love her as a best friend. You know what I mean?"

"Let me buy your drink," I said.

"No, I can buy my own drinks. I hope you understand what I said."

"I'm going back to the party now."

You're going to die with regrets, said death.

All those wonderful women, all those chances, my regrets and failures—I'm going to die with those regrets.

Wanda...

Chapter 14

Northbend, WA - A mountain town about 30 miles east
of Seattle.

Thick snowflakes had begun to drift down again upon
our necks and my body shivered next to Wanda's as we
clandestinely crept toward the house that loomed like a
lighthouse amidst a white sea. We had parked a ways off
down the road for every bit of anonymity, but the streets
were conveniently quiet, the snowstorm providing ample
cover.

House - A short hallway to a dimly lit kitchen, cupboards
next to window on left hand side, a sink, a refrigerator
with pictures hung by magnets. Opening up into kitchen,
a pantry on right hand side, a small dining room table, a
tack board with notes and pictures and various things. A
chandelier hanging from ceiling.

Kitchen - I was struck by the similarity of this kitchen
to my grandmother's. I went up to the refrigerator. I
stood in front of it. I opened it.

"Hungry, now?" Wanda asked.

"No, sorry—I was reminded of something. It would be
strange if I found liver and bratwurst here."

"What're you talking about?"

"Nothing, sorry. Whose house is this?"

"A friend of mine. They're out of town this weekend."

There was a picture of three children huddled around
a nice looking blonde woman and her husband.

"Does she know you're here?"

"Yes. House sitting."

Wanda set a paper bag down upon the countertop.
She reached in and took out a bottle of red wine. She
uncorked the wine and took down two goblets from the
cupboard. She moved around just as easily as if this were
her own kitchen; she obviously had been here before. She

poured fully the wine into the goblets, a fraction below the brim—unconventional, but to the point. She turned around and steadily offered me a glass. I took it from her and brought it to my lips. We sipped slowly, our eyes locking from above the rim. She set the glass down and looked out the window at the snow falling and I looked again at the family picture on the refrigerator. I set the glass down upon the countertop, picked it up again just as quickly and drank more readily. The wine tasted sweet inside my mouth and its effects were instantaneous: I felt my body warming and had that initial bodily shake when consuming alcohol.

"It's cold in here," Wanda said. "Could you turn up the thermostat? It's along the wall there."

Living Room – Where the kitchen's linoleum ends, the living room begins. Black leather couches sat alongside the walls, a large table in front and an entertainment center alongside the same wall as the refrigerator. In a corner, a desk with a desktop computer. Pictures hung on the walls.

Living Room – I went down the hallway and found the thermostat, turned it up to 76 degrees. I looked at one of the family photographs. They were a smiling, happy family. There was one with the kids sitting on Santa's lap, a picture of the husband, wife, somewhere tropical—they were on a boat, the husband holding a four-foot long fish, the wife a martini.

Kitchen – Wanda was pouring another glass for herself. She wore a knee length black dress and black boots. She stared straight ahead outside the window. I watched her sip her wine without saying a word.

"It doesn't often snow here," she said. "It reminds me of home."

"Where's home?"

"Kansas—there it snows for days at a time—covers everything. It's beautiful."

"You're beautiful," I whispered.

She turned to look at me. "Russ never looks at me like that." She set her glass down on the countertop and came up to me brusquely, almost bumping into me. She touched my arm and looked into my eyes, and all my nervousness went away. My body felt warmed, the wine, the heat. "Are you sure we should do this?" she asked.

"Yes, I want to. Don't you?"

"I don't have as much to lose. Russ wouldn't even care. He probably does it all the time. But you...."

I wrapped my arms around her waist and I felt the smoothness of her dress. I rubbed her back as a lover would. I was warmed from the wine and everything felt fine. I looked into her blue eyes and felt something rise in my soul—feelings of infatuation? No, it was love—but how could that be? But my heart beat and my head spun and my hands trembled when holding her close. There was nothing I wanted more than her. I kissed her softly on the lips.

"Hmm," she breathed.

Living Room – She took my hand and led me down the hallway, passed the pictures, and into the bedroom. Bedroom – Adorned plants on a dresser, a bookshelf, table with lamp. Bed, centered, white bedding.

Bedroom – She closed the bedroom door despite the fact we were alone and flicked on the lamp. I went to her and kissed her lips, her neck. She lifted my sweater up and off me and ran her hands down my chest, my stomach. I unzipped her dress and let it fall to the floor. I lifted her onto the bed. She unbuckled my jeans, and I kicked at them, struggling to get them off my feet.

I began kissing her calves, moving my hands up and down her legs. I kissed her thighs, her inner thighs, oh what lovely thighs. I kissed her stomach, her breasts, her neck. I kissed her lips as her hands ran along my body. It was everything I had been imagining for months: the lights were dim, her body naked, the snow falling gently outside.

144

We lay in the bed next to each other, the bed covers wrapped around our bodies. I thought I should be smoking a cigarette at this point.

I thought about the pictures in the hallway. I felt them watching me through the door. I felt their stares. The kids on Santa's lap, the wife, the husband. We were in their bed, a bed they used to make love to each other—real love, married life love. And Hadley was at home dozing and reading on the couch.

Car - I drove home to soft snow coming down upon my windshield. The night, halcyon, serene, and I couldn't get Wanda's body out of my mind. There was a connection between us. I thought about looking into those beautiful blue eyes. Oh Hadley...what a fucking idiot I am. I wasn't ready.

Living Room - Hadley was asleep on the couch, her book open across her chest.

Bathroom - I brushed my teeth.

Living Room - I went up to Hadley and kissed her gently on the forehead.

"Hi sweetie," she yawned. "What time is it?"

"It's time for bed," I said.

Bedroom - I set her down on the bed.

"Will you take my clothes off?"

I undressed her and put my pajamas on. I was Domesticated Slug Man once again. I lay next to her as she wrapped herself against me. "I love you," I whispered. But she was already asleep.

Car - I found parking inside the QFC underground parking lot. The streets were wet and black umbrellas bobbled swiftly down them like the shadows of clouds along a river in the moonlight. Everything was black tonight. My thoughts were black; the night was black; a black cat desperately sought refuge under an awning.

I tried to think of the audition, but I thought of Hadley. Hadley at home, sipping white wine, listening to Nat King Cole next to the lit up fake Christmas tree.

Why was she so good? How could she have been deceived into marrying a monster?—for that was what I was—not a man, but a monster. A man doesn't seek the refuge of other women and then kiss his wife on the lips and whisper love in her ears as she drifts off to sleep. I was a coward and a cheat. But I knew I wasn't going to stop; I knew I needed it. Wanda.

Theatre – Previously the Uptown Theater in the Queen Anne neighborhood, now called Sole Gemello. A wide foyer, dark, lit by two lamps mounted against back wall next to a small bar. Two ticket booths, right hand side, two restrooms, left hand side. A small door led to an antechamber behind ticket booths. Two large wooden doorways on either side of bar led to audience chamber and stage.

Theatre – It was dark, but I heard muffled voices coming from the antechamber behind the ticketing booths. I followed the voices.

Antechamber – Unadorned room with wood walls, a small desk with various books and scripts and an old couch.

There were two young actors talking quietly and shaking their soaking umbrellas. One was short and rotund, slightly balding with a healthy red beard and mustache, but the other...the other was Adonis incarnate, a gift from the gods to the women of Seattle, the kind of man loathed by the insecure.

He was tall, broad shouldered, and he spoke quietly, smugly without moving his lips, which protruded out as if in deep thought and his eyes were glazed with constant indignation at the lesser mortals before him. His hair was godly blonde waving perfectly to those many women who would (or would want to) run their hands through it. He wore black slacks, but his sheer black shirt was tight and afforded a glimpse of his tight midsection. His skin was spotless, a blended golden peach. He was a magnificent sculpture.

His eyes slowly roved into mine. And for that one instant, there was a look of surprise or fear, skepticism perhaps of his assurance to walk off with either coveted role. But it was brief, and his eyes once again settled into aloofness. The rotund man turned to me and smiled, the smile of a man not gifted with appearance, but with humor. Here was a man who could comfort a room with a quick quip or smile.

"Ah, just got here too. They haven't opened the doors yet so I suppose we wait here. What's your name?"

"Orville," I said.

"I'm Phil," he said. He offered his hand to mine and I shook it, heartedly.

"Patrick," the other said. I shook Patrick's hand. It was slack, hardly perceivable as a shake. A shake of indifference.

"The role of Jon," Patrick said, turning once again to Phil and away from me, "takes the utmost physical and mental prowess. Most actors do not take heed to the psychological factors and cannot adequately portray Jon's transitions of sublimity, to the anxieties of fear, to the afflictions of his heart. Only a handful of well trained actors can muster up the energy to pull off even a sub par performance, especially night after night. What role are you auditioning for?" He looked at me.

Jesus, I hadn't even read the script.

"I guess any that they find me suited for," I said. My mouth felt dry, loath to speak, the words barely able to come forth. I felt small next to this man, small and insignificant. "Have you been in this play before?"

"Yes, while attending ASU. I've met Mr. Belber as well and have spoken exhaustingly with him about the role of Jon."

"Must have been a lot of competition at ASU," I said.

"It's not a role for just anybody."

Theatre - We went back into the foyer when the main doors opened, and a woman told us we could enter. It was dark, but the stage was lit by one burning lamp.

147

There was a desk next to the lamp with a seated man behind it. The woman who opened the door for us took her seat next to the man. We went in. Patrick walked straight up to the man and woman at the desk and began shaking their hands. By the looks on their faces, it was evident he knew them both.

Phil and I sat down in the first few rows of the audience seats and began whispering to each other about what to expect. A few more actors and actresses shuffled in, offering their apologies for being late, and sat down in the seats.

I heard the door creak open once again and looked around. In the darkness of the hallway, I made out a tall, lithe figure of a woman. She stumbled up the stairs in an obvious effort to quickly apologize for being late. They nodded, and she took a seat near Patrick who, to my chagrin didn't even look in her direction.

The man at the desk stood up and addressed us with a deep, thick German accent. "My name is Henry Guttenberg," he said. "I am the director. To my right is Sally Frankovic, our patron. We appreciate you auditioning for our rendition of *Tape*. Let us begin."

There was a general stir among the actors, murmuring, the shuffling of papers, all the usual. I sat still, waiting for my turn to read. I was ready. I tried to think back to all the drama classes, feeling the nervous energy and going with it, using it to fuel the performance. I rubbed my hands together, shook my body awake. I was cold, the theatre was cold, but I thought of the glory of a perfect performance. They would raise their hands in salute, cast Patrick out of their minds, and say 'yes, yes, Orville is the Jon we're looking for'. What a joke.

"Patrick Swanson, Jon please. Phil Nelson, Vince please. And...Natalie Dogan, Amy please." Henry summoned the trio of actors. Patrick smoothly stood up, shook himself, and walked toward the stage. Phil sat up from next to me and went onstage. Natalie looked around her, apparently to see if she needed anything, realizing she

148

didn't, got up and followed suit. She looked like a mess—a sexy, sexy mess in a slim black dress.

Patrick stood in the light, the center of the stage, his body erect, ready to pounce. His right leg was bent rather posed than natural looking. He was an actor. He had a presence that made all eyes focus on him. He had a look that could kill, a look that could produce sweet tears, a look that said 'look at me, look at me, never take your eyes off of me, it doesn't matter what's happening on stage, it's me that you want to see'.

Natalie clambered up the steps to the stage and presented herself to Henry and Sally, took her place on the stage away from the action. Phil greeted her, but Patrick said nothing. Natalie's eyes roved the audience, her fellow actors, her body bore the signs of nervousness: her shoulders hunched up slightly as she leaned over the script, her back bent so that her height couldn't be fully perceived. She squinted at the small text in the darkness. I felt nervous for her; I found myself rooting for her. I wanted this gorgeous woman whom I hadn't ever met to be Amy as I knew I wanted to play the part of Jon.

She is a worthy trophy, said the great concubine.

You will never have her, said fear.

What an idiot you are Orville. She is up there with Patrick Fucking Swanson and you think you have a chance with her. What an idiot you are. He is an Adonis while you could hardly be his servant. He would fuck her into the wee hours of the night while you would have trouble even getting it up in her presence. Focus on the fucking script you insignificant and petty little worm.

"Tell me something, have you ever done something that you regretted?" Patrick began. They maneuvered through their lines like a dance, as if they had performed the very scene before, to each other. Natalie stood off to the side until it was time for her to enter. I could hardly watch. I sat in my seat with my hands over my face, my fingers spread so I could see through them as if watching a horror movie. I leaned forward slightly with my elbows on my knees in a position of defeat, of hopes shattered.

"Vincent!" Patrick's voice rang throughout the theater, and I could feel the heat of the audience as they would feel his agitation, his unpredictability when Amy knocked at the door, see their eyes bulge with wonder as to what he'd do next.

Natalie or Amy (I couldn't tell which at this point), had entered the scene, standing near Vince (Phil) and away from Jon as one probably would upon seeing the man who had raped her 10 years ago. Her voice carried malice as much as wonder. "Probably for different reasons," Natalie said.

"Okay, okay—thank you," Henry said. "Natalie, could you please stay and perform the same? Phil as well. And...Orville McFadden, could you please perform the role of Jon?"

I stood up solemnly as one would giving an address at a funeral. I knew I had to play the role opposite of Patrick Swanson. If I came close to playing the same performance, he would easily win out. But his performance was excellent. What could I do? Jon had just met up with his friend after 10 years and now suddenly, the woman whom he raped in high school shows up at the door and his confession has been caught on tape. How could I perform the scene any different? A good actor could. I clambered up the stairs.

I took the script from Sally. "Thank you," I muttered. And I went to the center of the stage. Natalie was looking over her script so that she could deliver her lines with more realism as she now had an idea what to do. I stood across from her. She looked up at me and smiled a beautiful full smile. She no longer seemed nervous, her first reading done. She stood erect, her shoulders broad and magnificent as she stood off to the side waiting to knock again. She pushed her immaculate curls away from her eyes and took a deep breath. I tried to breathe too, but the air was thick with tension. So many of us were competing for the same roles.

"Hi," she said.

I was only able to muster a smile as the growing knot in my stomach squeezed my intestines. Uh...I needed to use the restroom.

"Please begin at 'Tell me something'," Henry said.

I began the scene sitting on the floor. "Tell me something," I whispered, shrinking back away from Vince.

Phil responded to me as he had with Patrick, as if on cocaine and slightly drunk.

We continued down this vein until Vince and I had our little scuffle over the tape and the knock at the door was heard. With the scene played out, we three sat back down.

After those first couple of scenes, some other men performed with some other women, nothing substantial came of it—and that was it. It seemed to go well. The competition was Patrick Swanson. His resume was immaculate and impressive. There was no real way I could possibly be Jon as my resume was nonexistent. I only had college credits to my name, no professional experience to herald at all. I would be lucky to get the role as an usher for the play.

I left immediately after the audition, not joining the banter of the actors. I didn't need to hear everyone's lists of accomplishments that were the usual fodder for conversation. The rain was unceasing as I walked hurriedly to my car.

Car – I turned on the ignition, the lights, and the heat. I saw a figure cross the street and get into a car across from mine. It was Natalie. She, too, must have left right away. I'll never see her again, I thought. How strange it is when people come into your life for only a moment and yet if they stayed there, they could be everything to you.

I put the car in drive and drove home, the road sparse and lonely—I only heard the drip, drip, drip of the rain and the splashing of the water as cars passed me. The great lights of Seattle crested over the hill, and I took the exit to 85th Street. I pulled into the driveway and parked the car. I turned off the lights and the engine and sat back into the seat. The rain came down upon the little car as my thoughts came down upon me.

Your attempts at life are feeble and you fail at everything, said fear.

What was I doing?—acting? I was mediocre at best, had no significant roles on my resume, and had not performed a single role since college, not even in community theatre. How could I make it in this environment?

You are scared. That is why you got married—so that you wouldn't have to make the hard decisions in your life. You settled, said fear.

Everything I have ever done has been a failure. My entire life has been a failure: a failed baseball career, failed relationships, failed university experience, failed acting career, and now, and now I am failing again. I am failing at marriage. How could I ever have thought I was ready for marriage? Is it not the greatest sacrifice in one's life?—or close to it? What do I know about sacrifice? I am supposed to give my entire life to this woman, to Hadley, and here I am chasing other women, chasing fantasies with women. Sex. I want sex, sex, sex. I want women in thongs and dresses to spread their legs so that I can have my way with them; and then afterwards, go home to my little wife to a nice dinner and perhaps a movie. I wanted to conquer—have my cake and eat it too.

Hadley looked out the window through the curtains. I waved to her and opened the door to the car. I ran to the front door.

Living Room – "Hi, are you okay?" Hadley asked.

"Yeah, well, yeah, I'm fine. It wasn't great, but that's okay. I tried right," I said, taking my soaking wet clothes off and throwing them into the laundry basket.

"I'm sorry it didn't go well. Do you want anything?"

"Sure, maybe a cup of tea," I said. "I'm going to take a shower."

"Okay, I'll make you one. I bet you did much better than you thought."

"Hopefully," I said.

Bathroom – I turned on the hot water and let it warm up. I looked at my naked body in the mirror. I had gained a little weight since being married. My midsection was no longer the washboard abs I once had as a youth playing baseball every day. I leaned over and watched as the fat curled up into a glob of fatty skin. Disgusting. I thought of Patrick Swanson in his sheer black shirt, his abs tight, his skin taut. Jon?—ha, what a pathetic attempt at a career. An ugly body, a diseased mind, and no talent—what a wretch.

I climbed into the shower and let the hot water cascade down my body. It felt good, and I tried to blank my thoughts. It was over. It was time to move on. Nothing was in my hands now; I wash my hands of it. Hadley opened the door to the steamy room. She moved the shower curtain to the side.

"Do you want any company?" She said. She wore a light blue bathrobe, opened at the front so that her nude body could be seen.

I looked at her body, a body I once craved, desired. But something had changed. It was just a body now, skin, breasts, a stomach, legs. There was nothing there worth fantasizing about at night. I didn't think of her while at work, while out and about. No—I thought of all those other women passing by, in thongs and skirts, breasts bouncing freely behind soft blouses. This was marriage.

"No, I'm going to get out in a bit. I just want to think some things over."

"Okay," she said, tying her bathrobe back up. "I'll start making the tea then." She left the bathroom, and I sat down in the tub—a mass of pink, fatty skin, hair, a glob of flesh. And what a mind to run it all, a diseased mind on a path to the inevitable destruction of itself. The ultimate failure.

Everyone dies. Your mother will die, Hadley will die, and you will die, said death.

Someday I will die, be no more than a memory for some time in the minds of the people who knew me, until they too died off. How many minds have been forgotten? Never to be recorded and never really to have existed except in some haven in some far off place, if it really even existed at all.

What thoughts one thinks in the shower. I wonder how many of the best ideas came from taking a shower late at night. If only there were computers that were waterproof. Because that perfect line someone composes in the shower never has the same feel outside of it. Something always changes.

I wonder what Natalie is doing right now. Perhaps she is having raucous sex in the shower with some stud from Australia. Why not? She certainly wasn't sitting in the shower thinking about what I was doing. I got up from the tub's floor and turned the water off. I dried off, put on the pajamas Hadley had set on the towel rack.

Living Room - Hadley was pouring the tea into little teacups we had received as a wedding gift. This entire apartment was furnished with little gifts from the wedding. It was exhausting to think about. She smiled and handed me the teacup.

"There, feel better now?" She asked.

"Yes, thank you," I said.

"So tell me about the audition," she said.

"Not much to tell," I said. "There was a guy there who'll make a perfect Jon. And there was a perfect Amy to match him. I don't have any experience so how could I really think I had a chance? I hope now just to make it into the workforce."

"I'm sure you will. And what's wrong with that? You have to start somewhere right?"

"Always looking on the bright side of things aren't you?"

"Of course, like now I have my husband home with me," she said.

"And why's that good?"

"Because our bed is cold, and I was hoping you would help me warm it up."

Chapter 15

Restaurant - A hole in the wall at the base of lower Queen Anne hill on Roy Street. Eight tables in front, kitchen off to left hand side, two tables in back down a short stairway. Tables covered in white table cloths, red napkins, appetizer plate, knife and spoon on right, salad fork and entrée fork on left, water glasses, center table, candle, salt and pepper shakers on side. Dim lighting, paintings and pictures of Firenze on walls. A large marquee with the words *Occhi Belli* painted on it and two large, beautiful eyes hung above the entrance to restaurant.

Occhi Belli - Jack was in the kitchen.

"Perfect timing my friend, "Jack said. "This parsley is begging for your knife wielding skills."

"I don't work in the kitchen anymore," I said.

"At a small restaurant, we all work in the kitchen. We all serve, bus, and do dishes. We are the restaurant my friend."

"Yes, yes, capitano."

I took down a white cooking coat from the pantry and took the knife from him. I chopped the sprigs of parsley into a fine mound of greenery like a New Zealand hill. Jack went to the dining room through the swinging kitchen doors. He was a big man with a thick, red Scottish beard. He was a man customers trusted. When he said the homemade gnocchi with gorgonzola sauce was to die for, they believed him. He looked like a man who would endeavor to find the perfect recipe through constant trial and error. And he had tasted the world's cuisine backpacking extensively throughout Asia, South America, the United States, Europe, and he had lived in Italy. And through the fire and flames of many grills, woks, and stoves he eventually created Occhi Belli, a fine dining Italian experience named after his once Italian love.

"Marley or Dylan?"

"Breaking Benjamin," I said.

"You need a shot of whisky?"

"How about some coke?"

"I stopped dealing long ago," Jack said seriously.

"I meant Coca Cola," I mumbled.

"Whoa, you're in a bad mood," Jack said. "What's up?"

"Didn't get the part," I said.

"Ah well, *Hamlet*'s lame anyway," Jack said.

"It was *Tape*, but I take that back anyway. I didn't get *a* role. I got a part though, but it's not in the show," I said. "I'm going to be an usher—you know, black pants, black shirt, maybe a little red bowtie."

"Hey man, that's your way in," Jack said. "What about the mystery girl? Did she get a part?"

"I'll find out I guess. I have to head down there tonight after work to get a briefing," I said.

"A briefing? What're you doing?—launching a *Hamlet* strike?"

"*Tape*, but yeah, I know. How hard could it be right?"

I took a container out of the refrigerator, filled it with canola oil, olive oil, chopped garlic, parsley, red pepper flakes, salt, pepper, and stirred it evenly. I set it up on a rack next to a small bottle of balsamic vinegar (the secret ingredient). I chopped up lettuce for the Caesar salads and whisked together the dressing. I swept the floor and re-set the tables from the lunch goers of that day. I filled the water containers, checked the wine stock, and then began on the dishes.

"Pour one for yourself," Jack said. "And one for me."

The restaurant was home. No matter what was happening in the outside world, the restaurant was a refuge for the weary. Like Vegas, what was said at the restaurant stayed at the restaurant—it was the code. The restaurant never allowed for idleness; there was always something to do, which proved perfect for a preoccupied mind. Girlfriends, acting, wives, work all washed away when preparing a roasted beet salad or opening a bottle of Chianti.

I loved the kitchen. I loved pots and pans, cabinets with spices, containers filled with foods, empty containers from use (a sign that food was consumed and enjoyed). Cooking was creation, and I loved amalgamating disparate things into an artistic concoction. The plate was my canvas. Half the battle truly was presentation. I surveyed the clean kitchen as "Buffalo Soldier" blared in the background.

But the money was in serving and I had switched over once our one other server at the restaurant opted out for a chance to travel to Asia to teach English.

So *Tape* was out. I really didn't have a chance anyway with zero acting credits. I suppose I was lucky they offered me a chance at ushering. I'm sure that means I will just have to look at Patrick Swanson's gloating face every night. What a drag. Patrick will probably end up dancing the dance with Natalie too. Life seems to work out for guys like that. Not guys like me.

What could a failure expect but failure? said fear.

Everything I attempt ends in failure. My legacy, a failed life.

The fog, a stagnant, opaque pond rising above the still land, a castle loomed ethereal in the distance. Two sentries smoked cigarettes, shivering in black cloaks, just outside the castle's gates. They spoke of the Danish state of affairs, their children fair and strong, and the boredom of living a life waiting for something to happen.

I had played Rosencrantz. During rehearsals, we'd take smoke breaks outside the box, a small room with black walls and no heating inside one of the university's cold, cement buildings. The fog, thick and glowing with the lamplights like will-o-the-wisps on those frigid February nights hung about. Then, we spoke of the Bush administration, of Al Gore's sincerity towards the environment, and girls. We always spoke of girls—nine signs she wants to be more than friends, how to go from first base to home, that sort of thing.

The fog stills the land, quiets the living. It binds us— but in beauty. It gives us something to gaze upon and wonder. It leads the mind to produce inclinations to the profound—or to necessary evils. The earth tries to remind us of the magical and the fantastical, to keep us remembering that something unseen but felt is always around us. But we get distracted. We become numb. I remembered the silver bell from *The Polar Express*. Eventually, without realizing, we no longer hear the bell.

A four-year stint crowded with failure—a few minor roles in some plays and a theatre degree with neither talent nor experience—a waste of money and a waste of time. I saw the smiling faces of the women I once loved and lost, the moments of fogginess that seemed so clear once they were past and gone. The Sarah Marshalls, the Hannahs and the Megans seemed so cloudy at the time, but now I knew what they were—they were simply the failure to act. They were an amalgamation of confusion— do this or do that, *be* this or *be* that.

Ultimately you must choose Orville. Are you going to find some way to love her or are you going to leave her so that she can find true love? That's what you would be doing, leaving her so that you don't destroy her life. It wouldn't be the end for her. It was simply a mistake. We had rushed into this thing, and we were wrong. No—I was wrong. What was I thinking back then? How could I have made this decision? It all had happened so quickly. Everything had been so foggy.

You're lying to yourself. You could have stopped it. You knew what you felt, said fear.

Deep down in our hearts, our guts, our minds, the truth lingers. And we know it is there, albeit hidden. I knew it then. I played it off as cold feet and refused to succumb to the whims of my mind's desire to give up. I

159

fought against my own mind's desire for truth. But what I failed at was not having the nerve to speak up about what I had truly felt—to prevent the inevitable downfall of a woman I loved, but was not sure I was in love with—the common cliché.

I got married as quickly as possible so that I could never second guess myself because I knew that marriage was unbreakable. If I pushed those feelings deep down, they would go away. But they went and resided with the truth. And *now*, I'm second guessing myself. Marriage is not unbreakable. The truth lingers.

The truth was that I was 24-years old and dead. Fucking dead. I only had to look forward to a life of lasagna at home cleaning dirty diapers and wiping runny noses, a life of ennui. I was Domesticated Slug Man. And yet isn't this what you wanted growing up? To be loved and to be loved by someone in return? Then what was missing? I didn't love her enough...I love her—God knows I love her, but not enough. Do you remember those vows Orville? Sickness and in health, death do us part—you said those as one says tall white chocolate mocha, no whip.

Theatre – I opened the front door and a woman was leaning against the ticket booth shuffling through resumes and two others were standing at the bar.

"Okay, you must be..." the woman said.

I introduced myself.

"Well, I'm Donna, the theatre manager. This is Scott and Mark. We're just waiting on one more person," she said. "Oh, this must be her. You must be Natalie."

She came in offering apologies. She wore simple black spandex leggings and a black skirt with a black, sheer shirt. She was a disorientated, eclectic mixture of possibility.

Donna began the tour.

Back at university, the theatre was inside a massive building dark and eerie like a haunted house. I went in the evenings when nobody was there. Only a lamp glowed on the stage. I would stand in the center and look out at

160

the empty seats, the balcony above. I imagined an audience and I was a great actor. I performed brilliantly to lauds and applause. Behind the backdrop was a dark mess of props and cords and structures, a maze in the darkness. I would sit there for a full hour in peace. I would read or study in that small pool of light and transform myself to different times.

We came into the audience chamber. I fell in beside Natalie.

"I can't believe you didn't get the Amy part—it was amazing, spot on really," I said.

"Hi, thanks, but have you seen the girl who got the part? She's perfect for it I think. I remember you though. Didn't we do a scene together?"

"Yeah," I said. "When Jon and Amy first reunite."

"Yeah, your performance was great too. I felt really into the scene," Natalie said.

"Thanks, but I don't really have any credits to my name. No experience at all really."

"Have you done much theatre?" she asked.

"I was a theatre major, but not much outside of university," I said.

"I've done some minor stuff," Natalie said. "But not much either."

"Do you live in Seattle?"

"Yup, in Capitol Hill. You?"

"Ballard," I said. "I'm meeting my friend for drinks tonight at the restaurant we work at. It's called Occhi Belli. It's in Queen Anne. Have you heard of it?"

"Oh I've been there once I think. I loved it. Are you a waiter there?" She asked.

"Server, busser, cook, jack-of-all-trades really. I've probably made you something before."

"Really? You probably did."

"Anyway, I'm meeting my friend there, the owner actually. You want to go? I mean, if you don't have any plans or anything."

"Well, it is a Wednesday night, and those are quite full usually. Lucky for you this one is free."

"Perfect," I said.

"So, there will be an usher positioned here and there," Donna said, pointing to positions throughout the chamber. Donna went over the duties and responsibilities of the ushers, when they should arrive, how they should dress, etc. She gave us some materials to go over and then we left.

Occhi Belli – Jack sipped his whiskey on the rocks. His raised eyebrows upon our grand entrance were quickly recovered. He stood up ceremoniously with his arms outstretched.

"Welcome to Occhi Belli," Jack said. "Home of the strange and beautiful."

"He's the real actor," I said.

"I've seen you. You've come here before haven't you?" Jack said.

"Yes, I love this place. I'm Natalie."

"I'm Jack. I own it. What're you drinking?"

"Jameson—neat," she said. "Please and thank you."

"Gin tonic," I said.

While Jack busied himself making the drinks, I took Natalie's hand and led her back into the kitchen.

"Let me show you where the magic happens," I said.

Kitchen – "So this is the great kitchen," Natalie said.

There were still pots and pans from that night in the washing racks, and the countertops had crumbs strewn about.

"See what happens when I don't finish up?" I said. "I like a clean kitchen."

"Is that even possible?"

"I am a Virgo," I said.

"You can come to my house and cook and clean for me anytime," she said.

"Well, I don't cook and clean for free," I said.

"I'm too poor to pay," Natalie said.

"Okay, okay, one free dinner for you. But afterwards, no-can-do. Deal?"

"Is that a date?"

"It's dinner and wine," I said.

"Sounds good. I'll buy the wine and whatever food we need," Natalie said. "You cook and clean."

"I can handle that."

Dining Room – Jack was sitting at one of the tables sipping his whiskey, smiling as if privy to a private joke. We sat down opposite him. Natalie sat so close I felt the black spandex leggings she wore against my leg and the prickle of her arm hair against mine. It felt good to be close to a woman again.

The touch of a woman is a wondrous thing. A woman could hold an object such as a rope at the same time as yourself and you wouldn't feel a connection. But, if a woman's clothed leg is nestled next to yours, you would feel the extension of her body through the inanimate material, and a connection is created. The mind must create these connections through the sensations—it's the perception that the inanimate material is the very flesh of the woman.

A woman's touch, although not physically changed, could change against oneself. Natalie felt good against my body. She was new, mysterious—her touch reverberating. It was like a strange disease attacking the immune system. At first the body doesn't know how to respond; everything the disease throws at it is mysterious and it scrambles up the body's systems. The body either welcomes the disease or rejects the disease and puts up whatever defenses it can. Unless the disease constantly changes the mind's perception of it, the body becomes immune. I was immune to Hadley's caresses; they didn't jolt my system like when I had first met her. Natalie was a new disease, and my body liked her touch, her feel.

"And how do you like our little restaurant?" Jack said to Natalie.

163

"Looks good. I'm not unfamiliar with restaurants and kitchens. I work at Wasabi Bistro actually."

"The actors' and actresses' lives can be found in the kitchens and bars of this world," Jack said.

"Touché," Natalie said.

"I'll drink to that," I said.

We drank gin and whisky before moving on to the plethora of red wine at the restaurant. Our mood was light and the laughter filled the small restaurant from Jack's stories of travel.

My cell phone rang. I looked at the number. It was Hadley. I stared at the phone, hesitating. I got up from the table and walked to the front of the restaurant. I answered the phone and told Hadley I was drinking with Jack and his friend. Suddenly, a white car zoomed away down the street. I had seen that car before, but I couldn't place it. I instantly shook it off and went back to the table.

"A girlfriend," Natalie said.

Jack snorted with laughter. "A girlfriend of sorts," Jack said.

"Fuck buddy. Is she calling for a late night booty call?" Natalie asked.

"Oh, she's probably calling for a booty call alright," Jack said. "She hasn't got any for quite some time."

"Jack, shut up," I said.

"Who is she?" Natalie asked.

"She's...well, how do I say...it sounds so bad when I say it. I didn't know what I was doing? I thought I knew what I wanted, but I didn't know anything," I said.

"Is she...your wife?" Natalie said.

"Bingo," Jack said.

"Wow," Natalie whispered. "Really?"

I nodded my head. "It's not what you think," I said.

"I don't know that I'm thinking anything," Natalie said. "What could I think? I just met you."

"I mean," I stammered. "It's not real. It's not real at all. It's an unhappy nightmare. I didn't know what I was doing. I was young and dumb."

"Well, you're still young," Natalie said.

"And dumb too," Jack said.

"That's probably true," I said.

"So what're you going to do?" Natalie asked.

"Probably the only thing I can do," I said.

"I'm glad I'm not in your shoes," Natalie said.

Jack locked up the restaurant. Natalie hugged Jack warmly, and I shook his hand. He said his goodnight and left us standing there outside under the marquee. The fog had lifted, but it was still cold.

"So, I meet you and you find out my secret the first night," I said.

"I don't think being married should be a secret," Natalie said.

"Yeah, but it's not one I want to readily tell attractive women who I feel connected to," I said.

"Well, let's not think about it," Natalie said.

She looked at me with green, luminous eyes, the way a woman can look at a man and he will give her his world. A look that suggested many things, revealed nothing, but was impossible to ignore. I looked at those sweet lips protruding out, quivering in the cold, and I wanted to take her face into my hands and bring her lips slowly into mine. I wanted to feel her cold nose against my skin, her arms around me, mine around hers, her curly hair against my face. I wanted to touch her, to feel her.

She wants to be fucked tonight Orville. If you don't fuck her, she's going to go home, call a fuck buddy and get ravaged all night, said the great concubine.

You can't fuck her. She would destroy you in the sack. Go home and masturbate your life away, said fear.

"Well...dinner and wine still?" I said.

"Yup, dinner and wine," she said.

I hugged her softly, my arms wrapped around her body, and I felt her breasts press against me. I wanted to

165

stay there all night, but I let go. She smiled at me and went to get her keys out of her coat pocket.

"Well, ciao," she said.

"Ciao, ci vediamo presto," I said.

She went to her car and got in. I stood in the moonlight alone. She probably shouldn't drive home I thought. It was cold, but I didn't want to go home. I wanted to go to Natalie's and finish what I started. I sighed a great sigh, and it seemed to fill the city.

Car – I drove to Ballard. I parked the car in the driveway. The lights were out as I knew Hadley was in bed. This was my life. Here. This house. But I felt removed from it, that it was just part of a dream and wasn't real. This wasn't my life. This was just an episode. My life would begin soon. I had things to do.

Chapter 16

The gray skies loomed portentously over the vast, wooded heart of Seattle. There, at the Woodland Park Zoo, (one of the last refuges of the wolf) was no fear of annihilation.

Woodland Park Zoo - I bought two tickets at the western gate. Hadley pranced around in the rain puddles like a child in light blue galoshes coated with baby kittens and puppies holding up umbrellas and a rain jacket with a hood that covered her head. She looked adorable. We walked past the food court.

"Lunch time?" I asked.

"We haven't even started yet lazy," Hadley said.

"Right, let's wait a bit."

I picked up a trail map and we headed toward the Australasia and Northern Trail exhibits. We saw the sun and sloth bears huddled in the backs of their exhibits before coming to the tigers. They were magnificent creatures. One lazily slept against a rock and the other patrolled the elongated habitat. I imagined stumbling across a tiger in the jungle—the stealth of the tiger was incomparable, but it was those luminescent eyes that captivated me. Those eyes, glowing through the jungle leaves, watching, waiting, until the perfect time to strike— they were unbelievable.

The next exhibit we came to was the snow leopard. It looked up at us with disinterest—we were just two more people gazing upon its beauty. It began to rain when we came to the Australasia exhibits and the kangaroos and wallabies were huddled in the far corner of the habitat so we couldn't get a good glimpse of them. The emus were doing the same; their feathers were tucked in and they stood motionless and miserable under a large tree.

"Why aren't the animals happy to see me?" Hadley whined.

"They're happy to see you; you're cute. It's probably me."

"You're probably right. I can't take you anywhere without cute animals running away." Hadley sighed.

"Well, maybe the bears will want to play. Let's go see them."

We passed by the wolves' territory. I remembered coming to this very spot with my parents when I was younger and seeing the gray wolves running across the open field. Now they were nowhere in sight. They were becoming extinct in the wild and the zoo. The arctic fox was the same.

"It's probably because of the cold," I said.

"But it's an arctic fox—they live in the cold," Hadley said. "It's probably you again."

The snowy owl was tucked away inside thick tree cover. When we came to the bears, a great brown bear was wading a few inches in the stream that ran through the habitat. The brown bear wagged its great shaggy head back and forth waiting for a fish to pass by.

"It's just like in the wild," I said.

Suddenly, the bear smashed its great paw into the stream, and through the massive wall of water I thought I saw a large salmon shimmering within it, but the bear came up empty handed. I suddenly felt sorry for these animals. Zoos were a good thing: they allowed children and adults to see the glory of animal species and to teach many things that hopefully stayed with the children as to why it is important to share our world with them. But I could see the animals' faces, and I felt their boredom and sadness inside their glorified cages. They wanted to run free and wild, not held back by bars, gazed upon by inquisitive bystanders.

Everyday they went through a routine. They woke up, ate the food put out for them, performed a jig and dance for onlookers, and went back to sleep at night. Some didn't even perform anymore; some hid away in their cages or stood motionless as if already dead. It was sad what captivity could do to such magnificent beasts. They weren't supposed to live like this. They were supposed to be free, wild and free, running through the forests and fields. They were meant only to hunt and mate and sleep and eat and be happy with being a bear, or a tiger, or a raccoon, or a fish, or a bird. But we forced their hand. This was the last refuge of the almighty.

We went through the exhibits one by one, the rain coming down in big, fat drops. It felt good to be out in the rain, in the open. It felt like we were in the wild with the animals. We saw the orangutan, the elephants, the tapir, the giraffes from a distance, and then we came to one of my favorite animals, the hippopotamus.

"I love these fat blobs of gooey awesomeness," I said.

"You would," Hadley said.

"Look at those things. Look at those tusks."

"They live in ponds of water mixed with their own feces."

"But they're so cute."

"Oh brother...."

We came to the lion, but we could only see a bit of its mane through the thicket of trees.

"So, you're going to leave me tonight and hang out with Jack who you see all the time?" Hadley said.

"I see him at work," I said. "We rarely hang out just the two of us."

"What're you going to do? Drink and get drunk?"

"There's a good chance. You know Jack," I said.

"Yes, that's the problem. Where're you going to go?"

"Not sure yet," I said.

"And you don't want me to come," Hadley said.

"Well, it's kind of guy's night out," I said. "You know?"

"Is everything okay?" Hadley asked. "You've seemed different lately...like distracted."

"Everything's fine," I said.

"Orville...do you still love me?"

"Hadley, of course I love you."

"Could you love me more then?"

"I don't think that's possible," I said.

169

Natalie's Apartment - Living room ornamented with a rich, mahogany table, sofa and love seat set against wall, auburn in color, right hand side, inn table with lamp in corner next to sofa and love seat. Two large paintings hanging opposite each other, one a Salvador Dali, studio piano, black, underneath painting, and the other a traveler strolling along a lonely road towards a farm house, above sofa. Kitchen, glowing brightly with the embers of a wonderfully stocked warm wood stove, back of apartment. Hallway to restroom, art room and bedroom on left hand side. The Black Keys' "Strange Desire" was heard, coming from the kitchen.

Living Room - "So what're you cooking?" She said as she opened the front door. She wore dark blue skinny jeans and a black sheer long-sleeved shirt. I could just make out olive skin beneath.

"A surprise," I said. "If you'll show me to the kitchen and uncork some wine, I'll get started."

"Don't you want to see the place first?"

"Of course—quite silly of me."

"Yes, quite," she said.

"Acting has been good for you," I said.

"My parents have a little furniture store. This was the stuff that didn't sell."

Down the hallway was a small, bare room with white walls. The room drew me inside it. In the center of the room was an easel atop a score of newspapers. On the easel was a painting of a great tree with small villages within its branches. The painting drew me up to it as if it were the room's eye and the room swirled around it, mesmerizing. I felt Natalie's presence. I imagined her watching inquiringly, her lips aroused into an amused smirk.

"It's amazing," I whispered.

"I actually have someone buying that one," Natalie said.

170

"You act, you paint, and you actually sell your paintings?"

"Not many, but some."

"And that one in the living room...did you paint that?"

"Oh Jesus, long time ago."

"How much is that one?"

"That one's actually not for sale. It ties the room together."

"Did you...?"

"I did."

"Wow, I may be in love."

"That was easy."

"It's my favorite movie," I said.

"It's up there," Natalie said. "Well, that's it. My bedroom's a mess so I won't show you that. Bathroom's at the end of the hall."

Kitchen – The aroma of garlic filled the small, cozy space. Natalie popped open a red. She poured two large, round goblets and handed one to me.

"Cheers," I said.

"To the theatre," Natalie said.

The wine had a rich, oaky taste. It soaked like blood into my lips. I set the goblet down and began setting up everything I needed to cook dinner. Natalie handed me a baking pan, which I covered with tin foil and cooking spray. Then I salted two salmon fillets, sprinkled with lemon juice and set them aside. I whisked together Dijon mustard and brown sugar into a soupy mixture. I spread the glaze on top of the salmon fillets. Then, I started boiling red potatoes on the stovetop. I took down two plates and set spinach leaves down upon them. I sipped my wine.

"Now we wait," I said.

"The salmon fillets look amazing."

"Just wait until you taste them," I said. "So, the show opens tomorrow. What do you think of the cast?"

171

"I've only been able to see a little of their rehearsals, but it's tough to say without everything in place. You know?"

"Yeah, I don't know how directors can see the play as a whole when there's no set, no costumes, a constant breaking of ebb and flow with the lines and all that."

"They must have good imaginations. Or, they know what they want going into the rehearsal."

The potatoes were boiling and the oven had warmed to broil. I placed the salmon fillets inside. Within minutes, the glaze wafted from the open oven and enveloped the kitchen.

"I'm swooning," she said.

"Just wait," I said. "The best is yet to come."

"Do you cook for all the girls you know?" Natalie asked.

"Just the special ones." That was cheesy.

Natalie poured another glass for each of us. "And why am I so special?"

"Are you serious? You're gorgeous and you're talented—acting, painting, drinking wine."

She laughed. "Drinking wine makes me special?"

"Not all girls know how to make it an art," I said.

"Oh, and how do I make it an art?"

"Must I tell you all your secrets," I said. "Fine. When you bring the glass up to your sultry lips..."

"Ha, sultry lips?"

"Yes, sultry lips. Do you want to hear this or not?"

"Sorry, yes. Pray, continue."

"Okay, as I was saying before I was rudely interrupted, when you bring the glass up to your sultry lips, your eyes flash a brilliant green as if you're casting a spell on the wine. For what one might ask? Perhaps to bring out the taste, perhaps to give it the power to mesmerize—I don't know, but something for sure. Then, just before you completely enjoy what you're about to drink, you move your glass slowly and softly like a pendulum, and the wine breaks from shore to shore. Then you sip it like a queen, and your eyes dazzle in pleasure as I'm sure all your senses do."

"Oh this is a good story. Is this mine? Pray, continue sir," Natalie said. "What happens next?"

The oven's buzzer sounded off. "Next? Tune in next week. Now we eat what I hope is the most amazing salmon dish you've ever had." I put on two oven mittens and took the salmon out. The salmon's glaze sizzled. It had changed into a deep golden color. I used a spatula to put the salmon fillets onto the greens, mashed the potatoes and put them on each plate, and then opened a can of mandarin oranges and filled another third.

"It's all about presentation," I said.

"It looks phenomenal. Shall we have white?"

"Most definitely," I said.

I watched as Natalie took the first bite, a mixture of salmon and greens, watched as she chewed slowly. She swallowed, closed her eyes, and came back to after a moment. Her look was stony, impenetrable. I raised my eyebrows in anticipation.

"I don't have anything witty to say, nothing clever," she said. "Simply: my mouth is quivering with delight. I don't want to drink the wine, eat the potatoes, or even have one orange slice because I'm afraid it may ruin for all time that first bite. Orville McFadden, that was simply amazing."

"So...you're saying you like it?" I asked.

"It's okay," she laughed.

"Punk, you're a punk," I said.

"You like it."

After we finished eating, I put the dishes in the sink.

"Not now," she said. "We must celebrate this great triumph with wine."

"And what're we celebrating?"

"That amazing dinner made by one Orville McFadden," Natalie said. "And to hopes of future theatrical entertainment courtesy of us."

"I'll drink to that," I said.

173

Natalie poured the wine.

Living room – Chopin played softly, and we sat down on the love seat. This was the moment I had been waiting for. Everything had gone perfectly thus far, and now it was simply finding the right moment to kiss her. We sat close and talked about things of no importance, the type of talk people have right before something momentous, about the weather, about some sports game, anything that leads to that inevitable climax. We talked about the perfect color match of the oranges with the salmon fillets, about the various kinds of woods in her living room, the colors of the paintings on her walls. Natalie put her goblet down on the mahogany table.

"So what're you going to do?" she asked.

"I think I'm going to kiss you," I said.

She laughed. "That's the wine talking," she said. "I meant about your life."

"I don't know—something I guess. I have to do something," I said. I looked around me, at the walls and the paintings, at the glow of the lamp, and back at Natalie. This was where I wanted to be. This was where I wanted to spend my time. This was the woman I wanted to spend my time with. She was beautiful and talented. She was ambitious and clever. She had a contagious laugh and a mesmerizing smile, a smile that drew me close and sucked my soul away. I wanted her. I felt an ache in my loins for her. I wanted everything about her to be mine. I wanted her body; I wanted her mind.

"You have some hard decisions to make," she said.

"Some are hard; some are clear," I said, moving closer. She didn't move away.

"Do you love her?"

I stopped. I looked down at the wine goblet still in my hand and set it upon the table. Yes, I loved Hadley. I loved how she looked when she slept, how she breathed softly into my ear. I loved running my hands over her back and listening to her sigh, a sigh that was meant for me to know she knew she was loved. I loved twirling her

174

blonde hair into my hands and kissing her cheeks when it was cold. I love hugging her tightly and lifting her up into my arms. I loved buying her dinner and jewelry and flowers when I remembered. I loved sitting next to her warm body in the theatre or at a movie. I loved listening to her talk about politics with her friends, how she rolled her eyes at the imbecilic Russisms. I loved how she opened presents on her birthday, how she shook the box and guessed at what it was, but she was always wrong. I loved how she lost all traces of the real world when she sat down and read a book. I loved how sometimes she would sit in the shower for hours and think philosophical thoughts and I would sit against the wall and discuss them with her.

I looked at Natalie looking at me. I imagined lifting up her shirt and feeling her lacy breasts in my hands. I imagined unclasping her bra and taking her breasts into my mouth, kissing them. I imagined slowly unbuttoning her jeans and sliding them down off her. I imagined kissing her calves to her legs to her thighs to her soft black underwear. I imagined slowly sliding them off and sliding into her.

That's what I didn't imagine with Hadley. Why? I don't know. What I knew at that moment was that I loved Hadley and I wanted to make love to Natalie and spend my time with Natalie at night and Hadley during the day. I wanted the impossible.

I leaned closer to Natalie who fixed a quizzical stare into me. I put my right hand around her neck and drew her lips into mine. Ah how soft they were, how good they felt. I kissed her lips and brought her body closer to mine. She pushed me slowly away.

"Orville, listen to me," she began. "I can't be the one who pushes you over the edge. I can't do this when you're with Hadley."

"And what if I wasn't with Hadley?" I asked.

"I don't know. We can't think about that right now," she said.

175

Car – I drove home with a gnawing, sickening feeling in my gut. It had to be tonight.

My cell phone rang. It was Wanda. I answered. Come over to your place tonight? Yes.

Wanda's Apartment – Standard apartment—sofa from Ikea, a white table, television, a Thomas Kincaid painting against the wall.

I was disappointed to find her in jeans and a plain white shirt. We didn't say much to each other. It was understood that what we were doing was wrong, but greater forces were acting upon us. We undressed methodically. We sat down next to each other on her Ikea sofa. Our hands all over each other, my thoughts distracted, I kept seeing images of Hadley in galoshes at the zoo, then of Natalie in her black sheer shirt. And I had drunk a lot of wine. Nothing was happening.

"What's wrong?" Wanda asked.

"Nothing...something's just not working," I said.

"Oh...that makes me feel great."

"No, I drank a lot of wine tonight. I just can't feel anything down there."

"Are you not feeling me anymore?"

"No, it has nothing to do with you. I really think it's all the wine."

But it wasn't the wine. I didn't want to be there. I always found myself in these situations. I wanted to be at home with Hadley...I wanted to be with Natalie. I didn't want Wanda—it was over.

"*Who* did you drink wine with?"

Fuck her brains out you fucking fuck, said the great concubine.

Fucking failure, said fear.

"I should go," I said.

"Russ is gone tomorrow night. Can you come over then?"

"I'll try," I said.

"Don't drink so much wine."

Chapter 17

In early January, the rains poured down like the tears along the sides of my face. There was a woman I loved, but wasn't in love with, a woman about to have her life shattered for there was no going back now. The time had come. It had to happen tonight.

Car – I drove to work feeling like the only person who ever had to end the dream of the one he loved to consequently begin his own life. And for what?–the *chance* to sleep with Natalie and begin a relationship with her? Was it even possible under these circumstances? What was it I didn't want, wasn't ready for, couldn't find in Hadley? I didn't know, but I knew I could not keep up the charade.

Occhi Belli – I chopped the parsley, stony. I chopped the lettuce, methodically. I baked the bread, loveless. I cleaned the kitchen spotless, robotic. My thoughts were muddled with the paradoxes of life: I loved Hadley, but I didn't love her enough, I wanted Hadley, but I wanted Natalie more so, I loved Hadley's family, Hadley was comfort, the world was chaotic, but Natalie was adventure and I wanted adventure, Natalie was sexy and I wanted sexy, Natalie could drink wine and paint, and I wanted art. My whole life had been one large bowl of confusion soup. For every step I took, enigmas emerged, multilayered paths to nowhere. No answers were given. My life, my fate, was failure.

Jack moved about the kitchen in feigned concentration. There was no usual morning banter. He was constantly in the way. I knew what he wanted, but I couldn't talk to him. I couldn't talk to him because I knew the tears would come, and I had work to do. My saving grace–if there was one thing I could do well–was pushing aside emotions and feelings to accomplish work.

So I worked with the conviction of a man doomed to the gallows. Just before committing suicide, a man might wash all the dishes, vacuum the room, and pay a bill online. Men fated for destruction clean up with zealous fervor. It's one last ray of hope in a hopeless life. If the world destroys a man who can clean his apartment, pay his bills, walk his dog, then the world destroyed the man. A man must show the world that the world is in error. There is good in all men, and nothing shows that like a final act. My final act that morning was serving the finest lunch I could—and the customers would leave satisfied and not in want. Isn't the sacrifice of one worth having a world peopled with happiness?

"Hey, I can't stand you moving around like this," Jack said. "Although I definitely appreciate how the kitchen looks. Let's talk."

I looked at Jack, envious of the fat, jolly man who was my friend. I didn't deserve such friends. I deserved to be cast out to the farthest realms of space, alone and miserable for what I was going to do. And here Jack was asking how I felt, if there was something wrong I wanted to talk about. Have I deceived everyone? I am not a good person. I am a liar and a cheat, a wretch of a man. I don't deserve the life that had been given me—or perhaps I do. Perhaps this is the ultimate joke at my expense: a man given the ability to *almost* make it. That's what I was, an almost man. It was the cruelest joke God or the gods or fate or nature or some supreme thought could play. It was a game—when would the inevitable strike? I would rather be nothing and know it than a man hopeful of being something but fated to fail. I had deceived everyone because I had deceived myself.

"I think my relationship is over," I said.

"Okay, and this is what you wanted right?"

"I don't know. Yes I guess. Some parts just don't feel right."

"Man, I've kept my mouth shut for a long time because it was none of my business, but man, you need to figure out what you want," Jack said.

"I know," I said. "I know...but I don't know how to go about doing that."

"Man, I don't know, but you need to find it."

House - Hadley was not home.

Living Room - I sat down on the love seat where I had sat many times before, but I looked around the room like a guest now. I looked at the art on the walls, the entertainment center, the lamps, the coffee table, the computer—I didn't want any of it anymore. It was the stuff of a life I didn't want. It was Domesticated Slug Man's stuff. Not mine—my life was out there somewhere, waiting for me. It was not here, and this stuff was part of a life that was holding me back from achieving my dreams. And what were my dreams? I didn't know, but they weren't this. It was all an ominous fog. I was blind. I was blind because I was living a lie. The life of a lie blinds the truth. How can a person know anything in this world if they are not on a path to enlightenment? That's what I wanted, enlightenment. Hadley was not enlightenment—she was the darkness holding me back. How dare she marry me? How did she not see I was not ready? There were signs everywhere. We barely had known each other. This is just as much her fault as mine, more so even because she cajoled me into thinking this was what I wanted.

No, that was stupid. She didn't cajole me. She had been in her own fantasy world. She was ignorant and blinded by my lies just as much as I was. But was I? Did I truly believe the lies I told her and myself? I didn't know. I didn't fucking know. I didn't know anything.

Bathroom - I took a shower.

Bedroom - I dressed for dinner. Hadley came home while I was dressing with a bag from Anthropologie.

"Hi," she said.

"Did you go shopping?"

"Yeah, I just picked up a couple things," Hadley said.

"You look really nice."

"Thanks."

"I'll get ready straight away," she said, smiling.

She took a quick shower and got dressed. She came out of the bedroom wearing a dark blue sweater dress. It was beautiful. She had curled her blonde hair, had applied makeup, and wore red lipstick. What a wretch I was.

Anthony's Restaurant – Overlooking the Puget Sound with a beautiful view of the Olympic Mountains.

Anthony's – We were sat at a table next to a window on the lower level, eye level with the dark sea. The sun was making its way down into the sound, and the sky was filled with pinks and oranges and yellows, but I couldn't enjoy it. I looked out and saw a tugboat going out from the harbor. How I longed to be on that boat, alone on the sea without worries or problems—man versus nature. I wanted to be free. It was what I wanted most in the world, the freedom of a bird.

A server came by and I ordered an appetizer and some white wine.

"Are you okay?" Hadley asked.

"Fine," I said noncommittally.

"Okay," she said. "So, how was your day?"

"Fine, boring, the same as it usually is," I said.

"Okay," she said. "So..."

I looked out again at the dying sun. It rapidly sunk into the earth. Soon, the darkness pervaded and the silver, shining moon crept up into the night sky. The appetizer came, the wine came, and I ate and drank without tasting while Hadley sat across from me, dressed up and pretty, eating small bites and looking up to see if I would break from melancholia, but there was no breaking away from what I was to do. Only when I was free could I be happy. All my energies and thoughts worked their way toward freedom.

"I bought this dress today," Hadley said into the silence. "I wanted to surprise you."

I looked at the dress and saw outer garments making one last attempt to hold me down. A pretty dress on a pretty woman. But I knew I was lodging everything about this night into my mind. Her dress, her beautiful face, her worried looks, her loving eyes even in the face of her destroyer. I watched as her lip quivered when she spoke of trivial things like they were the last words echoing into the vacuum of life expiring. I watched as her body trembled with each passing moment of silence. She must have known then that I was going to unleash my demons. She looked beautiful in her dress, her makeup, and with her hair curled. She spoke so sweetly about life, meaningless, disastrous life. I didn't deserve such a woman. And I was going to make sure I was to get what I deserved that night.

"My mom told me she heard from John's mom," Hadley began, forcing conversation. "I guess he's had a rough time in Iraq. He won't tell the deals, but I guess he got into some bad stuff."

"Like what?" I asked.

"Not sure, but it sounds like he might have to answer some very difficult questions. I guess his platoon has been raiding towns or something. Nobody knows much, but innocent Iraqis might have gotten killed."

"Hmm..."

"Yeah...," Hadley said. "Scary stuff."

We finished our meal, drank our wine, and then I paid the bill, and we left.

Car – We drove home in silence, and my heart started racing, slowly and methodically it beat faster and faster like the beat of the drum to a crescendo. I wasn't ready. I couldn't do it. Not tonight. But it had to be tonight. I had been rehearsing what I would say to her all week, but all of it left me now. I couldn't remember my lines.

I parked the car beside the house. Hadley got out and ran to the front door. It was a cold night, and a chilly wind from the west had sprung up. I opened the door for her, and she rushed in.

Living Room – I went in slowly after her and took off my coat. I hung it up on the coat rack by the door.

"I'm going to get ready for bed," Hadley said. "I'm tired."

"Okay," I said.

She got half way down the hall when she turned around. She looked at me with sad, knowing eyes.

"What is it?" she asked.

I stood staring at her in silence. My legs knocked together back and forth, and my heart beat, beat, beat, and my lips quivered. I took a deep breath. Another. And she stood there waiting. She walked slowly back into the living room and sat down on the love seat. I couldn't look at her. I stood away facing the hallway.

"Are you happy?" I asked her.

"I was; I am. But I know you're not," she said.

"No...I'm not happy," I said.

She sat there waiting, but I didn't know what to say next. Why didn't she say something? Why didn't she say what needed to be said so that I could say what needed to be said? Why did this have to be so hard? Why did I have to break her heart?—to break my heart? I stood. I sat down on the sofa opposite her. She sat with her legs close together, her body leaning forward like a child sits listening to a fairy tale. But this was no fairy tale I was going to tell her; the fairy tale was over.

"Why aren't you happy? What can I do?"

Don't say that. Don't make it harder than it has to be. Don't you know this is over? Can't you see I'm done here? Just say you understand and that you want to be friends, that you will always love me and won't ever forget me. I will say the same.

"I don't know. I don't know why I'm unhappy. This isn't the life I dreamed of growing up. I always wanted to do more with my life."

182

"Wow...thanks. I mean thanks. So I'm just a roadblock in your pursuit of happiness. I'm not enough in your life."

"I didn't mean that. My work, this life, is just not what I want. I wanted to be an actor, and now I'm not acting at all, doing anything at all. I work in a restaurant as a measly cook and server; work at a theatre, but not even as an actor, but some puppet. This is not the life I wanted."

"Then why don't you go after the life you want?" Hadley screamed.

"How? Tell me how. How can I? What am I supposed to do?"

"I don't know, but I know that sulking every day and saying woe is me every day isn't the way to do it," she said.

"What about you? Don't you want more than this?" I asked.

"I was perfectly happy. I love you, and I'm happy with what I'm doing. I don't need to be famous or anything like that. I was happy with the life I chose, the life *we* chose. Don't you remember? We chose this life."

"Yes, I remember. Don't think I don't remember. And I don't need to be famous. I don't want to be famous. I just want to know that every day I'm working towards achieving something, and right now, I'm achieving nothing. Every day seems to be a waste."

"God, you can be a bastard. Every day seems to be a waste? Wow, you really know how to make me feel like shit," Hadley said.

"That's not what I meant," I said.

"Then what did you mean? Say what you mean damn it."

"I don't know. Let's just go to bed," I said.

"No. You have something to say. Say it; say everything you need to say."

"I don't know what I want to say. I just know I'm not happy."

We didn't speak for a full two minutes and it felt like an eternity. I just stared at her unmoving face. She waited there, waited for the brunt of the conversation to hit. Do it. Do it damn it. Be a man for once in your life. End her pain. End your pain. Do it.

Do it, Failure McFadden, do it, said fear.

"Hadley, I..."

"What?"

"I...I don't know. Things just aren't going well," I said.

"They aren't going well because you're not putting any effort into it. I'm trying every day to make this work, but you don't even seem to care."

"I..."

"You're such a coward. What do you want?"

And I said the most hurtful words ever uttered from my mouth. I said the words that pierced her heart, the strike that sucked her life away, sucked away her dreams as a wife, her dreams as a mother, her dreams as a woman loved and happy, a strike that sliced away her naivety, her innocence, a strike that killed a part of her forever. I said the words that were at once malicious, hateful, spiteful—I was her champion turned destroyer. I was the poison that killed her, an unsuspecting, loving, woman who only wanted to love and be loved in return.

"I want a divorce."

She leaned back in the love seat, a blow to the heart.

"This isn't the life I want. I'm sorry, but I can't live a lie anymore. I can't lie to you like this and pretend I'm happy. It wouldn't be fair to you or to me."

"Okay...okay...yeah, okay," she said.

She got up from the love seat and went down the hallway. She turned around.

"I gave you everything. You're selfish, and you're a liar. I hope you never, ever do this to anyone ever again."

She went into the bedroom and came out a few moments later with a suitcase.

"Where're you going?" I asked.

"You no longer have the right to know where I go, what I do," she said. "But I'm going to my parent's house."

"To Bellingham? No..."

"Don't tell me what I can or cannot do. You have given that up," she said. And she took her keys and walked out the door.

I watched her drive away through the open doorway. I took a deep breath.

Kitchen – I poured myself a glass of wine. I sipped it slowly. I looked at my cell phone. I picked it up. I dialed a number.

"Hey, how are you? Just seeing what you're up to tonight...oh yeah, that's cool. How long will that take? Do you want to get a drink afterwards? Okay, perhaps another time then. Okay, sounds good. I'll see you at work then. Have a good night."

I hung up the phone and put it back on the countertop.

Living Room – I tried to watch television, but I couldn't focus. I sat.

Some day she'll die, and you won't be there. And you'll die alone, said death.

Chapter 18

Bedroom – It was some Saturday in March when I awoke from a terrible dream: I relived the conversation, continually said those terrible words. I got up.

Bathroom – I took a shower, the room steamy and hot, and I saw her sitting against the wall reading Hemingway, asking me whether I thought his short stories or his novels were better.

"Indubitably," I had said in a mock English aristocratic accent. "Hemingway's tough, terse prose is skillfully mastered in the author's short stories so much more so than his novels. An exception, my good woman, would be *Old Man and the Sea.*"

"You're a nerd," Hadley had said.

"Yes, quite so, quite so—now get in here my little pumpkin."

There was only an echo now of what once was.

Bedroom – I put on sweats and my university sweatshirt.

Living Room – I tried to read some book on the sofa. I read the sentences, but their meanings were incomprehensible. I set the book down on the coffee table and looked at the black, blank screen of the television. Her ghost was next to me smiling and watching *America's Next Top Model,* eating popcorn, licking her greasy fingers—"Hmm...yum, yum". I saw her in the kitchen, dressed in an apron I had given her with a fat, rosy chef on it. She read over a recipe with one eye half-cocked. Setting the book down, she said, "Cooking is not about precision anyway."

She was everywhere: in the supermarket sifting through the vegetables to find the imperfect ones because she knew they would be last picked and wasted by the store, in the coffee shops sipping on vanilla lattes and reading Steinbeck. "Don't you sometimes wish we were

186

poor and bought jugs of wine to share with our friends and read literature all day," she said. "We are poor, we read literature, and we buy jugs of wine, but we don't share any out of embarrassment," I said.

I saw her in the bedroom sleeping peacefully, the room messy with lingerie, shoes, dresses, and books. Her ghost followed me from room to room. I looked out the front window and saw her in the garden trimming the flowers while I mowed the lawn. She was dressed in faded, holey blue jeans and a white shirt. I saw her chatting with the neighbor, an elderly man who brought over fruit from time to time and was in love with Hadley because she reminded him of his own wife who had passed away many years ago.

I sat on the sofa, doing nothing save dreaming of what I had had, seeing her move from room to room as a ghost in my imagination. I sat with my hands clasped together in my lap, my eyes staring straight ahead into the white walls. Hadley had given me all the furniture, but she took all the art. She had taken everything that resembled beauty. I wanted her to have everything, anything because I didn't deserve it. It was the least I could give her.

The house was devoid of meaningful life—only the mold growing on the dishes in the sink was thriving. There were stacks of miscellaneous papers, mail, all over the kitchen and coffee table in the living room. I didn't cook anymore; I ate out and made Ramen.

This was not the life I imagined getting. This was the hell I imagined growing up as a child, a lonely existence in the void. This was purgatory. Was this necessary to purge myself of my past sins before I could move on, move on to the life I was meant to be living? I sat and stared, looking at the clock, tick-tock, tick-tock, again and again and again until...

Death is knocking for we all must die. Why wait and watch as all your loved ones pass before you when you could easily enter the void on your own terms, said death.

...the thought occurred that a bullet to the brain would be the perfect ending to a life not worth living, a life of failure. No books would be written about this life because no one knew about it; it was just another miserable existence in a world that rotated on an axis of impenetrable confusion. A bullet to the brain. A bullet to the brain. It sounded wonderful off the tongue, a beautiful English phrase. What was that line, that perfect line I had heard many years ago? Cellar door—the most perfect English combination of words someone had told me. But now—a bullet to the brain. I said it over and over sitting on the sofa watching the wall.

I would have to write a note for Hadley. She must never suspect that it was her who caused the inevitable suicide. Her pure and sweet mind would agonize over it. No—she must know it was never her that pushed me over the edge—it was life itself, a cruel existence because it was the life of a man who had the gifts but fate played its cruel tricks to bring that man down. A bullet to the brain—it sounded so perfect, but my vanity whittled its way into that brain of mine. A bullet to the brain would cause a mess, an ugly mess. The coffin?—a hideous, ugly mess of a head. That wouldn't do. I must preserve my dignity in death. A bullet to the heart like Sean Penn in *21 Grams*. It didn't sound as sweet off the tongue, but the effect would be monumental, even more significant. The heart, the heart wherein all my desires raged and confused my brain. The heart wherein I could love a woman and yet cast her out of my life to sleep with another for five minutes of pleasure. Ha! A bullet to the heart would be the perfect symbol of my failure in life. That must be so.

I heard a knock. I looked at the clock in the kitchen. It was 11:30 in the morning. I had forgotten; it must be Jack. We were having lunch. I got up off the sofa and opened the door.

"You look like hell," Jack said.

"I feel like hell," I said.

188

I let Jack in.

Bedroom – I changed into jeans and a t-shirt.

"Is this place sanitary?" Jack called from the living room.

"Shut it," I yelled back.

The Viking – A small diner along 24th Avenue. Outside was a red sign that read, 'Since 1959'. Bar on left hand side, barstools alongside it. Booths on right hand side. Restroom, kitchen, and an area for darts and ski ball in back.

The Viking – When we walked in, there were five or so middle-aged men sitting at the bar, the perennial customer base. The woman who ran the place was the kind of woman who made you feel comfortable, like she knew you or someone who looked like you so conversation was easy. She came over to our table once we sat down.

"Well, what'll it be today boys?"

"A pitcher of Mac and Jacks will do nicely," Jack said.

"Food?"

"Two turkey sandwiches."

She turned to me. "I've seen you in here before haven't I?"

"Yeah, I think so, a couple of times," I said.

"Yeah, I remember. You had a pretty little lady with you," she said.

"That I did. That I did."

"Okay, pitcher of Mac and Jacks and two turkey sandwiches. You got it."

When she walked away, I looked at Jack.

"I need to move," I said.

"Bullshit. It's only been two months dude. Things will get back to normal."

"Yeah, but what's normal? I've been married for a year now and been with Hadley for a year and a half. I don't really remember what it was like being single."

"It can be fun," Jack said, then added, "and lonely."

189

The pitcher came, and I poured us both a glass. We quaffed the first pint down quickly, and I poured another.

"To new beginnings," Jack said.

"Right," I said. "So what's up with you?"

"Not a whole lot."

"You seem out of sorts. What's up?"

"You really think sleeping with this Natalie chick is going to make everything okay? I just think you may have thrown away a good thing. You had a beautiful woman who loved you completely. A rare thing."

What I thought was good at one moment, I wanted to run away from the next. How could I be sure? What if fifteen years down the line I realized it wasn't what I wanted at all? What if fifteen years down the line, I realized it was exactly what I wanted all along? How could anyone be sure of anything?

"Anyway, what're you up to tonight?" Jack asked.

"It's the last *Tape* show, and afterwards, we're having the cast party, which the ushers go to also—probably to serve wine and cater to the cast," I said.

Tonight you will do what you meant to do all along—you will finally fuck Natalie's brains out, said the great concubine.

Tonight you will do what you do every time—you will fail at achieving happiness, said fear.

House, Bedroom – It was early afternoon when I got dressed for the last time in the usher uniform. The sun was still high in the sky as I left the house for the final performance.

Car – It was strange, my life the last few months seemed a forlorn dream—just another day in the life of Orville James McFadden. Cars honked, zoomed past for I drove slowly when deep in thought. The sky was blue, the pines green, and my own hands pink and alive. I wondered why I ever felt melancholy in the first place. What did I have to feel melancholy for?—I was alive, free from responsibility, a new life was beginning to shape. I knew what I would do. I would double my efforts, triple my efforts in study: plays, scripts, monologues, and I would go to graduate school. It would be the beginning block to a new life. I had eight months to prepare, plenty of time. I would make a name for myself, get the proper training I needed to become the greatest actor the stage had ever seen, move into movies, and finally, finally live the life I had always dreamed about.

Natalie would be the first reward for my newfound faith. No more failure; no more timidity. I was a new person. Change comes from the mind. What a wonderful thing a simple thought can do—change one's view of oneself. Tonight, tonight, tonight, I would be laboring in sex because of my own mind's ability to change itself.

The room would be small and cramped with books and paintings, warmed from our bodies, incense burning, and a candle giving off a dim light that lit the walls with our flickering carnal images, two people expressing themselves through sensuality. Tonight was a night of passion.

I stopped to get coffee before heading to the theatre for I was a bit punctual.

Some Starbucks - I ordered a mocha latte and sat down by a nearby window. I watched the people in the café. There was a couple reading together and a few others mingling with friends. Hadley and I used to frequent coffee shops all the time. I would read scripts and she would read literature. But those days were over. Now there was no one in her life to lie and cheat her, to break her heart. I, was free.

I was free to retreat into my fantasy world. Like Da Vinci, I was not meant to live in this time. A life of failure, my only companion was death. My entire life had been a road with detours of death and failure. Or was this simply my road? I never had a choice. My life was destined for death and failure because I was living in the wrong time. I was born too early or too late, I didn't know. What is the message here? My life is a sick, cruel joke.

I was born out of time. I didn't know for when I was meant, but it wasn't now. What have I learned along the way? I delve into the fantastic because it is the only place I feel at home, away from real people and places, away from responsibilities. My friends are ogres and trolls, witches and wizards; my homes are enchanted forests and castles, mountains and rivers. These places—coffee shops, highways, apartments, are not my home. The theatre takes me home, but I am thwarted from constant failure. Why?—because I was born out of place. It was a great cosmic joke—Ha!

Soon you shall die, said death.

Soon it will be over. My epitaph will read, "The Life of Failure McFadden: A man who lived to die an insignificant, failed human existence, a man out of joint with time and place—an Almost Man."

Theatre – Natalie was there. I said hello and went to prepare for the show. Show goers started trickling in two-by-two, dressed in dinner jackets and slacks, little-worn dresses. I showed each couple to their seats with a smile on my face, the best façade I could muster. I was an actor—Ha!

Hadley and I had gone to the theatre quite a few times. Never again. Never again will I see her in a little black dress and high heels, linked to my arm, our faces jubilant. The nights had been alive, the wine had tasted sweet on my lips, the food extraordinary. Hadley had been life; I gave up living.

No. How could I be feeling this way? Natalie was across from me on the other side of the theatre, dressed in black, her long legs slender and tight, her curly hair whisking from side to side with the turn of her head. She was beautiful, sexy, and I knew that I had given up my old life for a chance at that. A new life: she was potential. My life, my all. With every thrust of myself inside her, I would have complete bliss, a happiness never foreseen.

Her green eyes would flash brilliantly as we clung to each other's bodies under the art of her brush strokes. Tonight was the night. I would tell her of my misfortunes, my bravery at giving Hadley back her life, my bravery at taking a new step towards happiness, and finally, Natalie, for us, I did this. Let's drink to us!

The lights dimmed, and the curtain opened. It was not long before Patrick Fucking Swanson and little Fat Phil gave the audience a performance to remember. I had seen the show many times now and just wanted it to be over so the real party could start. At long last, the lights went up, and the audience spoke in rapid concessions about the performance. I showed them the way out as was my duty. And when the last audience member left, I smiled. Now, the night would begin.

The party was at Phil's house in West Seattle.

Car – I parked a ways down the street and walked along the sidewalk, my stiff shoes announcing my arrival with each step. The night air was brisk, and West Seattle was quiet.

Phil's House – Living room jammed with people, kitchen off to right hand side, dark hallway leading to a bedroom on left, a restroom next to it, another bedroom on right hand side, door to deck at end of hallway. Miscellaneous art was along hallway and walls of each room.

Living Room – I didn't belong there. I was merely an usher, a wannabe actor. I was the bottom of the barrel. Only the thought of seeing Natalie prevented me from turning right back around and going home. I thought of Hadley—it was in our most uncomfortable times we think about when we were happiest. What was Hadley doing right now? It had only been two months, but it already seemed like my life with Hadley was but a dream. Now I awoke to real life, a lonely, meaningless existence, finding myself once again in situations I had no business being in.

I thought of Natalie; I thought of kissing her and touching her. But how to go about that?—wine and beer loses fear. I was a fool going in there. It was going to be a bunch of talented, egotistical people with inside jokes and years of togetherness. Who was I but a lowly usher? There were a couple set crew members in the kitchen.

Kitchen – "Hey guys," I said. "Awesome job with the set."

"Thanks," said one of them. "Were you at the show then?"

"I worked as an usher," I said. "Not in the show."

"Hey, without you guys helping out, they wouldn't have a show," said the other one.

I looked out into the living room. I didn't recognize anyone. It seemed like a cast party for all the performances before my time at the theatre. There was a tub full of micro brews in the kitchen. I took one into my hand and found the bottle opener. I popped the cap and drank down half the bottle. The beer instantly raised my spirits and a smile came to my face.

"Slow down man," Phil said coming into the kitchen. "You have the whole night ahead."

We talked for a while, and it felt good to begin the night with conversation. He gave me a quick tour of the house, and then we went onto the deck in the back yard.

Deck – The deck overlooked a narrow street and across from his place were nice little townhouses. He had a gorgeous view of downtown Seattle; the lights of the city blinked and flashed, and the skyline was clear. It was a beautiful night. There was a small crowd gathering around the woman who played Amy on the deck drinking and talking. I finished my beer and put the bottle in one of the recycling containers that had been laid out.

Amy (as I only knew her) opened up two bottles of wine and started pouring glasses. I was near the circle so a glass was handed to me. I took it and we clinked glasses and drank. I stood there listening to them talk of the performance, how the costumes were suffocating, the

194

lights burning, and the audience's lack of enthusiasm that night. They prattled on about the shows' trivial annoyances.

They were lucky to be in the show. What I would have done to be in that show. I remembered what it felt like to be behind the set as a show went on. The comradeship of being with friends in something special and the high levels of energy of a show was an experience never to forget. Everyone joked and talked and smoked cigarettes outside when they weren't on for some time. Nobody cared if the costumes didn't fit that great or the lights burned. It was being on stage performing something beautiful in front of an audience that made it all worth it. The trivial things remained trivial because they would never enervate the energy.

But I drank their wine and listened to their banter as one interested because there was no one else to talk to. I was an outsider trying to be an insider. They didn't pay any attention to me, and at the slightest break in conversation, I absconded away. I finished the wine in my glass.

Kitchen – I poured another glass of wine with mock enthusiasm...dum-de-dum.

Living Room – The music was blasting from the speakers, and more and more people trickled in, each making a scene as if they were coming on stage for the first time. With each arrival, the audience would clap and laugh and joke. I was a ghost haunting a house, invisible to everyone, but seeing everything. And there was no sign of Natalie.

Kitchen – I found Natalie pouring wine into a glass.

"Hi," I said. "Did you just get here?"

She jumped and then turned around. "Hi," she said. "You scared me. Yeah, I just got here."

"It was sort of hard finding the place," I said.

"Yeah, it's a bit out of the way."

We stared at each other in awkward silence. I expected her to be a bit more talkative. We hadn't talked much

195

since that time we had dinner a few months ago, but I assumed it was mostly because I hadn't ended my relationship with Hadley.

"Well...it's over," I said. "I couldn't lie to her anymore."

"Wait, so you're getting a divorce?"

"Yeah, it will take a while for it to be finalized, but yeah, she's moved out."

"I'm so sorry Orville," she said.

"No, no—it's okay. It's time to move on with my life. You know? It's time to become the person I want to be."

"Yeah, good. Good for you," she said.

"So, what're you going to do now the show's over?"

"I don't know. Audition for the next one I guess."

"Yeah, me too probably. Hopefully, my ushering days are over. Although I did get to meet you doing it," I said.

"Yeah," she said.

"So, do you know anyone here?" I asked.

"Not really, a few I guess."

"So, I've been working on an entirely new recipe. I was hoping I could make it for you," I said.

"Um...yeah, probably. When? I've been really busy lately."

"Um...I don't know. Whenever you're free I guess. What about tomorrow night?"

"I can't tomorrow..."

And then a shape materialized suddenly in the kitchen—Patrick Fucking Swanson. He rushed up to Natalie and took her in his arms. He kissed her fully on the lips. The wine in her glass swished to the sides and a bit fell onto his shirt.

"Don't worry about the wine," he said to her between muffled kisses. When he finally let her go, he turned around again. "Oh, sorry. I didn't know we had a voyeur."

"Ah..." I said.

"A joke man," he said and extended his hand out to me. "I'm Patrick Swanson."

"Yeah, I think we had an audition together," I said.

"Oh, yeah," he said. "Did you get a chance to see the show?"

"Yeah, a few times," I said.

"Orville was an usher with me," Natalie said.

"Ah, good. Good—you were taking care of Natalie while I was performing every night. She needs someone to look after her," he said, putting one hand at the small of her back and bringing her close.

"I want you to meet the director Nat," Patrick said.

"Talk to you later Orville," she said.

I leaned against the kitchen countertop and sipped my wine. I opened another bottle and poured another glass. A few others came in, and I poured them glasses too. They thanked me and walked away. I was once again a servant to the gentry. I drained my glass of wine and took two beers out of the tub. I opened them at the same time and drank from both, one in each hand.

I heard laughter from the living room and the boisterous voices of the actors and actresses. Everyone was so happy. I drank. I began to see things moving quickly around me. My body felt good as the wine made its way into my veins. Everyone's laughter felt good. They were all happy people living happy lives.

And you are a failure, said fear.

And Patrick Swanson is going to fuck Natalie's brains out, said the great concubine.

And you're going to die alone, said death.

Everything felt so good. I was the ghost haunting the house, and nobody noticed, but it didn't matter because they all were having a great time. This was their life, a life with parties and orgies and wine and makeup and costumes and facades. Good for them. I finished off the two beers and took two more. I uncapped them.

Living Room - Natalie was there sitting next to Patrick Swanson on the couch, listening as he related some hilarious tale. Everyone was laughing and swooning. I caught Natalie's eyes just as I went through the front door. 'I'm sorry,' they said.

I went outside.

Front Yard – "Double fisting," a guy said.

"Double fisting," I said.

I walked along the sidewalk to the clip-clop of my shoes up to my car, but then I stopped. I didn't feel like driving. I wanted to walk.

Chapter 19

West Seattle – The streets were silent, houses silent, street lamps lit. I stumbled down the sidewalk. I wanted to walk until my legs could not walk anymore. Everything was a blur. My life was a blur. What had I accomplished? Nothing; I had accomplished nothing. For twenty-five years, I had lived a meaningless, pathetic existence. Do people deserve to live if they aren't achieving any good for the world? What was my purpose here? If a person is simply eating, sleeping, and defecating on this earth, do they deserve to live? That's all I was doing. No—I was doing worse. A life of eating, sleeping, and defecating hurts the planet's resources, lacks meaning—my life, my life was hurting others. I destroyed Hadley's life because I destroyed her innocence, her ideal, her naivety. I destroyed the good she thought people were; I showed her that people were manipulative, deceptive, liars. I am a liar. I am a liar and a thief. I stole her dream and squashed it under my foot. Does a person like me deserve to live? You make me sick Orville James McFadden.

Failure McFadden, said fear.

Failure McFadden.

I stumbled on, delving deeper into the quagmire of depression. I didn't know where I was going. I didn't care. I found my cell phone in my pocket. I scrolled down and stopped at Wanda. I would release all this inside Wanda. I hit the call button.

"Wanda? This Orville. How you are?"

"Orville, why are you calling me?"

"What're you up to tonight?"

"Orville, you shouldn't be calling me."

"I've thinking about you a lot."

"Orville, I'm sorry...I told Hadley everything. I couldn't keep it a secret anymore."

"What? What the fuck? Great—that's fucking great. Thanks. What the fuck Wanda?"

"What the fuck Wanda? What the fuck Orville. You're the one who did this to her. You're the one who wanted this. Remember? You wanted to fuck me and then never talk to me again so you could parade around with some other woman."

"What're you talking about?"

"I saw you with her, at your restaurant. I stopped by to see if you were working. And you were drinking it up with her—you basically were on top of each other."

"Oh bullshit. That's fucking bullshit."

"You're an asshole Orville. It's not my fault your marriage ended. Don't call me anymore." She hung up.

"Fuck you Wanda."

I walked on. I called Sarah Marshall. After five rings, she answered.

"Sarah, hey, what's up?" I burped into the phone.

"About to go to bed," Sarah said. "What're you doing?"

"Partying, out for a walk, thinking of you," I said.

"Really. Why's that?"

"I think about you a lot."

"Orville, I heard what happened with you and Hadley."

"Well, the gossip train has started, hasn't it?"

"Well, anyway, I'm sorry."

"How bout you come out for a drinks?"

"Not tonight Orville."

"Ah c'mon. One drink. I'll buy."

"Orville, you sound drunk already." Someone said something in the background.

"Is someone there?"

"Yes. My boyfriend."

"Oh, you've a boyfriend."

"Yes. I have a boyfriend."

"So when you say you're going to bed, what mean you, hiccup, is you're going to spread your legs wide open and get fucked."

"Okay, we're done here. Good bye." She hung up.

"Whatever bitch," I said.

I called Hannah, Megan, no answer.

I called Hadley.

"Hadley, I'm so sorry."

"Yeah, I bet you are."

"What can I do make this better?"

"Make this better? Wanda called me. Wanda—you know, my friend who you slept with behind my back and who had to tell me because she felt guilty whereas you're perfectly fine lying to the person you say you loved. Well, fuck you Orville. Make this better? You made it better when you told me you wanted a divorce. Because I don't want you. I don't want you in my life. I don't want to talk to you. I'm deleting you from my phone and from my life. Good bye. So long." She hung up.

I stumbled along. I called Hannah again. No answer. I called Megan again. No answer. "Fuck you too you fucking sluts. You're out fucking your brains out you fucking sluts. Everyone wants to fuck someone else. What a bunch of fucking bitches. Stupid, fucking bitches."

You're a loser, said fear.

Fuck you Orville James McFadden you fucking loser. What a fucking loser. Why would they would want to fuck you? You're a fucking loser. You're a fucking disaster. Why would they want to fuck *you* when they could fuck superstars? What a dumb, mother fucking, moron, idiot you are Orville.

"Fuck you Orville," I shouted. "And fuck you too God, you fucking cruel son of a bitch. Jesus fucking Christ love, love, love—my fucking ass. What a dumb, fucking, idea. There's no love here. There's nothing here. You hear me god damn it?"

"Hey, shut up. We're trying to sleep," someone shouted from a window in some house.

201

"Hey fuck you too prick," I shouted back.

Ballard Bridge - Metal bridge across Salmon Bay connecting 15th Avenue to Ballard.

Ballard Bridge - I started across. Cars zoomed passed me with bright lights like bullets. I hated the constant cacophony. What would a world without cars sound like?—could we listen and feel close to nature once again? There is no spirituality within the city, only religion. Religion is the noise of the world, and spirituality is the quiet solitude. How I longed to be in a quiet safe haven. Magic: The Gathering—there was a card called Safe Haven where if a creature was killed, you could send it directly into the safe haven to be released later. I wanted to go to this safe haven to be released into another time, another world, one wherein I knew who I was.

I heard the metallic click of the metal draw bridge beneath my feet, and I looked down to the see the inky black water below. It seemed so far away. I wanted to sink my body beneath those black waves and drown out the sounds of this world, the cruising cars, the music, the cursing, the chattering, the people and their insignificant conversations. Why was it no matter where I went, I had to listen to the music of everyone else?—I cursed the invention of the iPod.

I came to the middle of the bridge and stopped. I looked into the night sky. Somewhere out there, there was a god—not in a physical place like sitting on Saturn in a hut, but out there out there, existing in some reality. This god, this one true god, maker of heaven and earth, of all that is seen and unseen, was out there, and this god had created me, a peon, a person so insignificant in the scope of the world to be, to exist, to do what? To do what? To destroy the life of another? To destroy innocence— because that is what she was, innocent. She was innocent of the horrible things man can do. Nobody compared to the horrible person I was to her. I lied to her. I cheated on her. I deceived her on the most important day of her life, my life, our life together. I destroyed all that she ever believed in, in what marriage was. And now there was no going back. What a worthless human being I have become...how did I become this way? Where did it all go wrong? I was destined to do great things. And all I did was deceive myself and the person I was supposed to love the rest of my life. I stood in front of her family, in front of my family, in front of her, and in front of God the Almighty and I said I would love her for my entire life, and protect her, and keep her in sickness and in health. I stood there, knowing I was a fraud, knowing I was sick in the head and a liar. And she loved me...and she loved me.

I don't deserve life. I abused God's most precious creature. And she loved every fiber of my being. What kind of person does that make me? I am worse than the worst criminal. I am the lowest being on this earth. And my punishment should be death. I only hope that she heals from this and learns to trust again, to love again. She deserves to be loved.

I wanted to curl up in a ball and let the world devour me. I peered down into the water where I wanted to go and end it all. For once in my life, I was going to make a choice. I chose to be a coward such as was my nature: cowardly, dishonest, vain, egotistical, self-loathing, self-righteous, ugly, ugly, ugly nature. I climbed up on the metal railing and wobbled. I had to say something to the God that created me. I had to explain to God why I was choosing to continue my cowardly ways and bequeath myself to the great unknown, to the safe haven.

"My God, my God, why hast thou forsaken me? All my life I loved you, and yet all my life I was scorned. You gave me so much only so that I could squander it. They say it is better to love and lose than not to love at all. I don't know. I didn't love and lose—I loved and lied and destroyed my life and her life. I didn't just lose Lord—I destroyed an innocent human being who loved me. She really loved me Lord. She had so much love to give, and I destroyed it. I took it and crushed it under my foot and said I wanted a divorce. I want a divorce. I don't love you!

I want a divorce. Those words, those ugly, hideous words I uttered to the most beautiful, loving human being ever created. I did that to your creature of love. I want a divorce. I don't love you. You see these tears Lord, you hear my sobs? I am a wretch. I am a filthy, ugly wretch. You made me. You fucking made me." The tears poured down, down, down into the water below, salt to salt, water to water. I only hoped they would find me quickly so that my family wouldn't have to identify a black, bloated ugly body. I wouldn't be found humiliated like the man who dies in bed, urine staining the sheets, his bowels still working long after his heart and mind have stopped. "I pray Lord that you take some pity on this wretched human being. You know who I am, more so than myself. You must know why I have to do this. How can I live knowing I destroyed another human being's vision of love and life forever? This is it Lord. Soon, so soon all this will be gone. To think, what will it be like to not exist in this world, not to be this person, not to feel all this pain and suffering? It's hard to imagine that Lord. Okay, okay..."

I looked down into the black bosom of the Puget Sound. Down there, waiting for me was death. What an ugly word, but what a grand adventure. Just a quick plunge down, it would be over quickly. I heard the cars scream by, but I was shielded by the bridge. To think that each one of them was driving by with no idea a man, a wretched man was about to jump from this bridge. They were going home, living happy lives, not plagued by self-loathing and hatred of one's own being. I hoped they were happy.

"To be or not to be, that is the question...what a fucking joke."

But my knees wouldn't do it—they stood erect and would not buckle. The will to live was strong. One had to choose—there was choice after all in this world. The tiny glimpse of hope that was always at the far reaches of my mind was pounding inside my head now. Be. Be. Be. Be.

Do. Do. Do. Do. Be what? Do what? I have tried and failed at everything. The last thing I was going to fail at was my own fucking death. It's my choice. If there was going to be one thing I was going to do right, it was my own death on my own terms.

Come to me, said death.

Your failure is complete, said fear.

Nobody loves you, said the great concubine.

I'm the victim now...I jumped straight up into the air and when I came down, my knees hit the metal railing's edge and I fell.

I fell down, down, down towards the water, so fast. The wind whooshed against my face and I screamed something unintelligible. I felt momentary goose bumps, and the water was coming at me quickly. It was not supposed to be like this. The alcohol was supposed to make this a euphoric plunge into the unknown. I wanted to close my eyes, but I couldn't. I became a thin stick figure and my feet hit the water below, and I felt stabbing pains strike up and down my legs, my stomach, my arms as I submerged deep into the black depths.

Chapter 20

I was strapped into some kind of wheel chair, my wrists cuffed to the sides. I saw bright light. One white coated being wheeled me through a narrow tunnel and I heard what sounded like automobile traffic above. And then the tunnel passed, the sounds diminished, and I found myself in an elevator. I was wheeled across a lobby with perhaps marble flooring and then into another elevator. The button for the ninth floor was pressed by what could have been a hand. I went up.

I emerged into a room with an office with fiber glass windows. Two long hallways were astride the office and they contained many different rooms. There were two women and one man inside the office and the woman wheeling me brought me up to the window. I was registered in; what possessions I had were taken from me, maybe a wallet, my keys inside my pocket, I didn't know. I was issued a blue nightgown and instructions were given to me, but I couldn't remember what was said. I just saw a mouth opening and closing, a language of sorts. I was shown to a room and was told to change into the nightgown and get some sleep—I had had a rough night.

I dressed sluggishly, lied down, and promptly fell asleep.

**

The night felt warm and the sky cloudless. I went to the graveyard. I parked and crept clandestinely through the tall juniper trees that surrounded the cemetery. The night watchman's light was on in the little house, and I felt exposed under the pale moonlight. I scampered across the lawn, ducking down behind gravestones to avoid being seen. I found his grave and sat against it in the shadow.

206

"Maybe you know, maybe you don't. I don't know how you could. It's ridiculous to think you are looking down from somewhere."

To think of my father, my once alive father who I could touch, who could talk and think and love, as now being no more than a skeleton being eaten by worms and whose entire being was nonexistent for eternity was sickening. But worse, to think he existed in a raging inferno for eternity, suffering endlessly for simply being human, angered me.

"Where are you?" I cried. Then more muffled for fear of getting discovered, "Where are you?" I couldn't tell if I was asking about my father or about God. "You took everything from me. You took my sister, my grandmother; you took my best friend, and finally you took my father. Who's next? You created me weak, afraid. You have shown nothing to me but hate. Failure McFadden. Every decision I had made had ended in failure. How could I have done that to Sage? How could I have done that to Hadley? And for what?—five minutes of superficial love? I must be a big disappointment to you...you who were so great and me, a wretch of a son. A baseball prodigy turned failure, a liar, a cheat—everything I ever wanted to be, you, I am not...but, I feel, somehow, I will become something. I have hopes dad. I will become something. That I promise you. For reasons unexplainable, I have hope."

***

"That was three weeks ago Orville," Dr. Fields said. "How're you feeling now?"

The walls seemed to move, inch closer every day and the claustrophobia was increasing. The hospital had been the haven from the dangers of the outside world, but now it was slowly transforming into a prison. Things had to be done. For three weeks, I had not left the ward, had not gone outside, had not seen my friends, and had only seen my mother once when she came in to see that I was alright.

"I can't come here again," she had said. "I can't watch as you destroy your life bit by bit. You have to find yourself, in here or out there, but I can't come here again. I just can't do it."

I didn't blame her. I didn't want her to come; I didn't want anyone to come and see me at my weakest, in my blue hospital gown and slippers, finding me in one of the classes with all the others on Suicide Avenue. The few friends I had, the very few, had emailed already and I explained to them the situation...the few friends I had. That was the sad truth of it all. I only had Jack. I had systematically destroyed all my relationships through lies and subterfuge. Cut them off before they cut me off was the name of my game.

And now only Jack remained—an older, wiser man than me whom I never feared—that is why our relationship survived. Brett, Clint—I cut them off years ago. They went down different paths, Brett into baseball, Clint into drinking and women. I don't know what happened to either of them. But Jack, good man Jack—I must keep him. What happened to my university friends? What does it matter? They were all liars and cheats just like me—a true theatre department. For twenty-five years, I hadn't made any real friends (save for Chris who was taken away from me) because I was, I am a liar and a cheat and a coward. Why? It was time to find out.

"Orville, some of this may be painful to hear, but if you're to recover, you must hear it and understand it," Dr. Fields said. "The greatest power one can attain on earth is to know oneself. You feel powerless because you don't know yourself."

"What do you mean? I know myself. I'm Failure McFadden."

"You're Orville James McFadden," Dr. Fields said. "And you know your history. But you don't seem to know what any of it means. I have been listening to you tell me your past for three weeks, and you haven't even seemed to recognize the patterns that you have fallen into. It's impossible to sum up a life in one session, but simply put, you from a very young age learned to fear the world and through that fear, you failed at all your undertakings, which have been many."

"I don't feel afraid. But maybe that isn't the truth. No, I've always been afraid. That's how I was made. I was born with a fear of the world. I was born with a fear of failure. I can't think of a time when I wasn't afraid. No, my entire life has been one large melting pot of fearful experiences."

"Why do you think so?"

"It's my lot in life," I said.

"Let's start there," Dr. Fields said. "For the past three weeks, you have been telling me about an Orville who had things happen to him rather than an Orville who chose those things."

"I didn't choose to have my best friend die or my father, or my sister and grandmother," I said.

"No, you didn't. But you chose how to interpret their deaths. You chose to believe that everything you have and will ever love will be taken from you. And that belief has forever affected your relationships—with lovers, with friends, family, and ultimately, with yourself."

"So, you're saying nothing should influence us, that we can simply ignore what has happened, choose to believe that everything is okay," I said.

"No, not choosing to ignore your feelings—never pretend everything is okay. And of course things influence us, but if you let those influences dominate your life, it's going to seem as if things happen to you rather than you having control of your life. I truly feel sorry that your life started under the circumstances that it did, but Orville, you are only 25 years old and still have your entire life ahead of you. If you can begin to understand yourself, I think you can begin to find happiness within yourself."

"Okay, so where should I begin?"

"When you were five years old, at your grandmother's house. This was a magical place for you. It was a sanctuary, a haven, and a place to explore your mind as a young boy. And then, without warning, suddenly and cruelly, this safe haven, this wonderful place to dream and imagine was torn away from you. Your sanctuary had become a place of fear and death. Everything you had believed to be safe and secure turned into a place of fear— a complete reversal. You were five years old. It's highly doubtful you saw it this way—if you had, you would have had the means to combat that fear, but instead, that fear influenced your life. The world was no longer a safe place. If even your safe haven could be turned against you, what would be stopping the rest of the world? That's not all you must have learned. It wasn't simply a place that became fearful; it was also that the things you loved could be snatched from you in horrifying and terrible ways. The ramifications of that loss must have been extremely heavy if you couldn't understand what they were at the time. I imagine your entire world changed—afraid of the dark, strangers..."

"Deathly afraid," I said.

"Yes, and horrible dreams. And those were just the external ramifications. Those were the things that would pass in time, but it's the internal ramifications that stay with us if we never confront them. The problem is that we aren't always aware of what they are. In your case, your entire world had become a world of fear so naturally it affected everything you did. And yet you were a gifted talent in sports, especially baseball. Even in this world of fear you lived in, your natural talents allowed you to succeed in baseball, especially when you were younger when your mind was less aware. And you loved playing back when it was simple. And despite your terrible loss at the hands of a madman, you and your family were able to move on enough to adjust to your new way of life—you met Chris and began lowering your walls once again. Baseball was fun and you were among the elite—you made all-star teams. When the big change in field size, pitching mounds, and whatnot happened, you adjusted and continued to thrive, to be an all-star. Your natural talent took over to propel you to the next level. Then what happened? In the midst of an all-star summer, suddenly fear struck again. The stakes were getting higher and higher—baseball was becoming more and more competitive. You had already established yourself as a great player, so you had expectations put on yourself by yourself, and inevitably, you assumed others put those expectations on you too. You developed this fear of failure—it may have started with baseball, but it continued on to other things as well. No longer did you play for yourself; you were playing for others. You put tremendous pressure on yourself and baseball was no longer fun. Constant failure, strike outs, whatever, was caused eventually because you believed it would happen. And this was in a sport where the athlete fails more often than succeeds and is still considered good. And then when you were struggling with your baseball career, your failed at-bats mounting up, the pressure mounting up, at fourteen-years old, your best friend, your self-proclaimed other half suddenly drowned in a boating accident. And then a few months later, your father died of a heart attack. And old fear emerges—your fear of losing everything you will ever love. You begin to alienate yourself in relationships—you believe your family will die, your friends will die. You have trouble making connections. You create facades, comforting facades. Your relationships are surface-level relationships wherein you only give the part that you think so-and-so would want to see. With your baseball friends, you gave a façade, a part or a part of you mimicked from other people. This was the part of you that wanted to be accepted, be a part of something you thought was valuable. Even if you didn't necessarily want to play baseball anymore, you still wanted to be a part of the team, the groups of guys who you thought were the people you wanted to be a part of. You hid the part of you that liked fantasy, Magic: The Gathering, reading, role-playing, etc. You hid from them the people who were a part of your fantastic world—Chris, the twins, even Sage. You knew, or thought they wouldn't accept this part of you so you hid it—but you refused to give it up. Why? Because this part of you was also a part that made you, just as athletics do. You hid from Chris and the twins your other parts. They didn't know about your drinking, your sexual relationship with Sage, how you talked to the baseball guys. You were virtually two different people with different mannerisms around each group because you feared the ramifications of exposing all the parts of you. Sage was perhaps the person who knew you best, and yet you even hid things from her. You hid very important things from her, things you didn't understand—and since you didn't understand them, you made assumptions about them. You acted the same with Hadley too. But, after four years of dating Sage, you felt you were beginning to fall out of love with her, that there was something wrong with her physically. She repulsed you at times. Why? I think there's something very troubling going on here. You began to have the same feeling toward Hadley, didn't you? Why? When did your feelings start to change about Sage?—after two-and-a-half years, you were completely sexless and happy. You began sleeping with Sage after that time and sex was a beautiful novelty—for a time. Then things started to change. The way you felt about Sage and the way you thought about sex with her started to change. I think the way you thought about sex started to change. Why? There's no easy answer. That's something you'll have to discover. But I think the beginning of that problem lies in what happened to your sister. I can't imagine what it must have been like to witness her rape and murder. But, there's a sexual element there that cannot be ignored. This may be difficult, but I think it's vital. You witnessed an angry, terrible and scary man rip the panties off your sister and then savagely rape her little body. What do you remember about that experience?"

"I remember blood. I remember screaming, fear, and blood—everywhere there was blood."

"And you couldn't watch. What did you focus on?"

"I remember seeing her underwear that had been thrown between us on the couch."

"Have you thought about why you lose interest in sex with your partners, but you end up being disgusted with them—and yourself?"

"I guess I always assumed I just wasn't interested in them anymore. The love had waned."

"And maybe that's true, but I think it's far more likely that that event so many years ago has traumatized you unfathomably. I think perhaps somewhere in your brain, in your subconscious, you equate sex with pain, death, sin, and guilt. Sex to you seems like a defilement of a woman and a defilement of yourself. I think it's possible you see yourself as an attacker, and your weapon is your penis. As soon as your relationships reach a sexual level, this mechanism within your consciousness is activated. Perhaps you experience a lot of sex in the beginning of your relationships, but it gradually wanes until you almost have no desire for that person whatsoever. And then you equate it with falling out of love. You are disgusted with the female body and the male body. So you want to cover it up. This is perhaps why you might only get sexually aroused when a woman is wearing clothes and especially lingerie. During sex, you focus on the feel of the panties in your hands, the colors, and the textures. It arouses you to watch yourself enter a woman, but you have trouble looking into the eyes of a woman during intercourse. And then afterwards, you want to quickly shower and get dressed. You are disgusted by the effects of sexual intercourse: semen, wet sheets, the smells of sex, and most of all, the nakedness afterwards. This isn't a question of love. Your love is clouded by your disgust of sexual intercourse. And I think it may go even deeper."

213

"How could it go deeper?"

"I think because of your past, a past you deemed filled with constant failure, you began looking for perfection. You strived to be perfect in everything you did, and yet this mentality ended every endeavor a failure. You wanted to be the perfect baseball player, the perfect son, the perfect friend—so much so you were constantly hiding your true self. And you wanted to be the perfect lover. But you were, are plagued by your own demons, which have constantly hindered you, and you are plagued by this idea of perfection, which simply doesn't exist. The perfect lover is not out there; what you see in the movies is superficial. Movies don't show the wet sheets, the premature ejaculation, the fat jiggling, the penis slipping out, the awkward transitions, or the use of condoms and taking them off once filled. That's real sex right there."

"So what can I do?" I asked.

"As cliché as it may be, you need to find yourself, who you are. The greatest power a person can attain is to know oneself. You need to learn, discover who you are and accept that person, love that person. You need to understand that failure is a part of life, but if you go into anything thinking you will fail, you certainly will. You need to challenge yourself. If you challenge yourself, you will discover yourself. Once you're aware of what has made you who you are, you can then begin to understand why and your road to personal power has begun. You are now, hopefully aware."

"Yes, I'm tired of being a failure."

"Orville, you never were a failure. You were a product of events, but instead of choosing to overcome them, you allowed them to shape you, to create a persona for you. You have this notion that *Fate* controls your life, that you are destined to fail. If you don't break this line of thinking, you'll continue believing you have no control. You'll continue to cheat on your lovers because you believe that only through sex with many different women are you powerful. You'll continue to fail because you

214

believe you're insignificantly weak, and a pawn in the universe. When you believe you have choice, your whole life will change."

"And the death of everyone I have ever loved?" I asked.

"Death is a part of life. Orville, perhaps this may burst your fragile bubble, but do you really think you're so important in this world that *Fate* would choose to affect the lives of so many people simply to cause you pain and suffering, to cause you to fail? That would suggest that the death of your father was simply to cause you pain and thus continuing your belief in your own inevitable failure. The death of Chris the same. The death of your grandmother, your sister. Do you really believe that all their deaths, from that of a seven-year old to a seventy-year old, were all caused only to affect your destiny?"

"I never really thought about it like that," I said.

"It's a bit pompous isn't it?"

"Yeah, it is."

"Imagine, Orville, a life full of choice. Imagine what that life could be like. Imagine if you decided right now to control your life. Obviously, we cannot control every aspect of our lives, but what if you could control how you reacted to a situation, choose how to look at the world, choose to overcome fear of failure and the unknown. Imagine the happiness and what could be accomplished. What do you think about a life like that?"

"I think it sounds wonderful."

Dr. Fields leaned in close to me and whispered. "Life *is* like that Orville. Now the secret is out. What're you going to do about it?"

"I think I need to leave this place and begin and start anew—a life where I'm in power."

"And how're you going to begin a life like that?"

"I honestly don't know. I guess I'll have to find my way."

I gathered the few belongings I had and changed into the black slacks and long-sleeved shirt I came here with three weeks ago. I walked down the ward's long corridor for the last time. I passed one of the rooms wherein some of the patients were taking one of the survival classes. Every one of them had their fixed blank stares. Every one of them had tried to commit suicide, some more than once. Every one of them believed their lives were not their own, that forces were acting against them. I had thought this way. I saw myself in that room, my face blank, my life one failure after another until I ended up in a ward like this for good. I was twenty-five years old. It was time to make some changes.

I passed the room. At the end of the hallway, Peter and Juan were playing rummy at one of the side tables. Peter looked up and smiled in that perverted way of his.

"You look like you want to play a game of rummy," Peter said.

"Actually, I'm leaving," I said.

"Leaving? When're you coming back?"

"I'm never coming back," I said.

"This is so sudden," Peter said, obviously agitated. He snatched at the pen and paper he was using to score the rummy game. "What's your address? When I'm out, I'll come see you."

"Ah...I don't think that's a good idea."

"No, I'll see you soon," Peter said.

"Probably not."

"Oh no, I will."

"Well, goodbye," I said and walked away. I turned around once and saw Juan sitting upright with his perpetual grin watching me. And then I took the elevator down and walked out of there forever.

Part III
Chapter 21

The day of my departure was halcyon with fat, cumulus clouds gently creeping along into the west—and that was where I was headed—Vietnam Airlines Flight 205 was boarding and I handed my ticket over as one does a get-out-of-jail-free-card. The Vietnamese stewardesses were dressed beautifully in traditional ao dai (long silk tunics with slits at the sides worn over transparent white, silk trousers) and after our plane left ground and was moving into the endless stretch of darkened Pacific blue to new lands and new beginnings, they began serving tea and beer and pho with either beef or chicken.

Everything was right in the world; the stars twinkling above were aligned with my wishes. I was a white beacon amongst a sea of black whose language I could not understand. I was a new man, a phoenix arisen from the ashes of failure. I was ready to light my chosen path afire. How strange that just a few weeks ago I was on suicide watch in a mental ward and now I was flying to Saigon, Vietnam. I chose this course. I chose to uproot my life from the fatalistic avenues of defeat into the life saving boulevard of dreams. This was a chance at redemption, salvation. I knew that. No longer would I be led, but I was to lead my life.

I had drifted off to sleep with these thoughts and when I awoke, the plane was descending over long stretches of green fields flooded with muddy water and pocked with water buffalo and tan pointy hats. Sleep quickly vanished from my eyes—it was the Vietnam I had envisioned. When the plane touched down, the eager Vietnamese hurried up and off. But I took my time, wanting to soak in every moment. I focused on each movement, each sight, each sound. I was a new life and I wanted to feel every sensation.

The Ho Chi Minh City Airport was a chaotic, cacophonous maze—daunting in every aspect: the sheer size of it was of some grand metropolis, not one sign in English about, blank stares of what could be construed as hostility, and bustling Vietnamese scrambling to get their luggage, to board their flights, to eat and to shop. I stood in awe at the chaos, but I was profoundly happy.

The customs official wore a stern face and a green, military uniform. She asked for my passport and looked at the photo and then me and then the photo and then me. She stamped it and I was free to enter the once hostile country (albeit the northern part). I picked up my single duffle bag from the luggage conveyor and headed toward the light of the day. I found, in my pocket, the directions to my friend Mark's apartment—'Don't pay even one dong more than 100,000 to get here' he had warned.

I stepped outside into the bright light of Saigon; I took the sunglasses off my shirt and put them over my eyes. I smiled.

There was a long line of taxis waiting to be of service.

"Sir you want motorbike." A short Vietnamese man approached me from a group of men standing around smoking cigarettes.

"How much?"

"Where you go?"

"Backpacker Street," I said.

"40,000 dong."

"Sounds good."

I got on the back of his motorbike, put on a shabby helmet, and we sped off at a death-defying pace—I imagined it was similar to racing motorcycles around a muddied obstacle course. We dodged and veered around the multitude of motorbikes on the roadway. This was a nation on the go quickly and cheaply—there was no place for the automobile here. And from what I saw, as we cruised up and down various side streets, was that this was a nation of leisure and people watching as well: every shop had three old women and two old men sitting and watching (people, the motorbikes, the children playing), young men and women eating ice cream and noodles hung about against store posts or sitting on white plastic chairs at small, hole-in-the-wall restaurants, and beside all of these people were little brown scraggly dogs hoping for any scraps to be thrown their way.

Backpacker Street was so named because it was filled with foreigners with backpacks and Vietnamese who catered to them with merchandise. I paid my driver (including a 10,000 dong tip) and headed passed the shops and cafes to a bar called The Crazy Buffalo. It stood out against all the rest and was perfect for stop number one. It was on a corner and had a massive, obnoxious red bull head (not a buffalo) protruding from the bar's façade, complete with horns and a nose ring and it swayed its head back and forth. I heard Michael Jackson's "Thriller" blaring from the open doors even before I crossed the street. It was my kind of place.

Inside were glass bar tables with stools. I saw the strangest sight I had ever seen and it wasn't anything Vietnamese—there were two guys each wearing French flags as capes and one other American-looking guy practicing what appeared to be the dance steps to "Thriller." I went up to the bar where three attractive Vietnamese girls leaned lazily against its railings.

"Join us," the American said.

"Might need a few beers first," I said. "What's good?"

"Saigon Bia," he said. I took his advice and ordered the beer and stood next to the American who stopped dancing momentarily. The two Frenchmen were now on their knees playing air guitars. They both wore aviators. "They've been here awhile."

"This beer must be potent," I said.

"It's not bad," he said. "I'm Tim. Je suis Americain. Picked that up from these two."

"Orville," I said. "Also American."

"You just land?"

"Obvious huh?"

"Well, if you hadn't had Saigon beer yet, you must have just landed."

"What about you? How long have you been here?"

"About a month. I'm touring Southeast Asia before heading back to the States. I was teaching English in South Korea this last year."

"Oh, awesome. Did you like it?"

"It had its ups and downs. Overall, glad I did it. It allowed me time to write a novel."

"What's it about?" I asked.

"It's about a guy who coaches a teenage Korean baseball player—sort of like *Mr. Baseball* with Tom Selleck, but coaching rather than playing."

I left the bar with plans to meet the two Frenchmen and Tim later that night. It was three in the afternoon. I walked a few blocks east to my friend's apartment. The streets were narrow and bustling, littered with old women selling vegetables and men playing dominoes. I walked with my head held high feeling fine. This was my new home; these were my new streets. The apartment was a three-story, white, gated building with a roof and a barbeque. Mark was just pulling up on his motorcycle.

"Hey buddy—long time man," Mark said, embracing me warmly.

"I don't even know how long it's been," I said.

"Since university dude—sorry I missed your wedding."

"Just because you were 14,000 miles away doesn't excuse you."

"Well, maybe another one will happen—hell, maybe here in Vietnam. Check out the place—it's awesome."

Inside the black gate and through a large, wooden front door was a sparse room, which would serve as mine, a kitchen, a dining room table, and a spiral stairway that led upstairs to more rooms and finally to the roof, which had a view of the city. Mark took me up to the second floor.

"This here is the pot-smoking room." The room had a small couch and some soft chairs, a guitar case with an acoustic guitar inside, a glass table with a bong, a pipe, some ashtrays, and a bowl of what looked to be stale chips. Ben's room (Mark's roommate from England) was next to the pot room.

Mark's room was on the third floor. A short stairway on a balcony led to the roof, which had a barbeque, a clothesline, and a small bed. Over the rooftops was an overhang that protected from rain—there were four other adjoining buildings to ours.

"Yeah man, we have some fun parties up here in the summer. Barbeques, dancing—it's a fucking riot," Mark said.

We heard a motorcycle pull up to the apartment from the rooftop. We looked over the top.

"Hey, thought I told you not to come back here," Mark yelled.

"Hey, I thought I told you to fuck off."

We went back down to the first level.

"Ben, this is Orville—Orville, this is Ben," Mark said.

"If you're anything like Mark, I'm going to hate you," Ben said.

"Excellent—I hate Mark too," I said.

"Oh, you guys are funny. You both can get back on the airplanes that brought you here."

Two Vietnamese bouncers and one extremely large black guy guarded the front door and a line of Vietnamese men stood waiting outside dressed in Hawaiian shirts and black sunglasses.

"I think just *that* guy would suffice," I said.

"The other two are there for translation," Ben said. "In case brawn and muscle don't translate."

I noticed white foreigners going in and out at will, some with small Vietnamese women linked to their arms. Cabbies flocked to the absconders, opening their cab doors with smiles. Mark and Ben walked passed the bouncers without hesitation as if they owned the place, but I slinked on in like a poser expecting a hand to reach out and grab my shoulder—'hey, where do you think you're going' and then I would be thrust back out alone in a city I hardly knew.

The Apocalypse Club had two floors and a back area with extra seating. The first floor had a pool table to the left of the entrance where men were competing in a billiards tournament. There was a dance floor to our right with tables of foreigners and Vietnamese encircling it. Upstairs was packed tight with people dancing and drinking—the music and people were suffocating though so the three of us stayed on the first level.

We shared a table with three attractive Vietnamese women dressed in varying shades of red dresses.

"The women here are gorgeous," I said. "Like these three next to us."

"Oh, they're gorgeous alright," Mark said.

I turned to the woman closest to me. "How's it going?"

She flashed her fake eyelashes at me, lit herself up. "Hi honey, I'm so-so."

"Why only so-so?"

"Oh baby I'm tired."

Ben and Mark cracked up behind me. I briefly looked their way. Ben leaned in and whispered in my ear—how tired was I? I looked back at the woman.

"You a handsome man baby—do you want put me to bed?"

Oh. Naivety 1 - Experience 0. "Oh, you're beautiful—gorgeous, but can't right now, with friends, meeting friends here, maybe later okay?"

"I'll be right here baby," she said.

"I'm getting a beer—you guys want anything?"

"Yup," Mark said.

"Yup," Ben said.

"Saigon beer then?"

"Yup."

"Yup."

222

"You guys are great conversationalists."

"Yup."

"Yup."

The club was crawling with beautiful young and old Vietnamese prostitutes. They hung around together at the tables or individually with old white guys and young black men. The young white men were too shy to approach them, but they gawked from afar and quaffed down their beer. I passed through this throng to the bar. And then I saw her—the most beautiful woman in the club, nay, in Vietnam was behind the bar counter. She smiled at me as I approached.

"What would you drink sweetie?" Her voice was sweet and melodic like the fabled Siren's.

"Three Saigon beers please," I stammered, looking down at the wad of cash in my hand to avoid those luminous eyes.

"Come again," she said.

I took the beers to the guys and sat down.

"I just met the most beautiful woman in Vietnam," I said.

"She's the most expensive then," Mark said.

"No, she works here—behind the bar."

"The only difference here between a bartender and a call girl is that the bartender will cost you more," Ben said.

"Words of wisdom to live by," Mark said. "Women here will wilt you away—financially."

"And emotionally?" I asked.

"Nah, boss them around a little," Ben said. "They respond well to that."

"You two are quite the dynamic duo," I said.

We went out on the dance floor and flopped around for a half an hour; then I went to the back area to catch a breath of fresh air and to find a restroom. She was back there, leaning against a wooden balustrade and smoking a cigarette. Orville, choose to talk to her—talk to her.

"I'll have three Saigon beers," I said.

"Oh, I'm on break," she said. "One minute okay?"

"I was just kidding. I just wanted to talk to you."

"You like this bar?"

"Yeah, it's great. Do you?"

"Yes, very fun. I meet many people."

"What's your name?"

"Tuyen Vo Mong," she said.

"Nice to meet you—I'm Orville."

"I must go back to bar. Come talk to me again okay?"

"Definitely," I said.

It was four in the morning when we made it back home.

"Well, you guys can talk, talk, talk well into the night about this or that, but friends, countrymen, Englishmen, lend me your ears—Tuyen Vo Mong is amazing, gorgeous, and I have a date with her tomorrow."

"Day 1—Orville seemed a nice enough fellow, a bit wet behind the ears perhaps, but seemingly alright. Day 2—Plundering the natural resources of Vietnam. Day 3—Caught up heavily in Vietnamese culture, Orville finds himself spending a lot of money he doesn't have. It starts out petty enough, a beer here, a haircut there, but then comes jewelry, a trip to Japan, condoms, condoms, condoms," Ben said.

"*You*, are funny," I said. "But you're right about one thing my good sir. I will have to buy a fair share of condoms."

Yes, fuck your way through Asia, the great concubine said.

I lied down in bed and stared up at the overhead fan twirling around and around. The fan twirls in circles, crossing over the same point again and again. The fan's blades don't make linear progress, but instead repeat their path. Progress is linear; stasis is circular. And yet there is movement in circular stasis. Where are you going with this Orville? The fan was built to provide comfort through circular movement—in a word, its *fate* is predestined. But the fan is static and never becomes more than simply a fan. The fan is life and its blades are circular. The fan perhaps provides comfort, but inevitably, the fan will eventually stop functioning—die. Only when going against its intended use can the fan progress. Orville, your life may have been intended to fail, but you were moving circularly. Now, you are moving linearly, progressing, and in that you are defying fate. You have moved into a life of choice. Fate is circular; chaos is linear.

Tomorrow you will fuck that little Vietnamese until she squeals, said the great concubine.

Tomorrow, I will experience this Asian persuasion I keep hearing about. No—enough of that. Don't you realize that that line of thinking is what leads to failure? Tuyen Vo Mong is not a sexual possession, something to conquer. She is a person. Take her to coffee, talk to her, watch a movie. Sex is the devil anyway—where has it got you but riddled with confusion and loss? Exactly. You should just become ascetic and asexual. Vietnam is where you leave your old life behind Orville—you are to emerge from this cocoon into a beautiful Asiatic butterfly, a metamorphosis of fateful failure to...to what?

"To what Orville James McFadden?" I whispered. "What do you want to become?"

That's the beauty of it—I had no idea. But I believed that whatever I would become through choice and the rejection of fear would be infinitely better than what I was before. The excitement was overwhelming.

Chapter 22

The Saigon sun bore down like a tanning bed UV light, and it was only ten in the morning. I walked along a side street somewhere in Phuong 1—the city was still a labyrinthine maze of curved streets similar in every aspect. I looked for an old, cracked yellow painted building that Mark had mentioned to me called *Miss Hoa English School*. I was in shanty-town. The buildings were old concrete boxes stacked atop each other that had small balconies with plants hanging off the sides. The only aspect that differentiated any one apartment from its neighbor was the colored wraps that flapped breezily between the small doorways. I heard laughter and the high pitched, clipped staccato of Vietnamese women going about their business.

I continued walking past the old women stacking vegetables into their buckets until I saw it—a building with a large white sign above the entranceway that had a large red lotus with a sun blooming from its center with a painted picture of a woman saying *Miss Hoa English School* in a bubble like a comic book. I went in. I came out an hour later with a job. I would start in a week.

I headed to Backpacker Street and found a three story coffee shop called Bobbie's Brewery. The first two levels had booths and small tables with chairs for people to drink their coffee, but the third level was a dark room with six cozy booths and a theatre screen. The room was elevated like a cinema, each layer rising just above the last.

I met Tuyen there just as the sun began to dive deep into the mountains of Dalat. I ordered two coffees and then we went up to the third floor—the café screened movies for free, everything from new releases to old favorites. We sat down in one of the booths and she snuggled in next to me. I instinctually put my arm around her. The movie screen flashed and a helicopter flew just above the tree line amidst a thick jungle—*Predator*.

When the movie had ended, we emerged onto a bustling Backpacker Street—every night was a Friday night here—there were foreigners sitting outside the bars drinking Saigon beers and a plethora of Vietnamese walking up and down the street selling everything: cheap watches, DVDs, bracelets, earrings and necklaces, key chains, bottled water, and sex. There were women in short skirts and shiny dresses going up to male foreigners to get beer and to offer quickies at nearby cheap hotels.

"You meet my family, okay?"

"Tonight?"

"Yes. My family like you to try real Vietnamese food."

We took Tuyen's motorbike to a restaurant loosely translated 'shimmering dragon.' I didn't know what I was getting into, but I found myself glancing over at Tuyen's shimmering, shiny green, form-fitting dress and wondering when I could get my hands under there.

No, no, no, no. Stop it. This was the line of thinking I needed to avoid. This was not a new world to compel old behaviors into fruition. This was not leaving behind the old world of Failure McFadden emotionally and physically so that I could continue what I left behind. No—this was a new start to a new life being a new man. Turn your head Orville. Turn your head.

The Shimmering Dragon was steamy and packed full of people. It was everything I thought an Asian restaurant should be: crowded, bustling with women serving drinks and steaming foods, wading delicately yet quickly through the throng of people serving as one does without the hope for a tip (efficiently and without splendor). It was warm and everyone was chatting incessantly with their neighbors. There was a large table at the back with a bunch of well-dressed men and women in black or tan suits and Sunday dresses.

Tuyen took my hand and led me to that table. Suddenly, the chatter stopped and Tuyen began introducing me. I was amazed—at least half the table knew a bit of English, and the other half, the elderly half, spoke rapidly in Vietnamese and smiled big, toothy smiles. I sat down next to Tuyen and across from a man who eyed me mysteriously. He didn't smile, but stared straight at me into my eyes as if he were judging me in some form or another. I just hoped I wasn't trespassing on anyone in the room.

Saigon beers were ordered all around. Large bowls of pho with beef, chicken, pork, and tripe were set in the middle of the table. Plates were scattered about—Banh hoi (a thin noodle woven together and served with spring onion and roasted pork), large portions of white rice, spring rolls, Cao lau, which was a dish of thoroughly cooked egg noodles topped with beef and chicken. There was a plethora of seafood and duck noodle soup with bamboo shoots (called Bun mang vit). My eyes grew large at the sights. Nowhere in the States would I have eaten a meal of this magnitude.

We raised our beer glasses and said, "Mot hai ba yo!" And then we drank.

"You are very handsome." The woman sitting next to me said.

"Cam on ban," I said.

"Oh very good," she said. She introduced herself as Hai Phan Thi Tu, but said to call her Phan. She was Tuyen's cousin and worked as a teacher in one of the private schools. "You should come work at my school."

"Maybe," I said. "I'm working at another school right now."

"I pay you better," she said.

The man sitting across from me was Phan's brother. He introduced himself as Steve. We talked a bit, and I found out that he had lived in Las Vegas for some time and learned to be a dealer and worked his way up into the major casinos. He had been back in Vietnam for six years and now worked as a dealer for one of the major hotels in Saigon.

228

"Only foreigners can play at my casino," Steve said.

"You get a lot of foreigners in there?"

"Every night," he said. "I work at the VIP tables."

"Very important person," I stated.

"Very important player," he said, eyeing me. "We created a new game called PBJ." *Peanut butter and jelly?* "It's poker and blackjack together."

"How do you play?"

"It's very simple." Steve began to explain the rules to me. His reticent and even morose manner metamorphosed quickly into a businesslike candor, which held even a suppressed cheery disposition as if he knew he had won something, but wasn't letting on to what it was. He obviously enjoyed his work and enjoyed sharing it with others. The rules were simple enough, but he looked at me with complete concentration, reading my face to see if I truly understood. He taught me as one would teach a child how to play a new game.

"The minimum amount a player brings to the table is five thousand US dollars, and the minimum amount the banker must bring to the table is one hundred thousand US dollars," Steve said. The banker was a player (a foreigner) who voluntarily chooses to be so and who plays the other players. "And the casino collects ten percent of all winnings."

"So the casino makes money without losing any no matter what?"

"That's correct," he said.

"Wow, nice setup," I said. "And there are players who come in and actually have that much money to gamble with?"

"Yes, many players," Steve said. "I would like you to come play at my casino."

"Oh, I'm not much of a gambler," I said. "And I definitely don't have that much money."

"It's okay. I will give you the five thousand US dollars," he said.

"No one just gives somebody five thousand US dollars," I said.

"You're right. I will only give you five thousand US dollars if I knew you would win."

This didn't make a lot of sense. If he thought he could teach me to play expert blackjack and to read other players and read the cards, he didn't have a clue as to my playing ability. It just wasn't happening. "How would you teach me to win?"

"I have a system," Steve said.

"What's your system?" I asked.

"I will tell you part of my system, but I cannot tell you one part so please don't ask. My system is very simple. I will deal you two cards. You will look at your cards. When I say, 'Would you like another card sir?' you will look at me. If I am looking at you, you take another card. Understand? If I am not looking at you, if I am looking away, then you stay. That's it."

I looked over at Hai Phan. She simply smiled. "That seems really easy," I said, but something deep down in my gut was telling me to get up from the table, use the restroom, and slink out the backdoor.

"Would you like me to show you right now?" Steve asked.

"Sure."

"Please shuffle the cards," he said. Steve handed over a deck of cards to me. I looked around and the Vietnamese were chatting away with their family members and not paying any more attention to me. Tuyen sat next to me intently watching my every move. I shuffled the deck five or six times, cut and handed it back to Steve. He dealt two cards to me and two cards to Hai Phan. I looked at my cards: a six and a queen, 16. Hai Phan looked at her cards and then back up at Steve. "Would you like another card sir?"

I looked at Steve. He was not looking at me, but a bit to the side. "No, I'll stay," I said.

"Would you like another card miss?" Steve said to Hai Phan. She looked at her cards again and said she would take another card. She busted. I won the hand. "Good. Easy, yes?"

"Pretty simple," I said.

"Let's practice more," he said.

We practiced some more, and I won every hand whether I stayed or hit. It was remarkable—I won by hitting 21, by having a higher number than Hai Phan and/or by her busting and automatically losing. I couldn't understand it. I won each and every time by getting the exact card or cards I needed and yet I was the one who shuffled the deck. I guessed that this was the part of the trick I couldn't know how it was done, but I couldn't see any way that it was possible. Not *only* must Steve have known what cards were dealt out, but he must have control as to what cards were dealt out. The only way possible was for Steve to somehow stack the deck (although I shuffled—a fact I couldn't get away from) or to replace the deck with one already stacked, but even that wouldn't work because he couldn't possibly know when every player at a table would hit and when one wouldn't. It was impossible. Yet I watched him do it each and every time.

"Do you think you could do this at my casino?"

"Well...I don't know," I said. I wasn't seriously considering this. There was no way I could walk into a casino and perform...but that was what this was—the ultimate performance. This was real, true life acting. I would be playing the ultimate role, my *Casino Royale*. Everything I wanted to become could be in this performance. Vietnam was a place to change destiny, to choose and to live, to live by God, to live. "How would it work?" I asked.

"I would set you up with a room in the hotel. There will be a safe in the room. Inside the safe will be five thousand US dollars in chips. You will come down to the floor level. You will come to my table in the VIP area.

The minimum play is twenty minutes. In twenty minutes, you will make two hundred thousand dollars. I will take eighty percent and you will take twenty percent. You will walk away with no less than forty thousand dollars."

"Wow..."

"Do you think you could do this?"

Tuyen took me home on her motorbike. The wind pulverizing my face felt grand in lieu of the Saigon beers we drank. She whisked down side streets and bobbed and weaved through the multitude of motorbikes. It was comfortably easy to pick out the foreigners along the way wearing white khakis and bright string strap shirts, men in board shorts and tank tops from Luang Prabang rafting trips. Tuyen tried yelling and pointing to things while she drove, but I didn't respond with more than a grunt; I was simply enjoying being alive at that moment, speedily cruising the streets on the back of an old motorbike.

She parked outside the front gate of my apartment and turned the key which stopped the bike's engine. She went up to the gate and waited impatiently for me to fumble the keys out of my pockets. Apparently she wanted to come inside. I unlocked the gate and we entered to a raucous party—Ben and Mark were thumping away shirtless on some bongos and there were three girls drinking beer and singing horridly.

"Orville mate, grab some beer and join our little fiasco," Ben said.

"Fiasco indeed," I said.

"Give that beer a girl," Mark said hiccupping and continuing to pound on the poor bongo.

Tuyen and I each took a beer and met the three girls who were neighbors of ours from England. Ben pulled me aside while Mark put some real music on. "Well laddie, I see you brought a female back to our hovel. That means only one thing to me."

"Are you Irish?"

"Irish descent, but that's not what I was talking about mate," Ben said, his arm draped around my shoulders. I had to hold him up using my quadriceps and he was a tall guy. "I meant the sexual reveling you are about to experience in this household, which I'm all for, but there needs to be some ground rules. Firstly, no prostitutes unless previously bargained for—secondly, we men of...of, this world, must share things. So, that means..."

"We must share things?"

"Yes, sharing. Everything you need to know you learned in kindergarten...hey, hey, you see that lass over there. What you think of her?"

"Yummy," I said.

"Yeah, yeah I know. My mission mate is to pillage and conquer. But even a little kiss would be nice from that one," Ben said.

"How could she say no?"

"I like you mate," Ben said. "This is a house of sexual reveling," he yelled. "Let the music play."

The three girls cheered—Mark continued playing the bongos despite the background music, and Tuyen pulled my arm to go into my room.

"Hey, hey, where you going mate?"

"Just following orders," I said.

Tuyen closed the door behind me once inside. She kissed me on the lips. I looked at her looking at me. She was beautiful. I wondered how I got so lucky. Ha! Luck—no fate, only choice, and a little luck. I could handle a little luck. I kissed her back, and she took me to the bed. She undressed perfunctorily and lay down on the bed, but I didn't care at this point (perhaps romanticism wasn't in vogue in Vietnam). I took off my shirt and threw it to the floor and slid down my shorts. I climbed into bed with her.

"Do you think you'll play the game?" Tuyen asked.

"I don't know," I said. "It sounds a bit dangerous."

You never learn, said fear.

"It will be fine," she said.

Chapter 23

A stone dragon spouted water into a fountain pool inside the hotel plaza. The luxurious hotel had more than eight white stone stories with large, wood-framed windows, gaudy balconies, and a wondrous display of international flags pointing towards the heavens from the rooftop. I stood on the sidewalk outside the black gates and stared up at the hotel. What was I doing there? This was not me. I was dressed in board shorts, a shirt with 'I Love Vietnam' on it, and fake Crocs. Taxis and rickshaws came and went incessantly in and out of the hotel's roundabout. Foreigners dressed in khakis and thin, white cotton shirts with their wives and girlfriends hooked onto their arms fearlessly stepped into the hotel foyer.

Coming into the foyer was stepping back in time: large candelabra hung from the ceiling and sparkled brilliantly with the light, a magnificent staircase with carpet the color of blood led up to the casino and guest rooms, an elongated service desk with immaculately dressed staff waited to be of service. Off to the left and right were staff doors leading to the first floor rooms: storage rooms, laundry rooms, break rooms, kitchens, and the staff rushed through these rooms to handle the every day details of operating a hotel of this stature. Rooms, rooms, everywhere were rooms.

The rain pounded against the windows, and the droplets slid down into the pools gathering in front. What a murder mystery this hotel could allow, I thought. I went to the reservation desk and gave my name. To my surprise, I was handed a key and a young Vietnamese boy showed me to my room on the fourth floor. He unlocked the door with his own key, said something I didn't understand, and promptly walked away. I wasn't sure if I was supposed to tip or not.

I pushed open the door farther without going in. I looked down at the key in my hand and smiled—James Bond I now was. I stepped into the room. I saw a large bed with maroon bedding and cream colored pillows to my right. There was a bar at the back of the room with glasses and miniature bottles of alcohol, and to the left was a large vanity area and bath with porcelain tiles, an open tub, and a walk-in closet across from it. There was a jukebox and a sitting room with two chairs and a table. At the back, in front of the curtained windows was a small safe.

I took out the key Steve had given me earlier that day. I held it in my hand—once I opened that safe, the game was on. I walked slowly towards it, capturing the images of the apartment like a cell phone camera: a painting on the wall of red and maroon abstract shapes—click, the park outside the hotel and the motorbikes whizzing by— click, myself, in the mirror, 25 years old, in Vietnam with a new life—click.

I went to the safe thinking once opened, the dream would end. There would be no chips, no instructions, only empty space and relief that I went for it, but didn't have to do it. I put the small key into the keyhole. I turned it. The door snapped open. There they were—five rows of ten chips at one hundred dollars apiece. There was a note:

Get dressed and come down to my table around 9 o'clock.

It was 7 o'clock. I jumped in the shower and sat down in the tub. The steam filled the room and I relaxed down into the water. I soaked for what seemed like ages, thinking of how I would pull this off tonight. I was going to meet Tuyen afterwards at my apartment around 10 o'clock and we would celebrate with pomp and circumstance. I leaned my head back against a wash rag and looked up at the water cascading down upon me. What a metamorphosis had occurred since one year ago, since six months ago, since even six weeks ago. My old life didn't seem my own. That was the dream and this was the

235

reality. And what a dream it had been. Where was that woman now?—that Hadley St. Claire?

I wondered about the strange thing that was life. Life was always directly moving forward as if on a string. Sometimes it moved quickly, sometimes slowly, but it never stopped. What was the driving force behind it? Time? If the string were only so long, then one could say that there was fate, at least in view of death. And if there was fate, then one could say there was no purpose because there was no choice—at least not a personal purpose, but perhaps a purpose in a grand scheme of things, as in a purpose for God, but I would rather not think I was simply a pawn in God's scheme. What about choice? I could live my entire life with choice, but would have to accomplish whatever it was that I had to accomplish in a select given time. But with that scheme, there would be no purpose because at the appointed time of death, if one hadn't accomplished what one was supposed to accomplish, then what one was supposed to do was not what one was supposed to do—assuming there were things we were supposed to do. It was a paradox.

But if the string never began and never ended, then there was no fate, and then I had eternity to accomplish what I needed to accomplish, which was a great many things. Then there could be purpose. And there must be a purpose. So, the string must have neither beginning nor end and there must be an eternity of experience and learning.

If there was no God, there was no fate, but only chaos. But there could never be the mystic forces that seem to affect ourselves and our world. What were those?— figments of our imagination? That, I couldn't believe. How was it that every day I woke up and felt deeply, unequivocally within my bones that acting was my future? This time, this *now*, was simply the experience I needed to accomplish the great future I had dreamed about and knew, knew, knew was coming to fruition.

This life, this dream I led before was 25 years of failure. After a quarter of a century, I had finally learned that fear resulted in failure and only through choosing life can one overcome that fear and failure conundrum. And that's what tonight was all about—overcoming fear and failure.

My mind raced with these thoughts as I dressed. Steve had told me to dress casually as I would if going out to the nightclub. I didn't know exactly what that meant so I put on a buttoned white shirt and nice jeans. I wore a band of beads I had picked up from a street vendor on my right wrist. I sprinkled some cologne (courtesy of the hotel) around my neck and wrists and looked at myself once again in the mirror. Casual but trendy—I wasn't quite James Bond, but I wasn't Orville James McFadden either.

I glanced at the clock near the bedstead. It was 8:50. It was time. My heart beat faster than it ever had before. I thought it was going to crash through my ribcage and shatter my breast bone on its way out. It wanted nothing of the body it was trapped in. It was a prisoner banging on the cell bars during a prison riot. There was no stopping it. Remember your lines; remember your moves. You can do this. This is your moment of triumph. You will write a screen play about this very scene once you get back to the States and your acting career will flourish. Perhaps you're dreaming a bit, but no harm in that. This is your defining moment, not only as an actor, but as a person breaking out of the mold of decay. Do it. Go.

I took an energy drink from the refrigerator, opened it. I took up the five thousand in chips. I took my room key. I took a deep breath and walked out that door.

The casino floor was spread out like a trade show. There were rows and rows of tables: poker, blackjack, craps, roulette, even solitaire. The floor was a sort of reddish brown with yellowed diamonds, and there was a stage at the far end with a Vietnamese band playing pop-

American songs. Petite Vietnamese women in short blue skirts and white blouses carried trays of beer around for tips.

I had walked into a sort of carnival. Everywhere, movement: people constantly shifted from one table to the next with the rise and fall of their chip stacks. It was loud. I instantly fell in love with the sounds—the hoots and hollers, the short clipped snap of chips being stacked upon one another, the language of the dealers (soft and formal). There were all sorts of people here—I heard Indian accents, British, Australian, American and Canadian, Korean and Japanese. This was truly a house of sin for the traveling elite.

I could do this. Steve had told me where the VIP tables were. I had to cross the floor strutting my chips as if I owned the place (or at least belonged there) to one of the back rooms at the far end of the casino. There were different rooms for different games. Steve's room was at the farthest end. I held my chips upon the pedestal that was my arm and calmly walked towards the room, sipping confidently on my energy drink. I reached the door. A Vietnamese man dressed completely in black smiled and said hello. He opened the door for me. It was that simple.

The room was small, cramped even. It had three tables with a dealer at each of them. There were cameras situated directly above the tables. There were two or three men at each table, some western, some eastern. The room was sparse, perhaps so that the players could focus entirely on the play. Steve's table was the middle table.

There were two empty chairs. I took the one in the middle across from Steve. I figured it would be easier to follow the plan there. To my right was a gregarious Australian wearing a cowboy hat. On his right was a Middle Eastern man dressed in a silk cashmere business suit. To my left was an Asian man from Brunei. And on his left was an empty seat.

"Gentlemen, we are waiting on one more," Steve addressed us.

238

I chatted up the Australian. His name was Turk, which I thought was odd. The man from Brunei was Mr. Azwan Sharif. He was soft spoken and friendly and his eyes gleamed with intelligence. The Middle Eastern man didn't speak much, but Steve introduced him as Mr. Muhammad Hamid. Finally, a beautiful Asian woman took the final seat. She apologized for being late and introduced herself as Kim, Sun-Young.

Steve introduced the game we were to play that night and explained the rules. Mr. Muhammid Hamid (a business man of some sort) would play the role of the banker. The play would be clockwise beginning with Turk, the Australian. He had worked in ranching, made some money, and then married a rich heiress of an Australian cigarette company.

"The best money to spend is free money," Turk joked. Turk took out a wad of one hundred dollar bills and set it on the table. "50,000 in chips please."

I organized my five thousand in chips feeling a bit daunted.

"If you can lose five thousand at your age, you're doing just fine mate," Turk said.

"Well, I hope not to lose that much," I joked.

Mr. Sharif exchanged one hundred thousand in chips. He, too, was some sort of businessman. Lastly, Ms. Kim exchanged twenty thousand. She said she worked as an executive at Hyundai. How was I here? I was about to be an English teacher making pennies compared to these people and I wasn't even using my money, and yet I was supposed to walk away with two hundred thousand dollars. If they took one look at me, they would know I was a fraud.

"Players, the game shall begin," Steve said. We each placed our $500 ante. Steve shuffled the cards and dealt one card faced down to each player and to Mr. Hamid. Then, he dealt one card faced up for Mr. Hamid and faced down to the players.

I checked my cards: a King and a 10 so 20 total. Mr. Hamid had a 7 showing. He bet $1,000 and stayed, which meant that he had either a 10-card or an Ace. Turk played first. He double-checked his cards, placed the $1,000 dollar bet and asked for another card. Steve dealt him a card. Turk took his card, checked it, and then stayed. It was now my turn. I already knew what to do.

"Mr. McFadden, would you like another card?"

I had 20—I knew to stay without checking in with Steve. I placed my $1,000 bet and stayed. Mr. Sharif placed his bet, took his card as did Ms. Kim. The four players each revealed their cards (Ms. Kim busted so Mr. Hamid automatically collected his winnings from her) and then Mr. Hamid revealed his cards last: An ace and a 7 so 18 total. Next, Turk had a total of 19 so Turk collected his winnings from Mr. Hamid. I collected my winnings. Mr. Sharif had 18 as well so he and Mr. Hamid collected their bets back. So, the advantages for being the banker were that the players had to reveal their cards firstly and if they busted then the banker would collect the winnings no matter if he busted his own hand. The disadvantages were that the banker had to have one card revealed from the onset and then was forced to hit when under 17 and forced to stay when 17 or over.

The next hand was dealt. I had an 8 and a 3—Mr. Hamid showed an Ace. He bet $5,000. Turk was first to act. He checked his cards. He sat back a moment and looked over at Ms. Kim and smiled. Ms. Kim smiled back and tilted her head as if to say *what will you do Mr. Turk* and that we were here to gamble, let's make this exciting. Mr. Turk put his $5,000 in and took his card. He looked at it and laughed. I was up next.

"Mr. McFadden, would you like another card sir?" Steve asked.

I quickly looked at Steve—he was staring straight back at me. I looked at my cards and then I looked at Ms. Kim. She was a beautiful woman who commanded attention. Why I looked to her I don't know, but everything I did was part of the ruse. I bet and took a card. It was a jack—21.

Mr. Sharif folded. Ms. Kim looked at her cards. "I suppose it's my turn to squirm." She put in her bet and took another card.

Turk revealed first—bust. Mr. Hamid wordlessly took his winnings. I revealed my 21 and collected my winnings—I was now up $13,000 or so. Ms. Kim ended with 19 and Mr. Hamid had 20, an Ace and a 9. After playing for an hour with selected losses and fantastic wins, I was up $220,000. Turk had already put in more money as well as Mr. Sharif's, but Ms. Kim ended up being up quite a bit herself. Mr. Hamid was a clear winner as he took most of Turk's money and Mr. Sharif, but I had taken a large chunk of his money.

I was glowing. It really worked; I couldn't believe it really worked. We decided to take a short break before resuming, and I walked around the casino and had a couple of beers while watching some of the other games. Turk came up to me while I was watching a crap game.

"Well mate, you're playing quite well. Have you played much before?"

"Yeah I learned how to play a little while ago, but sort of fell in love with this game. I used to play poker mostly. I've certainly never played a game of this magnitude though."

"Well keep it up mate and you'll be able to retire."

We resumed play at 10:30 pm. I had received a text message from Steve just before we began. It said I was to play three more hands and decide to move on. I was then supposed to cash out and meet in the hotel around 12 in the morning. Three more hands and I would be rolling.

In the first hand, I lost $20,000 with a bust.

In the second, I put up the $2,000 that was now the ante. Each player was dealt their first card. Then, Mr. Hamid was dealt a King for his second card, and the other four players were dealt their second cards. I checked my cards. I had a 3 and a 9 so 11. I drank down the rest

241

of my beer, and instantly a woman came over and offered me another one, which I took greedily and thanked her. Mr. Sharif and Ms. Kim checked their hands and betting began. Mr. Hamid bet an insane sum of money ($200,000) and took another card. Turk quickly bowed out. I checked my cards once again. "Mr. McFadden, would you like another card sir?" Since I had 11 I knew I wanted another card and quickly said yes. There was a pause that seemed like an eternity. I looked at Steve who was looking at me intensely. His eyes burned into mine and his face flushed with anger. He slowly gave me a card. I looked at my three cards. I had a 9, a 3, and a Queen—21. No, not 21, 22. No—no—no—no! I had 22, not 21. Not 21. What the fuck! I had busted. I had bet everything. I had lost everything. I had 22, 22, 22. Not 21. I didn't have 21. Oh shit...

After the hand, I shook hands with the rest of the players. "Difficult hand," Mr Hamid said, his bushy mustache twitching excitedly. The man obviously didn't need the money, but he certainly enjoyed the win. My hands were shaking and I didn't know what to do. I looked at Steve who nodded to me.

"Thank you for playing Mr. McFadden. We hope to see you again," Steve said, even toned and professionally.

I left the casino.

I gathered my clothes back in the room and shoved them in my backpack. I looked around. I wanted to stay the night there, to feel the glitz and glam, but how could I when had I lost it all? I had lost it all. In one moment I was rich and everything seemed magical and then the next I had been brought back down to my humble beginnings. What had happened? How did I calculate it so horridly? I didn't even check in with Steve. He's going to be pissed. Oh well. We could do it again tomorrow night. It was easy. Just keep a level head. I left the hotel.

"Going out for the night?" The concierge said.

"Just for a bit. I'll be back soon."

I hailed a motorbike and was home in fifteen minutes.

I opened the front door of my apartment to the buzz of a mini party. Tuyen was there with Ben and Mark, the European neighbors and some other people I didn't know. When I walked in, they cheered and bombarded me with questions—the who, the how, the what.

"So what happened mate?" Ben asked.

Tuyen came up to my side and snuggled into me.

"Well," I said. "I, ah...well, I actually lost it all."

"What? What you say?" Tuyen asked, her face horrified. "You joking."

"Yeah, it was going so well. I was up $200,000 and then..."

"What? No, this bad. This very bad Orville. Very bad," Tuyen said. She paced the room hurriedly. She put her glass of wine down, and ran into my bedroom.

"Dude, what happened?" Mark said.

"Not sure really. I saw my cards, but I didn't see them at the same time. I thought I had 11 but I had 12 so I hit and busted. I was all in."

Tuyen came out a moment later with her suitcase. "I have to go," Tuyen screamed. "They come for me."

"What're you talking about?" I said.

"You lost the money. My family owes money to bad people. We have to pay tonight. You supposed to win money."

"What people? What're you talking about?"

"Bad people. They kill people sometimes. We owe money. I have to leave. They will come after us."

"Where will you go? This is crazy. Why didn't you tell me this?"

"I don't know where," Tuyen said, great tears welling to the sides of her eyes. "What will we do? They come after you maybe."

"This is crazy. What the fuck? Why didn't you tell me this? I would never have done this. This is insane."

"Mate, you need to get the fuck out of here," Ben said.

"Tuyen, we have to leave. I mean we have to leave. We have to get the fuck out of here."

"Where? Where we go? You take me?"

"Yes of course. But you can't tell anyone. I don't know. We'll have to take a bus somewhere."

"Go to Thailand," Mark said. "You don't need a visa to get in."

"Yeah, we'll hide in Thailand," I said.

You're mine now, said death.

Chapter 24

The bus had spacious walkways and generous seating (large enough to hold approximately 90 passengers). It was a double-decker style with two large televisions on each level. The seats were leather and could extend back to form a sort of bed—James Bond transportation on a limited budget.

We boarded the blackened bus in the cover of darkness. I had quickly packed one suitcase and one duffle bag, and Tuyen had brought only what was with her at the time, which, luckily (since she had planned on staying at the apartment for a few days) was her utility kit and some extra clothes. We were assigned seat numbers near the back of the upper level.

Tuyen crashed down into the seat and slumped her head until it was nearly touching the bottom portion of the upright seat in front of her. I sat down next to her, excited and unfazed. We were free. We were getting away. We were about to embark on the biggest adventure of our lives. Tuyen didn't see it that way. Of course, how could she? Her family was in financial trouble—although if they would have been perfectly honest with me, I would not have so readily joined their scheme—and she was now running away from her own obligations. But it was difficult for me to think in those terms.

"What can I do? My family is in trouble. What can I do?"

"We'll figure out something. For now, though, we need to get out of here. I'm worried mostly about you. They'll come after you. I'm sure your family can take care of themselves."

The bus's engines started up and within a few short minutes, we were off to Siem Reap, Cambodia. Tuyen fell asleep within minutes—I admired the Asian ability to sleep anywhere, everywhere, and do it in a twentieth of what it would take me. Within a short time, we had made it out of Saigon. I tried to glimpse and remember the landscape for the moon was high and providing good light through the window. But I only could see obtuse shadows of what must have been banana trees. The never ending buzz of city life had not lifted and motorcycles hummed passed our bus and the other large vehicles on the roadway. Vietnam was busy. The Vietnamese did everything with equal attention. When they worked, they worked hard; when they rested, they rested leisurely. I couldn't sleep. The bus hit enough potholes to have one think the road had trenches cut out of it every few feet. I tried watching the movie on the large television screen, but I had seen *The Fast and the Furious* too many times now on the flight to Vietnam.

I could only think of my predicament and smile. I wished I could call up Hadley right then and tell her what had happened. She wouldn't believe me: casinos, mob gangs, rich Australians and stern Arabs, losing it all on one bet, hiding out in Cambodia, or Laos, or Thailand—I would have left out the part of Tuyen of course. But she would have simply said that was strange or nice and then told me about the book she was reading. This kind of world was foreign to her and thus impossible to imagine. But I had been drawn to Asia by its mystery and magic (and its adventure). And now I was reveling in it.

When we approached the Cambodian border, Tuyen woke up and stretched.

"What happened?"

"Well, Paul Walker crashed his car, and backstabbed his friends," I said.

"What do you mean? Who Paul Walker?"

"It's a movie."

"Anyway, where we are?"

"About to go into Cambodia."

"Cambodia's dirty," Tuyen said, wrinkling up her nose as if the stench of Cambodia was infecting her.

"We have to go through Cambodia to get to Thailand," I said, amused.

"Let's hurry."

Our bus continued on to Phnom Penh. Phnom Penh was rundown and dirty like Tuyen had said. The buildings were decrepit, and like Vietnam, the government buildings were the sights of the city. They were gated, built aesthetically pleasing with large topmost rounded windows and beautiful gardens. But even they were an eyesore in the midst of such poverty. Large gray baboons scaled the rooftops of the shanties and power lines. And there were power lines. The skies of Phnom Penh were crisscrossed with a massive grid of power lines.

It reminded me of the bus tracks of Seattle, but on a much grander scale. And whereas one could forget and fail to see the power lines and bus tracks there as they blended in with the trees and buildings, here, in Phnom Penh they were the sky. Tuyen wanted to rush onto another bus without exploring the city, and I had to admit I wasn't thrilled about walking around. We bought tickets to Siem Reap—I refused to leave Cambodia without seeing Angkor first.

We had a couple of hours before the bus departed so we went to a local market and had lunch at a restaurant with plastic chairs huddled around small tables. I ordered a dish called Amok trey, a fish dish with vegetables and fruit, and an Angkor beer. Tuyen had noodles and a coke.

"Did you see the baboons on the rooftops?" I asked.

"Yes, dirty animals," she said.

"Do you know the history of Angkor?"

"We should go," Tuyen said. "We should go to Thailand."

"We have another hour before the bus leaves," I said. "And Thailand is not going anywhere."

"What do you mean?"

"There's no rush to get there. Look, try to enjoy this trip."

"I can't enjoy," she said. "I need to call my family."

247

"Okay, call them right now," I said.

Tuyen took out her phone, dialed a number, and spoke a flourish of Vietnamese. I leaned back and watched the Cambodian people move about their daily lives. There was a stark contrast here in Cambodia than in Vietnam. This was a country scoured by the Khmer Rouge, and although the Vietnamese had endured decades of occupation by French and American forces, their economy was doing well, they were in control of their government, and they were a happy people. The Cambodians scurried quickly to and fro with sacks of food, sticks, and straw upon their backs. They were friendly and smiled to each other, but their smiles lasted only as long as they spoke and then they quickly diminished. Perhaps they did not feel quite safe yet from the Khmer Rouge who still had members scattered about the country. The air here was different. The skies were downcast, but the country was downcast too. I had never been in a country as poor as Cambodia, and I felt my mood change just by being there (and it had only been an hour). Tuyen hung up and seemed a bit more relieved.

"So, what's going on?" I asked.

"My family escape, but men are searching for them."

"What're they going to do?"

"They don't know, but think it will be fine."

On the bus to Siem Reap, we once again had seats located near the back. The bus took off about fifteen minutes after we boarded. It was a six hour trip. We didn't get to see much of the landscape because the cover of darkness was too much, but I could see that towards Siem Reap, the mountainous regions grew quite a bit. The land was shrouded with tree cover with sporadic open areas used for rice paddies. At some point I fell asleep and had strange dreams. I dreamt that a large wild cat, a liger of some sort was tracking me through the jungles of Cambodia. Tuyen was with me and at one point we were both running from this liger, and suddenly she threw a large tree trunk in my path and I tripped. The last thing I saw was her running away, without looking back to see what happened, and the liger pouncing down upon me.

I woke up and Tuyen was talking on the phone. She looked over at me as I stirred myself awake. It was still night out, and we must have been on some mountainous road—it was winding and we were moving along quite slowly. Tuyen hung up soon afterwards.

"This trip is taking long time," she said.

"How long was I asleep?"

"I don't know, long time. I can't sleep at all, and you fell asleep so I was bored."

"Was there a movie?"

"I don't know. It was boring," she said.

Maybe bringing Tuyen was not a great idea. I wanted to help her get away. She was in danger, but it didn't seem like she saw it that way. I thought it best if we hung low for a while in Thailand, go to the beaches, have a holiday, but it seemed she wanted to go back to Vietnam. She just didn't have the adventurous spirit. But she must have other things on her mind; of course she had other things on her mind. This was an adventure for me; this was a crisis for her.

"Hey, I know this is hard for you right now, but I think it is best if we lay low for a while, only a short time—two weeks or so okay?"

"I want to go back to Vietnam," she said.

"I know. I know, but for right now, it's not safe in Saigon. Just two weeks. We'll check out Angkor Wat and then head to Thailand, hang out on the beaches, and when your family thinks it's okay for you to come back, we'll head back. This just needs to blow over."

"Why did you bet? You weren't supposed to bet?" Tuyen asked.

"I don't know. It was a lot of things," I said.

"That was dumb," she said.

Siem Reap was an entirely different city than the capital, Phnom Penh. The streets were paved without potholes, and the buildings were kept up. Even the people walking on the streets seemed to have just a bit more life in them.

We took a tuk tuk from the bus station to our guesthouse, the Green Garden Home. It had a short porch where some people were eating a late dinner. Inside was a cozy foyer with a couple couches and a television. There was a staircase straight ahead and computers to the left as we walked in. A man yawned at the back counter and welcomed us.

We checked in and the man gave us our room keys and a basket of fruit which I thought was extremely welcoming. Tuyen said something about the fruit not being washed properly, but I knew she wanted to eat it. I had heard about Asian people being completely nationalistic and not all too welcoming to other Asian countries, and Tuyen was a prime example of this.

The room was well furnished for the price. It had a nice queen bed, a small love seat, and a television. The bathroom was small, but had a shower with a tub and a sink and toilet.

I went downstairs to ask about getting a tour to Angkor. I set up a tour for that next day with a tuk tuk driver. An all-day tour was just ten dollars for one. I went back upstairs and when I opened the room door, I found Tuyen naked in bed.

Take her, the great concubine said.

"Why you stand there and look me? Come to bed," she said.

"I'm sorry," I whispered. "Something was on my mind."

"Come to bed."

We got up early the next morning and had a quick breakfast.

The tuk tuk driver was already outside waiting. He introduced himself as Bill. Tuyen climbed up first and I followed. The tuk tuk was basically a wooden cart with three wheels, but fortunately, it had padded seats and

250

plastic windows and a canopy to ward off rain. Bill started up the motor, and we were off along the city roads and eventually into the country roads which were unpaved and potholed. The landscape quickly turned to dense forests, and the roads were windy.

Suddenly, looming before us were three massive, spiraled temples surrounded by smaller stone structures and a great wall. I looked at the map Bill had given me— this must have been Angkor Wat. It was a gorgeous sight. All my childhood fantasies and play acting were precisely in imaginative places like this. And now it was before me, physical and real.

"Let's hurry," Tuyen said.

We had paid for our tickets while still in town so Bill said he would wait for us at that location once we were done. We were off. We walked along the long bridge that led to the famous temples. The stones on the bridge were large and small, crooked and square. I thought of the millions of people who had walked along that same path throughout the centuries. It was a shuddering thought. Tuyen skipped on ahead wanting to get out of the rain, but a little rain had never melted me so I took my camera out and started taking pictures.

We walked along the outside corridors of Angkor Wat. Each had a story to tell—of battles, of heaven and hell, of religious practices. The symbols were fairly easy to decipher. I stood and perused over the corridor with the people ascending to heaven, to purgatory, and to hell. There was a line of people walking until they came to a three-way fork in the road. Some chose to descend into the depths, some took the middle road, and some took the highest road. Eventually, those who took the highest road stood on the ground that the middle road people took, and the middle road stood on the ground that the bottom dwellers took. Those in hell were filled with strife and pain from holding up the rest, and those on top were happy and content.

Which road had I chosen? Things were finally coming into place. Before, the path took me along, and I suffered from fear. Now, I chose the path and the world seemed the limit. But it still seemed difficult to decipher if the path was the right one or not. I still thought of Hadley— even in the midst of the Cambodian jungle traveling with an attractive Vietnamese woman who I had to protect from Vietnamese mobsters, I thought of Hadley. I certainly had not done right to her. I wondered where she was at that very moment; I knew she wasn't anywhere like this.

"We must hurry Orville or we not see the other temples," Tuyen said.

The next temple was Prasat Kravan. Tuyen and I were able to walk to a number of temples once they began to be clustered closer together. The architecture and craftsmanship that was put into each temple was simply amazing. Some, now, were more ruins than temples, but I enjoyed those the most because they came straight out of The Legend of Zelda. I only marveled that goblins and ogres didn't appear from within and without.

At the end of the day, Bill drove us to the last temple along the path: West Meban, which was just outside Barai Lake, a lake apparently built for a king who wanted an extremely large swimming pool. As happened all day, swarms of children accosted Tuyen and me trying to get us to buy bracelets and t-shirts and necklaces and paintings and music CDs and jewelry and scarves and hats and soda pop and food. The list continued on and on and on. Tuyen had already given up speaking with them, but I still politely said no, I couldn't buy it, I already had some, I'm sorry, I'm sorry, I'm sorry.

When we completed our tour of the temples, Bill drove us back to our guesthouse. I paid him handsomely. He thanked us and left to find perhaps another tourist looking for a trip that next day.

Back in the hotel room, Tuyen promptly lay down upon the bed. I took my shoes off and lay down next to her. I had to admit that the day was tiresome with all the children begging and pleading for money, to buy, buy, buy. It was sad. They weren't at school because they were out selling so it was an endless cycle of poverty. A dollar wasn't going to make their lives change all that much.

"I'm famished," I said.

"What?"

"Starving—hungry—I need to eat."

"You need sex with me first," Tuyen said.

We took a long shower together and then got dressed to get some dinner. The streets of Siem Reap were always bustling and the atmosphere raised my spirits despite my fatigue. I felt a cold coming along; perhaps from being out in the rain all day. Tuyen seemed fine and chatted incessantly about what to eat. Her element was in the cities obviously. We found a restaurant with an open deck with a few people there.

We sat outside and drank red wine from South Africa. I ordered a noodle dish and Tuyen had fish (reluctantly despite her hunger).

"We should go to Thailand tomorrow," Tuyen said.

"Yes, I actually agree with you," I said.

Chapter 25

The next day, Tuyen and I went to the bus station early to purchase a trip to Thailand. It was a seven-hour bus ride; we got on the bus and were off to Bangkok in less than half an hour.

The trip was smooth and the landscape beautiful as we traveled down from the mountainous jungles of Siem Reap into the stumpy mountains and river valleys of eastern Thailand. At the border, we paid an exit fee and were quickly whisked into the country with a quick stamp of our passports. The Thai were friendly and welcoming and had an air of joviality about them that came from perhaps a lot of sex, drink, and drug use—I couldn't tell which, but I was excited about the prospect.

I took to Thailand instantly. It was completely different than Cambodia yet they were neighbors. But I suppose that wasn't so odd considering the United States and Mexico were neighbors. I guess my ignorance of Asian society was apparent. I thought people that looked alike must act alike. Certainly that was a ridiculous notion. Even Canadians and Americans could be told apart...well, to an extent at least. But the Thai were nothing, at least, not in culture, like the Cambodians. I couldn't put a finger on it, but they had something the Cambodians did not. I ventured it must have something to do with their history, their cultural influences, their religious practices, their...

"Yes, of course. All those things," Tuyen said.

"Sorry, I was thinking out loud," I said.

"Why would you think they the same? The north Vietnamese and south Vietnamese are different," she said. "It's obvious."

"Yes, yes of course," I said. "How silly of me."

"You Americans always think you're special," Tuyen said. "Nobody is anything like you Americans. All Asians are same."

"Yes, like all Hispanics are the same," I said.

"Who they?"

"You know: Spanish speakers."

"They *are* the same," Tuyen scoffed.

A festering city of abandoned buildings, roaming dogs, homeless men with amputated legs, skyscrapers, smog, rickshaws, imported cars, and sin was Bangkok. The city was a morgue throughout the morning and a hive throughout the evening. It was truly The City of Sinful Night.

Tuyen and I walked from the bus terminal into the city that was awaking from its long morning slumber. We were famished and the smells engulfed our senses—pork on a stick, pad Thai, fried vegetables, rice, beef soups, an entire arsenal of aromatic delights. I wanted to stop at each vendor selling his goods from little carts along the sides of the roads, but Tuyen was on a mission to rid herself of the baggage she had brought with her so that she could enjoy a meal in comfort. A part of me agreed, but I found myself leering over the counters and smiling incoherently at the vendors who smiled back with big, toothless grins, saying ten baht, fifteen baht, only twenty baht.

The hotel we chose was a three-story hotel in a back alley somewhere in the middle of the vast city near Chitlada Palace. Our room was small, unadorned with art of any kind, and had simple white walls, a bed, a small bathroom, but furnished with toilet paper and towels rather than the rag on a stick most Thai used instead. Thank God for small things.

Tuyen reluctantly put her things on the bed and quickly walked around the room looking in the corners and on the walls, apparently for cockroaches. She went into the bathroom and I heard a terrible scream a few seconds later. I rushed in there. A large beetle of some kind was upside down, dead, in the sink.

"I have to admit that's pretty disgusting," I said.

"We can't stay here," she said.

"It's only for one night."

"Let's eat," she said. "I'm flour-ished."

"Famished," I said.

"Yes, what I said. Let's go."

Later, we jumped into a nearby rickshaw and headed to one of the famous night markets. There were long crowded corridors filled with tourists and young Thai teenagers meeting their friends, rows and rows of booths selling everything from t-shirts to Tupperware, and in the center was a large seating area with a stage with two rows of food vendors selling every known dish in the world: American, Thai, Japanese, Mexican, Middle Eastern, Indian.

I wanted to try them all. It was like going into a grocery store purposefully famished so that you would be sure to buy as much as possible. There was nothing worse than going into a store with the idea to purchase a week's worth of groceries only to buy a couple things because nothing looked appetizing. Not this time; not in Thailand. I was famished and wanted to eat the world. I decided on Indian, and Tuyen ordered a huge burger and fries with a beer. I had a Tiger beer with my saag gosht.

We ate and drank. The beer was so cheap I had four of them. Tuyen wanted to go back to the hotel, but then I told her about what I heard—Soi 4, the Sin Street of Bangkok. She feigned sleepiness, but I could tell she was interested. We wandered around the night market for a time and then took a rickshaw to Soi 4. As soon as we began walking down the street, I was accosted by lady boys. They were easy to spot, even in my semi-tipsy, hazy-eyed state of being. Tuyen laughed at my plight. It was amazing; they simply walked up and asked where I was going, come out with them. No woman had ever been so blunt. It was unfortunate that they were actually men.

The lady boys were much taller than the short Thai men, which I found a bit strange. Did tallness genetically predispose Thai men to want to dress up as women? That couldn't be right.

We walked passed a square that had a string of bars and strip clubs. I wanted to go see what they were like.

"For experience," I said to Tuyen.

"You better not leave me," Tuyen said.

"Leave you? No, you better not leave me. I don't ever want to be alone while I'm in there. Okay? Even when you use the restroom, I want to come with you."

"Huh? You're funny."

We went into one that was said to have real women. There were perhaps twenty or so naked Asian women perusing the customers at the bar. The place was filled with white, western men in business suits or nice jackets and ties. They were sitting around a small stage in the center. We found a seat near the back. A few of the naked women turned to our direction. I was thankful Tuyen was with me.

We ordered drinks and then suddenly all the naked girls went into the backroom area. The music was loud and the place abuzz with various languages. I distinctly heard a string of Russian being spoken at the table next to me. I also noticed that none of the Thai men who were there were talking with any of the women. Did the girls know they wouldn't pay? Were they simply there for the show?—the atmosphere? I suppose that was what I was there for.

Suddenly the music flared up and there was a lot of chatter, Thai chatter, over a loudspeaker. Then a line of scantily clad women in transparent camisoles did a sort of catwalk around the stage. I was thoroughly enjoying myself (because I knew I was in no position to get accosted by naked women perhaps expecting something, which doesn't sound like a horrible situation, but it could have been), but Tuyen was watching me like a mother hawk watches the eagle trying to get to her babies.

Then, a naked woman came out onto the stage as the other women retreated to the backroom. The woman had two eggs with her and a cup. She wasn't an attractive woman in the slightest, but she had an air of confidence about her, if that could be said for a woman who strips in front of men for a living—well, she didn't even strip for she was already naked. She toured the stage and then made her way to the center. She put one of the eggs in her mouth and performed a sort of sucking motion. Apparently this was to show off what she could do if, say, it wasn't an egg.

"What she doing?" Tuyen asked.

"Um...not sure," I lied.

Then, she spread her legs and slowly slid down to the floor like a ballet dancer. She leaned back and put the other egg straight into her vagina.

"Yuck," Tuyen said.

The woman then propped herself up on her legs with the egg still in there. She started touring around the stage again to sporadic claps from the Thai men—the Westerners didn't know whether to clap or what. What was to happen next? That was quickly answered. The woman went back to the center of the stage, spread her legs and then suddenly dropped down to the floor. There was a huge thud and a crack—I thought she had hurt herself, but she sat there, legs outstretched, comfortable and meeting every gaze in that room. Then, she propped herself up once again and went over to the cup. She hovered over it. A slow clap began in the rear of the room by one of the workers. It quickly turned into a raucous clap from all the men in the room, but nobody knew what they were clapping for. Then, suddenly, the egg yoke and white came out like a slow moving waterfall directly into the cup.

"Wow," I said.

"You like this?"

"No, but I must say, I've never seen anything like that before."

The next morning, Tuyen and I took an early bus down south of Bangkok. We took a ferry to Koh Chang, an island in the Gulf of Thailand. It was a beautiful morning, the sun emerging out of the Gulf like an eye slowly appearing over a table. The waves gently rocked against the ferry, and we sipped coke and leaned against the railing. This was the life—a life on the run with moments of picturesque beauty. It seemed so fantastical.

We docked and took a cab up the road to our hotel. We were staying in some bungalows right on the beach. We walked along the beach to nearly the last row of bungalows—Pens Bungalows.

There was a short porch with cushions surrounding small tables. A woman lay against one of these cushions drinking some water. The dining area was just behind the porch. There was a bar there, and a man was at the bar looking out across the gulf. Behind the bar and dining room was a small staircase leading up towards the bungalows, which were numbered up through 29 or so.

Tuyen and I did not have a reservation, but we stepped onto the porch and dropped our luggage down. I went up to the bar and asked if we could get a room.

"Ah, no English. Talk her," the man said, pointing to the woman lying against the cushion. The woman put her water glass down on the small table and got up to greet us. She set us up with a room with air conditioning for 150 baht per night.

The room was completely made of wood and unadorned. It was small with a single bed in the center of the room with a mosquito net wrapped around it. The bathroom was next to the room and it had a shower head and a toilet and sink, but there was no tub.

"That's what 150 baht gets you apparently," I said.

"We can't stay here," Tuyen said.

"It's only for a couple of days. This island looks amazing doesn't it?"

"Yes of course. I need call my cousin."

Tuyen took out her phone and dialed a number. They spoke in Vietnamese while I went out on the porch of the bungalow. Through the trees I could see the ocean water. I heard the waves crash against the beach and wanted to go down there. I told Tuyen to meet me when she was finished.

The sun had fallen and the stars looked like twinkling eyes up in the night sky. I sat against one of the cushions and looked out at the ocean. A few tourists walked by, lovers holding hands, or friends going out for dinner. The woman from the bar came over and asked if I wanted to have some food or have a drink. I ordered a beer and sipped it slowly. This was grand. I didn't want to leave this place.

Tuyen met me a few moments later. I was feeling quite jovial from the beer on an empty stomach. I asked her if she would want to go out for food or to eat there. She wanted to eat there. The woman came back over and we eat and drank. I had a pad Thai dish with shrimp and Tuyen had some soup with coconut sauce and mushrooms. Even she admitted it was amazing.

That night we slept together to the sounds of the waves and the crickets chirping outside our bungalow. It felt like we were a fairy couple in a far off land—we were surrounded by the mosquito net, which seemed very Snow Whitish and the ocean put Tuyen to sleep soon afterwards. But I was wide awake. I couldn't help but wonder where this strange ride was going. I had no plan. I had had a plan—going to Vietnam, finding work, enjoying myself—but now that plan had been gambled away. That was okay, but now, in Thailand, in Southeast Asia with limited resources, I had to form another plan.

I had a coughing fit just before I went to sleep. I went to the bar to get some water, but even that didn't help much.

"Sick eh?" The woman asked.

"Just a dry cough," I said. "Probably something in the air."

"Who is your friend?"

"Ah, my girlfriend—we came from Saigon."

"Oh how nice. I've never been there."

"It's a nice place," I said. "A bit chaotic sometimes though."

We talked like that for half an hour or so and I started feeling tired. All the traveling was finally catching up with me. I felt fatigue drifting upon me. My body was sore and I had a slight headache. It's amazing. Once you get to a relaxing destination, you're body finally tells you exactly how it felt when you were out and about gallivanting through the jungles.

I crawled back into bed and finally fell asleep. I had bad dreams about a rabid elephant rampaging through the jungle sniffing me out. I awoke the next morning to red mosquito bites along my arms and legs and noticed a small hole in the netting. Tuyen slept peacefully next to me without a bite on her. My blood was obviously sweeter than hers.

Chapter 26

I got up sometime around 7 am that morning. I went to use the restroom and felt my entire body ache. I must have exerted too much energy last night. I was wide awake so I took a quick shower. The most unfortunate aspect of cheap travel in Southeast Asia was the lack of comfortable washing facilities. Sure, there was a shower with a nozzle that trickled down moderately warm water, but that could never compete with a nozzle with high pressure, warm to hot water aided by a bathtub wherein one with a hangover could sit down in without worrying about paying for the heating bill or having the water go cold such as in a hotel. I quickly dressed in board shorts and a sleeveless shirt and went to walk along the beach.

I walked along in the soft sand. There were a few couples lying on towels touching and kissing each other. They ignored me as I walked passed, which I found comforting. Thailand was a place to enjoy oneself and the one you loved. I strolled by them trying not to disturb their loving embraces. The ocean waves crashed thunderously against the shoreline.

What a beautiful world we lived in. Looking out to the great expanse of blue under that bright morning light, I wondered how a creature, an insignificant creature such as me, could have any impact on this world. What was I but a gnat, a microbe? And yet I thought, I moved, and involved myself within it. I was a part of it. I was born, was living, and would some day die and disperse my atoms into the cosmos once again. And everything I did here would be remembered by a few, but only until they, too, dispersed their own atoms. And then my existence would continue to fade until it was almost as if I had never existed at all. But then, at that point, I would be elsewhere, and the things I did here would mean nothing to me.

It made one think about the reactions we have to this world, to the people in it, to our very existence. Everything I had done thus far would some day mean nothing to neither me nor anyone in existence. Unless I changed history somehow—or, rather, created a history that altered the lives of billions of people such as a Hitler or Alexander the Great. All the depression and sorrow and even happiness would some day mean nothing. Does that take away the severity or pleasure of it? Or the reality of it? Pain still hurt even when knowing it doesn't last forever—pleasure still feels good. No—we are subject to our feelings and have a limited ability to look to the future when all this would mean nothing. Nothing would matter. That thought was a pleasurable thought. One day, I would exist differently than I do now. Happily, I thought of that day.

I continued walking along the beach and picked up the seashells that drifted onshore. I threw them back despite the fact that the creatures inside had already passed to the great beyond. It was the act of throwing that was pleasurable. It always had been—my baseball days in hindsight were the best days of my life. Nothing could beat the simplicity of that life back then. School was easy; food and lodging were paid for; there were no girls to complicate things. I could never go back to that time, but I was tired of living in the present wishing to be in the past. Now was the now and now it was time to live in the now.

It was around eight in the morning when I got back to the bungalows. I snuck into the room without waking Tuyen who could sleep through World War 3 and took my book out to the pillowed tables on the short porch. I was reading the short stories of Ernest Hemingway and found a true gem in *The Short Happy Life of Frances Macomber*. My initial thought was that Margot did Francis a favor when she shot him in the head. I read until about nine thirty and then I set the collection down and watched the people slowly trickle along the beach.

The bungalow woman came out and asked if I wanted anything for breakfast; I told her I would wait for Tuyen. I looked down at my arms and saw four or five red spots— last night's feeding frenzy. I wondered what we would go do today—perhaps an elephant ride through the jungle. Tuyen would probably hate riding elephants, but that's something she would have to get over.

At ten or so I was getting a bit restless and went back up to the bungalow. I opened the door and found Tuyen talking in hushed Vietnamese on the bed. She was startled at the door opening and jumped up and quickly hung up the phone.

"You scared me," she said.

"I thought you were still sleeping. Who were you talking to?"

"I called my cousin to see what was happening," she said.

"And what's happening?"

"They very scared."

"So what's happening?"

"I don't know. It's scary. I need to take shower," she said, getting up and going into the bathroom.

That was strange. Something was amiss. She was hiding something. Or maybe she really didn't know what was happening. Either way, it was a long ways away. But it was her family. How would I feel if my family was being chased by Vietnamese gangsters? And here I was in Thailand wanting to ride elephants through the jungle as if this was a peachy vacation. But it was a peachy vacation. I couldn't be bothered with doom and gloom. Everything would be fine. In this newfound world of choice, everything would be fine—it would be fine for me and whoever was with me. Tuyen had nothing to fear; I had nothing to fear. The sun was shining, the waves crashing against the coastline, the people happy, the food and drink fantastic, and all was well. This was Thailand, the land of gold and happiness.

When Tuyen emerged from the bathroom, she began to dress and asked what I wanted to do that day. I told her about the elephants and she quickly said yes. Now I knew something was not right.

"Really? You want to go ride elephants through the jungle?"

"I never was on elephant before," she said while dressing.

"And you know what an elephant is right?"

"Yes, big, gray, big ears."

"Couldn't have said it better myself."

We had breakfast in the front, and I had a couple Tiger beers with it because it was my vacation and on vacation it was never too early to have a beer. Hell, it's never too early anyway, but this was more kosher. After breakfast, we took a taxi down the road to the elephant camp.

There was a party of people huddled around a large tree near a picnic table. A group of elephants was being harnessed in a barn. And there was a baby elephant in a pen just inside. It was swaying left and right to the music in its head or something like that.

Tuyen paid the taxi driver and we went into a large building near the back of the camp. The group ahead of us had already left and no other groups were preparing to go so Tuyen and I would head out alone (with the tour guide of course).

Our guide was a small man aged fifty or so. The three of us went to the barn together and took a ladder up onto a plank way. The man guided the first elephant into the departure area with successive clicks of his mouth. The elephant slowly trudged in, and the man harnessed a wooden seat just behind its massive head once it was in position. Tuyen stepped onto the seat cautiously and sat down quickly to avoid falling over. The man bolted her in, and she looked at me with wide eyes and I laughed. She did look a bit ridiculous on that gigantic beast—she was no fat Maharaja. The elephant took a few steps forward and another followed it into the barn. The guide went through the same process and within minutes I was bolted in and the three of us were waddling off towards the jungle.

It had rained quite a bit the night before and it was extremely muddy. Many elephants had already traveled the path that morning as was evident from the large, round footprints filled with rainwater. Tuyen's elephant was a few yards ahead of mine when I suddenly heard her scream. I instantly thought of tigers. The guide turned around nonchalantly and laughed, but kept going. Then I found out why Tuyen had screamed. My elephant began walking down a small hill and it felt like we were going to tip over. Just before I had fleeting thoughts of the elephant squashing me into a flimsy pancake, I remembered a horseback riding trip I had gone on when I had been much younger. I had been riding an old horse that, at one point, had begun walking downhill. I had tried to stop it, but it was like a computerized, robotic animal programmed to follow the course. I had been terrified and had never gone on a horse since, and now I was putting my life into the balance of an old elephant.

But, as the old horse before it, the veteran elephant made it down the hill without incident. We had decided on the hour tour and did not see any wild life within the first forty-five minutes. Near the end of the tour, our elephants came to a splashing hole. It cost extra to take a shower with them, which Tuyen flatly refused to do, so instead the elephants simply waded into the water up to their torsos. After that, we crossed a road and came back to the barn. We disembarked our wonderful beasts and took a taxi back to the bungalows.

I wanted a shower after riding through the jungle on an elephant. Tuyen's phone rang as the water heated up. It was her cousin. The water felt wonderful against my skin. Life was certainly funny. There was a time when I had contemplated suicide and subsequently jumped off the Ballard Bridge only to be rescued. And now, I realized that life was continuously moving forward. The future was unmapped territory. Never back then would I have dreamed of being in Thailand (or Vietnam and Cambodia for that matter). So, now, the future looked refreshingly bright. What did it hold? I didn't know, but it was certainly intriguing.

I stepped out of the shower and went into the bedroom. Tuyen was laying on the bed in just her underwear. I smiled at her—

"I'm starving," I said. "We must eat."

"I want sex," Tuyen said.

"Seriously, I'm so hungry."

"Come in the bed."

I waited for some voice in my head to say something, but there was nothing. I climbed into bed with her and began massaging her legs and kissing her neck and lips. But, that nagging thought was there—I wanted more than this, more than perfunctorily taking our clothes off and simply sleeping with each other. This wasn't what I wanted. I wanted passion, romance. Was there such a thing that could last?

Afterwards, we lay in bed next to each other, but Tuyen insisted on getting dressed and then snuggling. We lay there for a few minutes when we heard a knock at the door. I grabbed some clothes and ran into the bathroom.

"Answer the door, okay?" I said to Tuyen.

While I changed in the bathroom, I heard Tuyen talking animatedly in Vietnamese. I opened the door. There were four men standing in my room, including Steve, Tuyen's cousin.

"Sorry," Tuyen said.

"You come with us," one the men said.

"We're going back to Vietnam," Steve said. "To finish what you began."

"What're you talking about?" I said.

"No mistakes this time," Steve said.

Suddenly, the other men began shouting in rapid Vietnamese. Steve shouted quickly back and the others quieted down.

"No mistakes this time," Steve reiterated.

I looked at Tuyen. Her head was down; she didn't dare look at me.

The trip back to Vietnam was stressful as one could imagine. I kept looking for opportunities to escape or at least use a phone or the internet, but I was being heavily guarded by the gangsters or whoever they were. Tuyen didn't come close to me, but she looked even more uncomfortable than I did. At lunch the next day, I got a chance to sit down next to her.

"Let me use your phone," I demanded.

"I sorry. Really, I sorry," she said.

"Not as sorry as I am. Let me use your phone."

"My cousin said no."

That night we crossed into Cambodia. We traveled from bus to bus without staying in hotels presumably because it would have been easier to escape. One of the men would sit next to me on the bus so the trips were long and silenced. I was left to my thoughts. As we neared the Vietnamese border, Steve sat next to me.

"We must go over the rules again," he said. "And no beer drinking."

He went over the signals and we practiced together. I was confident that everything would go well enough this time.

But as we came to the border, my anger towards Tuyen, Steve, and these thugs had increased ten-fold. How could Tuyen betray me? And the way she did—using sex and seduction. Ah, how could I blame her? But these criminals were idiots as-far-as I was concerned. They thought their fear tactics would cause me to bend over to their will without a fight. Ha—this was the newly evolved Orville James McFadden.

The bus parked outside the border patrol terminal. We got off and I took my backpack with my valuables with me, but left my duffle bag with my clothes on the underside off the bus. Our group went into the building and began the paperwork process. I was already the target of intense scrutiny as I was an American in Vietnam, but traveling with five other Vietnamese who obviously looked hostile gave me added attention. This could aide me.

We stood in line with our passports, but then we were separated into nationals and foreigners. Tuyen and the thugs hadn't really anticipated this. In Cambodia, we all were aliens and went through together. Tuyen and her group passed through quickly and waited for me on the other side. I was surprisingly calm as I waited my turn.

Finally, it came. I walked nonchalantly up to the militarily dressed woman and handed her my documents.

"I have a problem," I said calmly to her.

"What's your problem?" she asked in perfect English.

"Don't look yet, but I'm being kidnapped for money by the people behind you," I said without looking at Tuyen. The woman looked at me seriously and then at one of her comrades. She looked back at me. I nodded to her. She picked up the phone and said something softly into it. She looked through my passport and asked me about Thailand and Cambodia. I told her how they had come to Thailand to find me. I looked over my shoulder to see three security personnel approach them. They began talking and waving their arms frantically. One of the guards came over and whispered to the woman helping me.

"We will have to take you into custody," the woman said.

The man came around with handcuffs and put them around my wrists. The two other guards followed by two more who had come to their aide put handcuffs around Tuyen, Steve, and the others. We put on quite a show for the onlookers in the building. The gangsters were screaming madly in Vietnamese. I simply smiled as I was being led away.

But Tuyen got the last word.

"I give you AIDS!"

I got the last word, said death.

Chapter 27

Can one know a man who doesn't know himself? What was I but a man, a multi-faceted man constantly changing to the tune of the world, but I could not recognize the tune. The evolutionary process, through experience and thought, had metamorphosed my very being. But what was I before?—what was I now? I couldn't keep up with my own self. After facing the many microcosms of life, the one discernable conclusion that I could draw was that I was a fool. But knowing is half the battle, isn't it? Isn't awareness the necessary first step to self-actualization?

All I wanted, all I ever wanted was love. What was it inside me that needed this? Recognition, praise, love. There was a big, black void inside me that needed to be filled with the love of others. This desire had driven my life. My performances all for others; all had ultimately resulted in failure. It was that fear of rejection, that fear of rejected love, that fear of failure that had damaged my ability to simply live and be. I had craved a little touch, a soft word, a smile and a laugh. I had needed it to feel complete. I exploited it when I could; I ravaged it to feel powerful. Why?—because I was weak in spirit. I needed the love of others because I didn't love myself.

I was blind and could not recognize this and even when I did, I was a fool because I believed that things would come out differently each and every time. What was it that I had heard?—a person who does the same thing over and over again expecting different results was crazy. But I knew that I wasn't crazy. Therefore, I was simply a fool. I had expected the world to change with each endeavor. I had thought that the people should change. I had been fooled by life. It was I who had to change; I had to change my way of thinking if I was to survive in this world.

I had been sick for a couple of weeks upon my return
from Vietnam: chills, itching, vomiting, muscle soreness,
fatigue, I had developed rashes under my arms, feet, and
groin area. I had Googled the symptoms and sure
enough, in big, blue capital letters was AIDS. All the sites,
all the information pointed to a period of six months to
know for sure. So I waited.

I lived with my mother upon my return. I helped her
around the house, did some gardening, did some reading.
And then one day, I opened a script, *Art* by Yasmina
Reza, and thought of the future. But what future could I
possibly have?

"You've been down lately," my mother said.

"I'm okay."

"Perhaps you should find a job."

"I'm applying for graduate school."

And that was when I began studying scripts to find the
monologues I wanted to tape and send in to get a Masters
of Fine Arts in theatre. I sent my tape off a month later. It
was strange to believe you were dying and at once prepare
for the future. A paradox it was.

At six months, I went to the Reliance Medical Facility in
Richland. I was called into a room, and a nurse
nonchalantly explained the blood drawing procedure,
when I would receive the results in the mail, there was
nothing to worry about, everything was safe and secure.
She drew my blood and a part of me left in a little capsule
from the room. As I was being taken away, I wondered if
that little vial of blood contained my death.

I thought of Hadley at that moment. She was out
there, somewhere, doing something, living. It was strange
to think she existed outside of my own world. I seemed to
think that when away from me, people stopped moving,
thinking, existing independently of myself. Did all twenty
somethings think the world revolved around them or was
it just me? No longer could I think that way. What was I
but a dying man?

I was tired of living as Orville James McFadden. It was too much work. Constant bombardment of depressive thoughts, constant failure in all aspects of life—when would it all end? What did it all mean?—ah, to hell with that question. That question was always basking its ugly head from behind the gray rock. And frankly, I just wanted to shoot it down in a blaze of glory. With the shotgun cocked, a spray of pellets would surely end it once and for all. Can you truly imagine waking up every day plagued by hideous thoughts of self-basement, loathing at the sight reflecting in the mirror? But, I was past that phase. I was tired, ready to throw in the white towel. And not in a dramatic display of fireworks as one reaching out for attention. No—I wanted to simply slip away into the night. I didn't want tears and bellowing. I was simply tired, perhaps a little bored. Life wasn't all that exciting. Without love, the eternal romantic is in hell.

How would I do it this time? Something dramatic like jumping off a bridge was ruled out immediately. No, a quick bullet to the brain would suffice. None of that romantic bullet to the heart shit either. There would be no symbolism this time around. No, just a quick end. I was tired.

I called Hadley and was surprised when she answered. We decided to meet that week at the Verite Coffee in Ballard where we used to go on Sundays.

I drove across the desert wondering what it would take to accept the outcomes of my decisions. I had decided to sleep with Tuyen. If it was true that I had contracted AIDS through her, could I ultimately make the decision to live with it? To live with death—there was an oxymoron. Would that not be true courage though? Would I not have learned something, finally?

Once on Snoqualmie Pass, I saw and remembered how beautiful Washington State was. The trees glistened as the sun shrank down through them. The *sun*. That's what I wanted to be: I wanted to be a shining, glowing sun that could spread its light throughout the world and inspire. But what would that take? Certainly not suicide. Is there a future and a life while dying?

I was a tad early when I arrived at Verite so I ordered a coffee and people watched. Every person I saw went about their business, smiling, happy, holding the hands of their children, kissing their husband or wife, helping an old man in a wheel chair, ordering coffee, walking their dogs, going to the movies next door. The simple act of living is what life is all about. The daily routines. It doesn't have to be constant excitement at all times. That's what I had thought when I was married to Hadley, that marriage was supposed to be an exciting, end-all path. Oh how wrong I had been.

Hadley came through the door. She had cut her hair short and was wearing simple blue jeans and a shirt. She was beautiful.

"You look beautiful," I said.

"Not really, just wearing regular clothes."

"But *you* are beautiful."

"Thank you."

I bought her a coffee and we sat down in a corner.

"Why did you want to meet up with me?" Hadley asked.

I smiled at her, but I didn't know yet what quite to say. "I...might be going somewhere soon. I wanted to see you, and...I wanted you to know that I know now that I hurt you, that I was wrong. I was very, very wrong."

"Yes, well, you hurt me, but I've moved on."

"Yes, I believe you have. You're a strong woman. I need one last thing from you. I know you don't want to be friends, but...I want to ask for your forgiveness."

"I forgave you long ago. I don't know how, but...I knew you had problems. It doesn't make what you did okay. No, but I've forgiven you."

"Thank you. I can't thank you enough. I want you to know that never again will I ever hurt anyone again. You're an amazing woman and I lost my privilege to see you and be with you, but I want you to know that never again will this happen to anyone else. I've seen what I could've become, and I don't want to become that person."

"I hope you never do this to anyone again. You'll be hurting her, but you'll be hurting yourself perhaps even more."

"Yes, I believe that."

"In order for the both of us to completely move on with our lives, this will have to be the last time we see each other. I'm no longer angry with you, but I must move on without you."

"I understand that."

We embraced, and I kissed her one last time on the cheek. Then she left, and I knew I would never see her again.

I drove home. I arrived just as the mail carrier was dropping off the mail. He drove off and I went to pick up ours. There were two large envelopes addressed to me. One was from the Reliance Medical Center, and the other was from Boston University College of Fine Arts. I stood there staring at both envelopes in my hands— Reliance in my left, Emerson in my right. How fitting they showed up at the exact same moment—death in my left, life in my right.

I went into the house. My mother was not yet home from work so I could relax in the living room while opening the envelopes. But my heart was beating increasingly fast. Which one to open firstly...I took a letter opener from the kitchen and used it to open the Reliance envelope. Then, I stopped. I then used the letter opener to open the Boston University envelope. I would read them both at the same time.

Your last failure, said fear.

You're mine, said death.

I'm done fearing failure. I'm done fearing death.

I took out both contents. My future was in my hands. I skimmed both quickly as I was too excited to read each individual word.

I found what I was looking for on both pages.

I smiled.

Timothy Ross McDonald

Timothy Ross McDonald makes his home in Seattle.
He avidly enjoys traveling, wine, and playing softball.
This is his first novel.

Made in USA - North Chelmsford, MA
1078134_9780988356900
04.13.2020 1550